आ नो भद्राः क्रतवो यन्तु विश्वतः ।

Let noble thoughts come to us from every side

- Ṛg Veda I - 89-i

BHAVAN'S BOOK UNIVERSITY

TOWARDS THE SILVER CRESTS OF THE HIMALAYAS

by

G. K. PRADHAN

BHAVAN'S BOOK UNIVERSITY

TOWARDS THE SILVER CRESTS OF THE HIMALAYAS

G. K. PRADHAN

2024

BHARATIYA VIDYA BHAVAN
Kulapati Munshi Marg
Mumbai - 400007

Bharatiya Vidya Bhavan
Kulapati Munshi Marg
Mumbai - 400007

First Edition : 1963
Second Edition : 1975
Third Edition : 1982
Fourth Edition : 1988
Fifth Edition : 1993
Sixth Edition : 1998
Seventh Edition : 2007
Eighth Edition : 2011
Nineth Edition : 2013
Tenth Edition : 2015
Eleventh Edition : 2018
Twelfth Edition : 2020
Thirteenth Edition : 2022
Fourteenth Edition : 2024

Price : ₹ 475/-

Typesetting by Samir Parekh,
at Creative Page Setters,

PRINTED IN INDIA

By Nilesh Parekh, Paras Prints, at Gala 32, Singh Indu. Estate-3, 1st floor, Ram Mandir Road, Goregaon, Mumbai - 400104 and Published by P. V. Sankarankutty, Director, for Bharatiya Vidya Bhavan, K.M. Munshi Marg, Mumbai - 400007.
E-mail : publications@bhavans.info
Website : http://www.bhavans.info

KULAPATI'S PREFACE

THE Bharatiya Vidya Bhavan–that Institute of Indian Culture in Bombay– needed a Book University, a series of books which, if read, would serve the purpose of providing higher education. Particular emphasis, however, was to be put on such literature as revealed the deeper impulsions of India. As a first step, it was decided to bring out in English 100 books, 50 of which were to be taken in hand almost at once. Each book was to contain from 200 to 250 pages and was to be priced at Rs. 1-12-0.

It is our intention to publish the books we select, not only in English, but also in the following Indian languages: Hindi, Bengali, Gujarati, Marathi, Tamil, Telugu, Kannada and Malayalam.

This scheme, involving the publication of 900 volumes, requires ample funds and an all-India organization. The Bhavan is exerting its utmost to supply them.

The objectives for which the Bhavan stands are the reintegration of the Indian culture in the light of modern knowledge and to suit our present-day needs and the resuscitation of its fundamental values in their pristine vigour.

Let me make our goal more explicit:

We seek the dignity of man, which necessarily implies the creation of social conditions which would allow him freedom to evolve along the lines of his own temperament and capacities; we seek the harmony of individual efforts and social relations, not in any makeshift way, but within the framework of the Moral Order; we seek the creative art of life, by the alchemy of which human limitations are progressively transmuted, so that man may become the instrument of God, and is able to see Him in all and all in Him.

The world, we feel, is too much with us. Nothing would uplift or inspire us so much as the beauty and aspiration which such books can teach.

In this series, therefore, the literature of India, ancient and modern, will be published in a form easily accessible to all. Books in other literatures of the world, if they illustrate the principles we stand for, will also be included.

This common pool of literature, it is hoped, will enable the reader, eastern or western to understand and appreciate currents of world thought, as also the movements of the mind in India, which, though they flow through different linguistic channels, have a common urge and aspiration.

Fittingly, the Book University's first venture is the *Mahabharata,* summarized by one of the greatest living Indians, C. Rajagopalachari; the second work is on a section of it, the *Gita* by H.V. Divatia, an eminent jurist and a student of philosophy. Centuries ago, it was proclaimed of the *Mahabharata:* "What is not in it, is nowhere." After twenty-five centuries, we can use the same words about it. He who knows it not, knows not the heights and depths of the soul; he misses the trials and tragedy and the beauty and grandeur of life.

The *Mahabharata* is not a mere epic: it is romance, telling the tale of heroic men and women and of some who were divine; it is a whole literature in itself, containing a code of life, a philosophy of social and ethical relations, and speculative thought on human problems that is hard to rival; but, above all, it has for its core the *Gita,* which is, as the world is beginning to find out, the noblest of scriptures and the grandest of sagas in which the climax is reached in the wondrous Apocalypse in the Eleventh Canto.

Through such books alone the harmonies underlying true culture, I am convinced, will one day reconcile the disorders of modern life.

I thank all those who have helped to make this new branch of the Bhavan's activity successful.

MOST HUMBLY DEDICATED

TO

THE GREAT YOGIRAJ,

SHREE SADGURU SHANKAR MAHARAJ,

THE GURU AND GUIDE.

PREFACE

Towards the Silver Crests of the Himalayas is being presented to the public in an autobiographical form.

The radiance, the grandeur, and the beauty of the Himalayas is known to the whole world. The Silver Crests form that part of the Himalayas which slopes towards Tibet, the so-called roof of the world. It is in this part that many Spiritual Seekers and Seers have taken their abodes in its snow-covered caves.

The Supreme, the Unknown, the Ultimate Truth is their objective. To offer any opinion on their work and worth, is not the aim of this book. These spiritually perfect personages with their immense and uncanny spiritual powers are always trying to help mankind as a whole, to attain the highest levels of evolution, if not complete transformation. This is the faith of all Spiritual Seekers. The title is meant to symbolise this faith.

The names in the book are imaginary and have nothing to do with persons living or dead. I have only attempted to illustrate my personal experiences while in the presence of my Spiritual Guide and Guru, as well as in company of other Seekers. The situations have been selected either to explain or state some everlasting truths, my own experiences and convictions.

I leave it to my readers to judge the success of my efforts.

I am highly indebted to Dr. D.G. Vinod, M.A., Ph.D., Nyaya-Ratna, Darshanalankar, who has also the honour of being a Fellow of the Royal Society of Arts, London. An Eighty-Nation Conference of World Pacifists at Tokyo, Japan (1954) has elected and honoured Dr. Vinod as 'World Peace Ambassador.' He has kindly contributed a masterly Introduction to this book. His Sadhana in the Himalayan Mantra-Tantra lore is well known. His achievements are great. I feel proud for his deep affection for myself and for my whole family. I hardly find words to express my sense of gratitude for his Introduction.

Had it not been for the valuable help rendered to me by my daughter Mrs. Sumitra Mohan Parulkar, M.A., Mr. D.G. Brahme, and Mr. S.P. Karve, this book would not have been completed. Last but not the least, I have to thank Mr. S.A. Deshpande and Mr. S.G. Nevatia for their help in getting the book printed early.

- G. K. PRADHAN

Gokhale Road,

Thana (Central Rly.)

PREFACE TO THE SECOND EDITION

We have great pleasure in presenting to the readers the second edition of the book written by our revered father, the late Shri G. K. Pradhan.

In fact the need for its publication was pressing us for the last two years as we were regularly receiving number of enquiries about the book from readers as well as booksellers.

We must acknowledge that, being too inexperienced in the field of metaphysics and being too much engrossed in our worldly affairs, we were unable to evaluate the greatness of the inheritance left to us by our revered father. However, better late than never. We have, therefore, decided to rectify the mistake by publishing the second edition of the book.

The book is being published in a paper-back edition at a low price suitable for everyone's pocket so that anyone desirous of spiritual attainment can get guidance from it.

We must acknowledge the generous help of Padmashri D.M. Dahanukar, who has donated Rs. 5,000/- from Shri Dattatraya Dahanukar Charitable Trust as a token of appreciation after reviewing the book when it was first published. We should also make a special mention of Shri Arvind N. Mafatlal who donated Rs.500/- as a token of appreciation after reviewing the book when it was first published.

We must also acknowledge the letters of appreciation received by our father from the late Shri P.K. Atre, Padmabhushan Shri P.L.Deshpande and Shri F.A. Fazalbhoy, which have encouraged us to take up the publication work in hand.

This publication would not have been possible without the partners of Messrs. Laxmi Syndicate coming forward to advance the necessary finance for this publication.

Lastly, we are thankful to the Bharatiya Vidya Bhavan for undertaking the publication.

- G. K. PRADHAN'S FAMILY

B/32, Pandurang Society
Juhu, Santacruz (West)
Bombay

November 14, 1975

PREFACE TO THE THIRD EDITION

I am grateful to the Bharatiya Vidya Bhavan for publishing the new edition of my father's book *Towards the Silver Crests of the Himalayas.* They had already published the second edition and it was out of print for a long time. There has been persistent demand for this book from readers all over India and abroad and I am really sorry that, due to personal problems, I have taken a long time in giving my consent for the printing of the third edition of this book. My sincere apologies to all the readers who have been anxiously waiting for the book.

Looking back *Towards the Silver Crests of the Himalayas* after a period of twenty years I feel very peaceful and happy.

When we, my father and I, started writing the book in the year 1953, I had hardly dreamt that the book would be so much acclaimed by the public. Today, it has been translated into four Indian languages, namely Marathi, Hindi, Gujarati and Tamil (which is under print).

Over a period of time, as the readership gathered momentum, we - the author's family members and publishers - have received numerous letters from readers showing tremendous inquisitiveness about the author's personal and spiritual life and various aspects discussed in the book. I take this opportunity to place before the readers some information to satisfy their keenness.

In the first place, this is not an autobiography of the author or any member of our family or his friend. As stated by the author in the Preface of the first edition, it is "presented in an autobiographical form and names in the book are imaginary and have nothing to do with the persons living or dead." However, at the same time he says: "I have only attempted to illustrate my personal experiences while in the presence of my spiritual guru as well as in the company of other seekers." This conveys that the various incidents in the book as well as the philosophical concepts and elucidations thereof have been experienced, witnessed or conceived by the author in his spiritual life or journey toward seeking the Supreme, the Unknown, the Ultimate Truth. They may or may not have been in the same chronological order as the life of Madhav, the central figure of the book, and similarly, may not have happened in the same family. All these gems - rubies, diamonds and pearls - have been beautifully strung into the necklace of the imaginary life-story of Madhav, a promising, bright, athletic youth from our educated middle class family. Again, as the author rightly says in the Preface: "The situations have been selected either to explain or state some everlasting truths, my experiences and convictions."

Many of the readers have asked me the question: "When had he been to the Himalayas? The description of the places mentioned in the book is so realistic that unless a person goes to these places such description won't be possible." To the best of my knowledge, my father was a widely-travelled person but had never been to the Himalayas. He might have visited these places in his astral travels to which his Gurudeo occasionally used to take him.

Lastly, as regards my father's personal achievements in this field I can only say that he never used to talk about himself and that we came to know about his spiritual achievements, only after his death, through his co-disciples.

Six months before his death he used to tell us that his ticket was ready in his pocket and that he would bid farewell as soon as he would get the Divine Call.

It did happen that way. On 7th November 1963, he went to his office as usual. He was in a very happy mood that day.

At about two o'clock a cup of tea was offered to him. He went to wash his face, came back and sat down to have tea. He just bent down near the photograph of his Gurudev on his table. The late Shri K.K. Asher, his business partner and co-disciple, was opposite him and asked him as to what had happened. He just complained of a little pain in the chest. By the time Shri Asher approached him he put his head down and collapsed. That was how the self-realised pure soul ended his life-journey. The end was very peaceful.

I hope whatever little I know about my father and about the book would be sufficient to satisfy the curiosity of the readers.

The interested readers may visit the Samadhi of my father's Gurudev Shri Sadguru Shankar Maharaj. It is situated at Pune-Satara road - off Swargate, opposite Padmavati. It is a very quiet and peaceful place.

- SUMITRA PARULKAR

B/32 Pandurang Society
Juhu, Santacruz (West),
Bombay

August 29, 1982

INTRODUCTION
By
MAHARSHI Dr. D. G. VINOD
Nyaya-Ratna, Darshanalankar

I

THIS book by Shri G.K. Pradhan is both a document of personal experience and a parable. It begins with a dream, apparently simple and normal. Towards the end, however, the contents of the whole dream become a reality.

This raises several problems for the students of psychology and para-psychology. There is little light available from Freud and Adler. Dr. Jung's view of such a dream might be useful to some extent. In terms of his Depth Psychology, the Dream in this book is the Projected Ideal which always has a germ for self-actualisation. Dr. Freud could have interpreted it as the distorted shape of some sex-inspired longing!

Dr. Jung was himself an advanced spiritual seeker. He often used the word "Shadow" in the sense of the past Karmic influence. He had himself confessed it to me, in August 1951, at his home in Zurich (Switzerland), that the Karma theory of the ancient Indian thinkers is "the only possible rational approach to the several Imponderables" involved in any effort towards understanding the Human Personality.

In modern science, there are some Imponderables, which are accepted as such and there is no further "Why" about them, since results conclusively justify the existence of such an Imponderable. An instance in point is Max Planck's Constant which has proved to be one of the most fundamental Constants in Nature.

On some theoretical ground Max Planck happened to conclude that each physical quantum carries an amount of Energy given by the equation E = hv, where E is Energy, v is the frequency of the Radiation and h is the Constant, discovered by himself. The Constant is a very, very small but a precise and inexorable number, equal to 26 zeros followed by 6624. How does Max Planck arrive at this number? He does not know it himself, nor does anyone else. It is only on the basis of this Constant that almost the whole progress of Physics in the last fifty years has taken place. Einstein himself had told me in November 1953, at his home in Princeton, that he had continuously used this Constant since 1905.

I am mentioning this Constant here because it is an Imponderable, frankly accepted by modern science. In his reference, Sir Arthur Eddington has observed that "Any True Law of Nature is likely to seem irrational to rational man." The Law of Karma might appear irrational to rational man but it need not be really irrational, since the results logically justify its existence. Super-Sense, E.S.P., Sixth Sense, Intuition or whatever name we give it, justifies its claim to validity, because the results they produce become rationally acceptable.

Dream experience has a Coherence, a cause-effect continuum of *its own.* This proposition may be readily acceptable. But that the dream experience has also a kind of Coherence and continuity with the actual, wakeful world of experience, is a proposition which it is rather hard to digest. Here is another Imponderable which we could never reject since actual results can validate its truth.

This book is a suggestive study in the complexities of the Law of Karma, and also of the Dream Dimension of Experience.

II

Two volumes by J.M. Dunne come to mind: "An Experiment with Time" and "The Serial Universe." In these two rather remarkable books of our time, Dr. Dunne has pressed under service, highly complex, mathematical formulae to prove that Reality is always there in a finished form of its own, and that Time is only a Screen, projected by Human Intelligence to comprehend the Reality, with a severely limited apparatus of understanding. Man can never perceive Reality *as a whole* and exactly as It is. He is able to understand It, only in improvised Constructs. Time is a convenient Projection to facilitate Man's "Adventure of Ideas," so as to have Reality mirrored in his mind, at least as much as needed to make his life on earth possible and worthwhile. The past, the present and the future are only our own Constructs. They are not, out there, as genuine parts or even aspects of the fundamental Reality.

In terms of the ultimate Reality, the contents of our Dream experience are the same as the contents of our wakeful experience. We view them as separate order of experience, because we have evolved the Construct of time and the three areas of past, present and future. According to Dr. Dunne, a dream and its actualisation has nothing mysterious about it. Indeed every dream is nothing less than its actuality or its material manifestation. Dr. Dunne has given even historical data to prove his thesis.

Two girls, sitting in a public garden of Paris, could see and describe what had happened there, twelve hundred years before; The battle, the bloodshed, the corpses, etc. Of course, the two girls were in a trance and had transcended the time-space limitations, completely. Whatever they saw and said had been recorded, studied, and compared with the old historical documents. Everything tallied marvellously. Likewise a glimpse into future could be equally accurate. A farmer, also in trance, had uttered a prophecy: "A palace will be built beyond some few yards, after seven years." This also came true, to a word. I have presented Dr. Dunne's thesis here, because it offers a scientific authentication of the whole *background* music of Baba Pradhan's thought-provoking book.

III

Here is a brief story portraying the spiritual evolution of the Human Individual. It has been told in an intimately personal manner, and yet the constant content of its meaning and message is purely objective and universal. The whole presentation is so picturesque and realistic that sometimes the vivid phrases of the author seem to turn into colours and paints, his pen frequently revealing the hidden brush inside itself!

The logic of its inner ideology, as the story unfolds itself before the mind's eye of the reader, becomes inexorable and compelling. Any other alternatives to the experiences and events detailed, delineated in the book, seem altogether impossible. Everything that happens has a must about it. It can never be otherwise than what has actually taken shape. When a reader feels the must-ness, the compulsion, the inevitability in the emergence and succession of the events and occurrences, it is certain that the story has achieved a remarkable degree of structural excellence. This book certainly fulfils the test. The reader turns page after page till he reaches the end, and throughout his perusal he has a strange longing that the actual end should never arrive! The simplicity, the sincerity, and the spontaneity of the author keep the reader's heart attached and attuned to the moving rhythms of the soft and smooth unfoldment of this great tale.

Shree Baba Pradhan, the author, does not decorate the treatment of his theme by weighty quotes and an ostentatious drapery of style and phrase. Everything is so simple and so natural. Most of the characters involved are perfectly normal, eminently rational persons. Together they are a fine and acceptable set of people. This atmosphere is a grand asset to the Hero's Extra-Sensory pursuits and also to the Superhuman sunshine of the Gurudeva. Both the normal and the supernormal in human life seem to have intimately coalesced, as if to make the whole presentation a lovely and intriguing picture.

IV

Baba Pradhan wrote this book as an expression of the great creative crisis in his personal life. At such a crisis, man has to make one supreme choice from amongst a million alternatives. Every serious crisis involves a near-death point. A creative crisis means that the challenge of total ruin has been accepted but turned into a new beginning, a fresh rebirth.

It is out of our own ashes that we have to create the golden image of our highest Ideal, our truest God.

Baba Pradhan has presented here, in these pages, his sufferings and struggles and revealed his strategy for peace: A complete surrender at the feet of the Master.

He thought and thought, he sought and sought and he fought and fought! He *felt* dimly and deeply; he *willed* weakly and savagely. He played like a child, and also worked like a monster. Then came finally the Moment of stupendous discovery, and supreme delight. He discovered that all his straining and struggling had landed him at the very starting point. Like the Chinese philosopher Laotze, Baba Pradhan came to conclude that the best, and indeed the *only*, way to purify the muddy water *is* to leave it alone. Baba left himself severely alone. He ceased to do everything and anything about himself! He achieved a freedom from slavery to his own will. He burnt all the books, stopped his prayers, jettisoned all his tin-gods and entered the Great Silence and the Grand Nothing. It was then and there, that the Master came to him.

Baba offered, at his feet, all what he was and all what he had!

V

In this age of long-distance missiles, thermo-nuclear weapons and the outer space travels which could encircle the entire globe, this book, like just a few others of its kind, has an urgent message for the modern man. For western readership in particular, this book should prove of great assistance and inspiration.

Are we conscious that there is something like an Inner Space of which the present man is not even dimly aware?

In this ancient land, the Inner Space has been explored and even conquered, to an astonishing measure. The Inner Space Aeronauts, the Master Scientists and Seers, have discovered the Laws and Truths, the facts and realities which are far more significant, far more fundamental, to the evolution of Man, and to the process and progress of his self-perfection.

Baba Pradhan is anxious to strike a new note for the attention of the present man. He wishes the human world to turn its gaze inward. He is trying to impart a corrective to the modern deification of the sensuous and the successful. He has himself discovered that true success lies in the achievement of "Peace that passeth understanding." He has passed through the trials, tragedies, and tribulations which beset the path of every Sadhaka and Seeker. In his case the Master had some special considerations. Baba could bear the burden of trials with enviable ease. Why the special considerations for him? In my view, and I must say it out, now and here, Baba Pradhan's self-surrender to his Master's Will has always been of some superior strength and quality.

In this book, there is much to be discovered in-between the lines and around the words. I sincerely offer my fond appreciation and affectionate admiration for dear Baba's great performance. He stays mirrored in this book. I recommend every one to have a close look into the reflected image of his ever-aspiring Soul.

It will be a richly rewarding experience.

- D. G. VINOD

CONTENTS

PART – I

CHAPTER I

I WAS climbing a hill; visibility was poor. All around me there was thick fog and though it was late dawn, the sun was hardly visible. All was quiet but the calm was occasionally broken by faint whisperings of the birds from distance. Despite the intense cold, I was feeling warm, due to exertions of the walk which was difficult owing to steep ascent. Humming a popular note, I reached the top.

By now the sun had risen and the enchanting view round about thrilled me with joy. It was really wonderful and worth all the labour I had taken. All around, the mountain peaks were crowned with golden snow; the plains were under the snow-white mantle designed by green spots where the snow was thin and melted by the heat of the sun. The beautiful sight round about, the tender rising sun, the soft breeze, the perfect calm, made the whole of it so fascinating that for some time, I completely forgot myself. In spite of cold, I was feeling buoyant and energetic. A thought of going over the top of another hill nearby thrilled me; I had hardly taken two long strides in that direction when I became aware of some movement behind me. I knew that I was all alone in the hills away from the humanity, enjoying the most beautiful scenery without the danger of being disturbed. I therefore turned round with a start to find that I was not alone.

A towering figure with very broad shoulders, a most captivating smile on his half-parted lips was standing hardly a yard away from me. He was a sanyasi in saffron-coloured robe. Here was the most attractive personality I had ever seen. His skin was soft white-red, had a most handsome face, sparkling big eyes with overflowing kindness in them and a muscular figure that seemed to possess super-human strength. A profuse growth of golden hair was tied with a knot on his massive head, strings of rudraksha-beads adorned his full white neck. He carried in his right hand a big three-pronged spear and had put on wooden sandals. I always considered myself sufficiently tall, being a little over six feet; but he seemed at least eight to ten inches taller than me.

My turning with a start, staring at him with a surprise seemed to have amused him. In a sweet but firm voice he said: “Don’t you step forward. There isn’t any way there. What looks to you a heap of snow is nothing but a crevice thousands of feet deep under the snow. Nothing will be left of you if you take a step further. You are not acquainted with these hills and it is dangerous for people like you to move about without a guide. The idea of fun may cost you your life. Now like a good lad, follow me and I will see that you are safe on your way home." A feeling of gratitude came over me; I bowed down with a sort of reverence and said: "Sir, whoever you may be, I shall ever remain grateful to you for saving my life." He laughed loudly exposing his perfect white teeth and said: "Hurry up, we are already late. The melting snow will make our descent dangerous." Without a word, I followed him. The way down was easy but at places made perilous by the melting snow that made the ground under the feet slippery. The Sadhu was walking with perfect ease and helped me now and then over the risky points. We must have walked a good distance when he stopped near a snow-covered rock. He crossed it with ease and I followed him with some difficulty.

To my surprise I found that we were at the mouth of a cave. He softly whistled and out came two ferocious-looking dogs that fell at his feet as if with human understanding. He fondlingly picked them up in his strong arms and said "Don't be afraid of them; they are harmless though a little naughty." We entered the cave which was spacious, cosy and comfortable. It was warm inside. Pains seemed to have been taken to keep it spotlessly clean. Tiger, stag and deer skins were spread on the floor with an eye for taste. Woollen blankets were neatly folded and kept in one corner while a square fire-place with fire burning in, was in the other. Through the openings at the top, enough light was received in the cave; but no snow or water seemed to be coming through them.

A sweet delicate perfume pervaded throughout. The whole set-up had such a superb blending that it created a celestial atmosphere, which even a staunch atheist could not deny. He asked me to sit down and said: "You are tired; have some rest. I will see if I can offer you something." He spread his hands and before I could understand how it happened, he produced a bowl of hot steaming milk. He placed the bowl before me and said: "Drink the milk. It will refresh you. There is nothing refreshing like a cow's milk in the world." I was feeling tired and thirsty. So the hot milk was not only desirable but was a God-sent. It was sweet and delicious in taste. I drank the whole of it and put the bowl down empty. Smiling he said: "Look here my dear child, the cave belongs to you and one day you shall come here." I had no inferiority complex in me but somehow the superior personality of the Sadhu and the atmosphere of cave silenced down my otherwise inquisitive and talkative nature. I, therefore, did not ask him any question, though I did not understand what he said. He saw a puzzled look on my face and said: "You won't understand what I am saying but one day you will realise the truth. It is already late for you to go home and I need not detain you any more." With these words he asked the dogs to take me down the hill. I got up, bowed down to him with reverence, thanked him for all the kindness shown to me and followed the dogs out. It was late morning; the sun had fairly risen and the snow outside was fast melting; while avoiding a rock my foot slipped; I tried to regain balance but came down heavily instead. I must have fainted because when I opened my eyes there was dark all around. I tried to feel my head to see if it was injured. I was surprised to feel something soft under my head. Full consciousness rushed unto me and I sat up. Oh, I was in my room sitting in my comfortable bed with a soft blanket on. I switched on the light, consulted my watch. It was 4 o'clock in the morning. I had experienced a wonderful dream. It was rather early to get up. I switched off the light and tried to sleep. Sleep was impossible. The dream had started a train of thoughts in my mind. After an hour of futile efforts I got up, prepared a cup of tea and left my room with a racket in hand for the tennis court.

CHAPTER II

BORN with a silver spoon in my mouth, I belonged to an old aristocratic family. We had large estates and number of properties. Ours was an educated family that occupied a place of importance in society as well as in Government. Though Hindu by religion and Brahman by caste, we prided ourselves in being called reformers and performed no religious practices at home. Not only that but it was more observed in breach than in practice and we displayed our intolerance towards such things whenever possible. We firmly believed that religion, its practices, castes, different creeds, innumerable temples with gods, idols and other images have been responsible for the downfall of India as a whole and the degeneration of the entire social order in the country in particular. The damage had been done to such an extent that it had been possible for a handful of foreigners to rule our great country and shackle this vast population in fetters of slavery.

My father in his later life became member of Brahma Samaj or something like that, but I think it was partly due to his friends and partly as a fashion in those days. He, however, never brought his faith home. I was thus born an atheist and never offered prayers or visited temples.

My father was a distinguished pleader and my mother was fairly educated, being in college when she was married. She, too, belonged to a well-known Brahmin family and had inherited good fortune, being the only daughter of her parents. I had two elder brothers who were well settled in life. The eldest was called to Bar and the elder was a highly qualified Doctor passed from London College of Physicians. Both of them were practising in Bombay and had earned a reputation in their own sphere. Ours was thus a happy, compact family. I was a student of Deccan College, Poona, studying in Junior B.A. class and staying in the College Hostels. We looked upon this College as our family institution as all the members of our family had received their education here. Being more inclined towards sports, I had no claims over scholarships but was considered an intelligent good student. In the realm of sports I had done good and was considered above average in various games. I was little over six feet in height, athletic in build and was considered handsome. I was good at shot and a trained wrestler.

After playing a couple of sets at the tennis court, I returned to my room, had my breakfast and went to college. Inspite of the daily routine I could not forget my dream, particularly the sadhu and his cave. We were to play final of the Inter-University Cricket Championship match next week and I was expected at the field in the afternoon for practice, but I excused myself on the plea of headache. Though in excellent health, I was in a way in disturbed state of mind and was unable to concentrate on any work. As an alternative I decided to take a long walk or boating if available.

I had hardly turned towards the river when I heard somebody calling me from behind. I turned round to meet my friend Ramesh who fell in step with me. He said: "Madhav, how is it that you are in mufti instead of your cricket outfit? Are you going for any special work or to keep any appointment?" I said: "Nothing like that. I do not feel like playing today and have decided to take a long walk or boating if a boat is available." He informed me that the college boat was under repairs and would take about a week more to be of any service. He further informed me that he was going to the city to attend a lecture being delivered by a famous swami on the Synthesis of Hindu Philosophy at Servants of India Society. He said: "If you have no particular work, why don't you come with me to the lecture? We will sit if it is interesting; otherwise leave early."

Ramesh was in the same class with me but he was a student of Philosophy while I was that of Economics. He was a first class student and had many scholarships to his credit. He was a good debater and was liked by all for his jolly good nature. Inspite of our different tastes and temperaments, we were great chums. I thought his company would cheer up my spirits better than a lone walk on the banks of the river. I, therefore, agreed to accompany him to the lecture. I do not deny a thought in mind to see if there was any resemblance in the lecturer Swami and the Sadhu of my dream.

The hall was packed to the full when we went in. We secured a place with difficulty from whence we could see and hear the lecturer. After the usual formalities of introduction were over, the Swami got up to speak. I was, however, disappointed to find no resemblance between the speaker and the Sadhu of my dream. He was a good platform speaker and seemed to have mastery over the subject. He quoted profusely with ease various Indian as well as Western philosophers while establishing infallibility of non-dualistic (monistic) theory so ably expounded by the great Shree Shankaracharya. He was not only an exponent of it but substantiated it so ably with masterly arguments that everyone of us felt convinced about its absolute truth. Ramesh was very highly impressed and said that it was a treat to hear him. Philosophy was not my subject and I did not understand much of what he had said. After the lecture Ramesh went to see some of his relations and I was left alone. I thought of going to cinema to see if I could get some entertainment there. I visited various theatres on the way but there wasn't any picture that could be called interesting. I cursed the theatre owners as well as the public for their low, out of date taste and returned to my room at about 9 P.M. I had hardly opened my room when our hostel peon came running and handed me a yellow envelope.

It was a telegram. I opened it hastily with curiosity as well as with a little nervousness. I do not know why, but I always feel a bit nervous while opening telegrams. I think, partly because of the urgency of the message and partly due to ignorance of the nature of contents. I heaved a sigh of relief. It was from my father intimating that he was arriving early next morning and I was asked to meet him at the station. Just then the hostel bell rang announcing the last sitting of the dinner and I hastily went to our mess. I had no appetite but found Ramesh at the table waiting for me. He had just returned and had made straight for the mess on hearing the bell. He was talking about the lecture in superlative terms and was surprised at the Swami's profound study of Philosophy. After dinner I returned to my room with an idea of going to bed immediately to make up for the last night sleep. I set alarm at five o'clock in the morning to be in time at the station to meet my father. I was about to switch off the light when I heard knocking at my doors. Rather reluctantly I opened the door. The Captain of our cricket team entered my room with two members. He enquired about my health with concern. We discussed at length about the final cricket match due next week. Everybody including our Principal was interested in the match as the reputation of our college depended upon it. The Principal had particularly asked the Captain to enquire about my health as I did not attend the practice. It was past eleven when he left and I went to bed. I was rather doubtful of sound sleep, but hardly I had put off the light and adjusted my pillows, my eyes were closed.

CHAPTER III

I WOKE up with a start; it was five in the morning and the alarm was ringing. I must have had a sound sleep as I felt quite fit and fresh when I got up. With a cup of tea I left my hostel for the station. It was not possible to get any conveyance so early in the morning in the vicinity of our hostel which was situated at a great distance from the railway station as well as the city. I always enjoyed long walks and had ample time on hand. At the station I learnt that the train was late by about forty minutes; so I made for the newspaper stall for buying a morning paper. I bought a copy of the *Times of India*, a Bombay daily, that had just come. While I was paying money, my attention was drawn towards a book titled "Mystics of India." Ordinarily a book of that sort would not interest me, but surprisingly enough, I asked the price and purchased it. I thought my sub-conscious mind was very active and the suppressed curiosity impelled me to go in for the book. With the morning paper and book in hand, I marched towards the waiting room, which was empty and I was the sole occupant. The porter told me that no train leaves Poona so early and hence the waiting room, otherwise packed to the full during the day, was deserted then.

I spread my paper on the big round table, pulled a chair and started scanning the news. I read the paper; folded it neatly and was about to open the book, when I felt somebody standing at the waiting room door. I raised my eyes and saw Hari, the driver of uncle Gokhale, smiling at me. He came in and said: "I had thought sir, you would come. I am here to receive your father; my master has sent his car."

Mr. Gokhale, a famous Poona pleader, enjoying a large lucrative practice was my father's friend almost from his boyhood. They were in the same college and were graduated together. They were moreover in the same profession and worked together on many cases. Mr. Gokhale was known to us as uncle Gokhale almost from our very birth. There were no formalities between our two families and whenever in Poona, we stayed with him. Inspite of my being in the college hostel, I had to go to his place for meals every now and then and particularly on holidays.

The station bell rang announcing the arrival of the train. We hurried to the platform. The train had leisurely crawled in. All on the platform were alert to find out the people they had come to receive. My father in his usual calm way was standing fully dressed in the door of his compartment. He saw us and smiled. We hurried towards his compartment. He stepped out and Hari took out his luggage. I bowed down in respect; he patted me on the back and asked me how I was doing. I found him in excellent health with a radiant face lit up with smile as usual. Even in late fifties he looked handsome; walked straight and carried himself aristocratically. He had a sort of magnetic charm about him. We came out of the station talking to each other. Hari, in the meanwhile had drawn the car to the station steps. We got in and were speeding towards uncle Gokhale's bungalow.

Uncle Gokhale had just returned from walk when we entered his compound. He was at the door along with Mrs. Gokhale to receive my father. I left my father in the hall and went in search of Shrikant, the second son of Mr. Gokhale and Malati, his only daughter. Shrikant was almost ready to come down for tea and Malati on hearing my voice came out of her room to greet me laughing. We all went down together and joined the elders at the table, where hot dishes and tea pots were waiting for us. We formed our group and allowed the elders to talk themselves out.

Mr. Gokhale had two sons and a daughter; his eldest son was sent to England for further studies in medicine but he did not return after taking his M.D. from London University. He settled there and was said to be doing nice. Shrikant was in the second year of the college, preparing for the intermediate examination and Malati was to appear for Matriculation. Shrikant was tall and strong but because of his reserved nature, he was not very popular. Though a clever student, he was supposed to be a bit proud by his fellow students but, with us he was free and we found him to be of amiable nature. Malati was blossoming into a striking beauty, possessing attractive figure and radiant health. She was in her early teens, talkative and of jolly disposition. She was an intelligent student and was fairly accomplished in fine arts.

Soon after tea my father told me that he would look me up at the hostel, as soon as he was free from his court work. I took leave of uncle Gokhale and left.

Late in the afternoon when I returned to my room, I learnt that uncle Gokhale and my father were waiting for me in the hall. I was just thinking of going to the hall when I saw them coming towards my room. My father, on entering the room, looked about in a way parents do. Both of them asked me how I was getting on with my studies and as to my health, they were pleased to see that I was keeping fit. While I was changing for going out with them, my father lifted the book lying on my table and was bit surprised to read the title "Mystics of India." He asked me how I came about the book and did not say anything when I told him that I purchased it in the morning. He smiled when I hastily added that I did not get time even to open the book. We left together in Mr. Gokhale's car and after a good ride, were at his bungalow at about six in the evening. It was too early for dinner and I knew that Shrikant would not be at home; but I was sure to find Malati playing on violin. A servant told uncle Gokhale that he had a visitor and so I left both of them and went upstairs to find Malati. As expected Shrikant was not in and I was informed that Malati was talking to the visitor in her father's room as Mrs. Gokhale was out. I, therefore, made myself comfortable in Shrikant's room and picked up a book to read. Just then I heard my father's voice calling me down. On coming down I was surprised to see the Swami who had delivered the lecture last evening at the Servants of India Society, sitting there, chatting amiably.

CHAPTER IV

I WAS introduced to the Swami by my father who it seemed knew him well. Swamiji was an entertaining speaker and everybody was listening to him with interest. It was a light talk and no serious subject was under discussion. I told him that I attended his lecture yesterday. So he asked me how I liked it. I promptly told him that philosophy was not my subject and I did not understand it to a measure I should have. Everybody in the room including my father looked at me with astonishment; showing thereby as if I had done something which was not expected of me. I had, therefore, to explain that I had accompanied Ramesh known to all of them who was interested in subjects like philosophy. Just then Mrs. Gokhale who had returned, entered the room and joined us.

My father asked Swamiji his personal experiences in mysticism and whether there is any truth in what is said to be supernatural powers. He further asked whether he had met any person who could be said to have realised and attained perfection.

Swamiji looked at me and said that in his young days, he was an atheist and never believed in God or in any form of worship. He had a brilliant career at the University and after obtaining his master's degree, he was appointed a professor. Accidentally he met Gurudeo, a perfect Saint; who entirely changed the course of his life. He said that he did not praise Gurudeo only because he happened to be his Guru, but he was one of those few, who had realised and attained perfection. He naturally possessed what you call supernatural powers, but does not consider it as an attainment of any particular significance. Swamiji added that it was a stroke of good fortune that Gurudeo accepted him as disciple which normally he does not do. Swamiji was unmarried and had no encumbrances. He lost his parents when he was hardly ten years old. The small fortune that his father had left for him enabled him to complete his education. None was affected when he took Sanyas and changed his worldly life into that of an ascetic. He spent years with his Gurudeo, following his instructions and practising various things told by him. He was now happy and perfectly peaceful. He had no attachments, ambitions, desires and therefore no disappointments, frustrations or sorrows. Physical ailments, he said, are unavoidable and did not disturb his peace of mind. He had no fixed abode and was a constant traveller. He had visited Poona number of times and had a large number of acquaintances. This time he was requested to give a talk and that is how he came to address people the other day at the Servants of India Society. He was leaving next morning for Bombay and was there to see Mr. Gokhale and his family before going. He did not expect to meet my father, but was pleased to meet him as well as me. My father invited him to Ahmednagar and stay with him for a few days. He thereupon promised to look up when next in Deccan.

I said: "Excuse me Swamiji, what has made you to believe in God and what has your aimless wanderings throughout the length and breadth of India to do with it? Is it that you are not allowed to stay at one place by your Guru? Have you acquired any powers? I would consider it all nonsense had people of your education and calibre not taken to it. Even then I fail to understand its importance and consider it a waste of time and precious energy." Swamiji laughed loudly displaying his perfect white teeth. He said: "You are still young to understand it, but believe me that the present mysticism is an outcome of practical experiments, that are being carried out for the last ten thousand years or even more. It is not merely a product of guessing or fancy, merely condemning a thing without understanding it, is nothing but vanity. Broadly speaking, whole humanity is toiling for attaining peace and happiness in life. Just observe the life round about you. You will find nothing but conflict, the entire energy directed towards becoming something, running after ambitions, acquisitions and so on. There is no peace, satisfaction and happiness. One has, therefore, to seriously think before condemning whether it is possible to be peaceful and happy by following the teachings of saints and prophets. You would not understand the gravity of the problems unless you apply seriously to it. You can only condemn it, when you are convinced that it serves no purpose and is bogus. Intelligent persons like you should fathom the mysteries to find out the truth and advocate it for the guidance of the people. You should substantiate your arguments by your own experience and should not be led by the opinions of others." Mrs. Gokhale said: "Swamiji, next time you should stay with us and narrate to us your personal experiences in this field." It was getting late and Swamiji had to see somebody. He, therefore, rose to go and uncle Gokhale asked Hari to take Swamiji where he wanted. We all rose and saw him off at the porch.

CHAPTER V

YEARS rolled on and I was out of college with Master's degree in first class. My father had grown old and had almost retired from practice. Opinions in my family were divided as to what I should do in future. My brothers wanted me to proceed to England for further studies either at Oxford or some other University. My father had left the choice to me, while my mother said she would be happy in whatever I do. Personally I had not arrived at any decision, mainly because during the last three or four years, I had developed philosophical tendencies in me and wanted earnestly to probe into the secrets of metaphysics as well as mysticism. During this period, I had formed a sort of intimacy with Swamiji and had read lot of philosophical books written by ancient and modern, Indian as well as foreign, philosophers. For this purpose I had to devote a good deal of my time to study Sanskrit scriptures and the books written by ancient philosophers. To be candid, a sort of urge had developed in me that was driving me towards something unexpected as well as unknown. Physically I was keeping fit, had regular physical exercises and mentally I was undisturbed. I had received offers for service from Government as well as for professorship from my own college. I, however, decided not to engage myself in any serious work for some time;

but to travel all over India in company with Swamiji whenever possible or alone. There were proposals for matrimonial alliances but I did not consider them at all as I thought that it was too early for me to settle in life. Uncle Gokhale had suggested to my father that as I had completed my studies, I should now join his daughter Malati in wedlock. Malati had by now grown up into a beautiful young damsel and was studying in senior B.A. class; while Shrikant had passed his Bachelor of Law in first class. Uncle Gokhale or rather Mrs. Gokhale was not inclined to send him to England for calling at the Bar as she was afraid he might also settle there as his elder brother had done. To the proposal of Mrs. Gokhale, neither myself nor my parents had anything to say against the girl or the family. Uncle Gokhale in one of his letters wrote to my father that my growing interest in philosophy had alarmed him. He was afraid that I might follow Swamiji with whom I was coming into close contact and may turn a Sanyasi one day. My father, however, was not worried and wrote back that I was now fully grown up and it was now my affair to decide the future course of life. He further stated that he had given me the best of education and had sumptuously provided for me for the rest of my life. He was satisfied that he had properly discharged his duties as a father. "It is upto Madhav to decide his career or rather vocation in life. It is no use asking him to marry before he settles in life and he would not consent to any such suggestion even if we were to make it." "I am," he said, "aware of his growing interest in philosophy but I do not think that he will turn a sanyasi; supposing that he finally decides to follow Swamiji's footsteps, it would be sheer folly on our part to ask Malati to marry him, as that would ruin her life. I would consider it a sin to ask her to gamble with her life even for the sake of my son or our family relations. Madhav at present is doing nothing, but let me assure you that the life of an idler will never suit his nature. He has planned an extensive tour of south India and he will be leaving for South soon. I am sure the tour will do him good and also bring him round to the decision about future. Malati has still one year to complete her degree course. It is, therefore, no use hurrying the matters over."

My tour of South India was a success. I visited many places of historical importance as well as those that were famous from the point of view of sight-seers. This part of India is lovely. Though financially poor it is enriched by nature. With its huge forests, great Nilgiri hills, vast plains, beautiful sea-shore, it does make up for its deficiencies in other realms. I came across a hunting party and had quite an exciting time in the forest. I also enjoyed tennis and badminton at some places. Time flew fast and I was now in Mysore. Mysore, the capital of the state, is a city worth to be proud of with its beautiful palaces, extensive well-laid-out gardens and avenues; silk, artistically carved wooden material, sandal oil, sandal wood, etc., occupy a place of importance in the state.

For a long time I was not able to contact Swamiji. I had a great desire to meet him. It was difficult to locate his whereabouts as he was constantly moving from place to place, being an untiring traveller. One evening while returning from walk, I had a pleasant surprise in meeting Swamiji in the street. He was very happy to meet me and was in excellent health as ever. He told me that he had arrived at Mysore that very morning and was trying to contact me. I asked him how he knew that I was in Mysore. He replied only in smile and I understood. He asked me where I was putting up and whether I had chalked out any definite programme of the tour. I told him that I was on aimless tour; had come to Mysore from Ootacamund, down the beautiful Nilgiri hills and had decided to go to Madras. He gave me his address where he was putting up and asked me to see him in the morning at his residence. He was staying in a temple and when I went to see him, he was ready to meet me. It was a big temple of God Shiva built on grand style in which south Indian temples are built. It had a number of stone arches and spacious verandah running on all the four sides of the temple. Number of pilgrims and sanyasis were using it as a resting place. The temple and its surroundings were kept spotlessly clean. He told me that he was on his way to Rameshwaram to meet his Gurudeo who was expected there. He casually asked me whether I would like to accompany him so that I might get a chance of meeting the great Saint as well as visiting Rameshwaram, which from his point of view was worth visiting. By now I had developed a great liking for Swamiji and was naturally curious to see his Guru of whom he always spoke in superlative terms. I also thought that the company of Swamiji would be entertaining; so I decided to avail myself of this opportunity and to visit Madras on my return.

Swamiji was to stay in Mysore for a day or two

and then leave for Rameshwaram. For most of the time during these two days I was with him busy visiting various places and meeting his acquaintances. He told me many interesting things about his Guru and I found him to be in excellent mood. I could attribute that to the prospects of meeting his Guru for which he was so eager. I could understand Swamiji's love and respect for his Guru; but I failed to understand how a man of his education, culture and experience could consider his Guru to be a supernatural being almost like God. By now I had read sufficiently in the line of philosophy and metaphysics but even then I was not in a mental state to accept such a position having been attained by a man. I had explained my views to Swamiji many times over but he always said that I should be patient enough to have my own experiences so that I could base my findings on them. I believed what he said; but convictions I had none, which I must admit. During our discussions, Swamiji tried to convince me with his intellectual arguments based on experiences as well as references from Eastern as well as Western philosophers but those, too, were unable to give me satisfaction. He fully knew of this but never cared about it as he said that one should get one's convictions only through experiences and not by reading books or intellectual understanding. Swamiji's work in Mysore was over and we left for Rameshwaram. Our journey was comfortable, as Swamiji was a good conversationalist and he narrated various incidents in his life, which were vivid as well as interesting.

He was an untiring traveller who had travelled all over India number of times and had acquired mastery over various languages. When we reached Rameshwaram, he cautioned me not to be hasty in forming opinion about Gurudeo but to be patient and observant. At Rameshwaram, we stayed at the house of a Brahmin known to Swamiji who seemed to be a well-known figure there, as I saw everybody that met us wished him. At the house of our host, on making enquiries we learnt that Gurudeo had not come; nor was there any news about his coming. I was disappointed but Swamiji seemed quite unaffected. He said: "Gurudeo is definitely coming and we should be ready to receive him." We had our bath in the sea and went to the temple of Rameshwar for darshan. It was for the first time that I visited South and had no occasion before to see so big a temple. Standing for centuries over acres of lands is a solid huge building, which could easily accommodate thousands of persons. It is very nicely built, well kept even to this day. I further learnt that it is a very wealthy temple, has ample funds at its disposal from large donations given by various Rajas in India and has a steady income of million or over. People from all over India visit the temple and pay respect to Rameshwar; whatever may be its historical or mythological significance, even to this day. Swamiji took me around, showed me various things and explained to me the importance of the temple.

We passed the day moving about in the soft sands on the sea-shore. At night Swamiji explained to me some passages from Shankar Bhasya, the most authoritative treatise written by the great Acharya Shankar on Brahma sutras. I had studied the treatise myself some time back but the style of Swamiji in interpreting as well as explaining it was original.

He also explained to me the various controversies that existed when Acharya wrote this memorable thesis. Before and during the time of Acharya the sutras were being interpreted in various ways and that is how controversies on its interpretation had arisen which necessitated Acharya to write the thesis. Swamiji's mastery over Sanskrit was unquestionable but that did not surprise me so much as his powers of explaining as well as giving the correct idea of how and in what circumstances this world-respected thesis was written. I considered it a treat to hear Swamiji on philosophy. I wished he was a professor in my college and I was sure that Scholars of world repute would have come out of it under his tutelage. So difficult a subject was handled by him in a way that listeners would never forget or miss anything important. I said: "Swamiji, student world would benefit immensely, if you think of giving the advantage of your knowledge to them." He smiled in his normal way and said: "It is all the grace of Guru. I can't stick to any profession or place and teaching cannot be my vocation in life."

It was late at night when we retired. In the morning on our way to the temple after bath, I asked Swamiji whether he had received any information as to when Gurudeo was coming. Swamiji said: "I have a definite message from him and we must wait till he comes, which will not be long. I will also know if there is any change in his programme."

CHAPTER VI

TWO days passed without any news from Gurudeo. Swamiji was calm and self composed. He was in excellent mood and talked a lot. I hardly knew how time flew in his company. It was early morning. I opened my eyes in the bed to see Swamiji standing near me. With sparkling eyes and face beaming with joy he said: "Madhav, get up. We have to go to the temple early. Gurudeo is due at any moment and we should be ready to receive him." I finished my bath etc., and we set out for the temple. After the darshan we came out of the temple and had hardly turned towards the beach when I saw number of persons coming towards the temple in a group, talking loudly. Before I could ask Swamiji what it could possibly be, he caught hold of my hand firmly and started running towards them. As we went near, I saw a person round about whom people had gathered. Swamiji left my hand and rushed to the person on whose feet he put his head and I could hear sobs escaping his mouth. Tears of joy ran down his cheeks. I knew that he was his Gurudeo. He lifted Swamiji and blessed him on head. Swamiji quietly stood aside with respect and I folded my hands and paid my respects to Gurudeo. To me Gurudeo looked a very ordinary person and I could see nothing surprising in him. He was hardly five feet six inches in height, lean in build but had very long arms, broad forehead, skin which could be called fair and eyes which were remarkably big and full of lustre. He had long hair but not well kept. His clothes consisted of a big white gown and white cloth that was wrapped round his head. Both of them were dirty and needed washing. He had a charming way of smiling and easy manners. He casually looked at me and smiled but did not say anything. I thought he was not interested in me. The news of his arrival had spread like a fire in the town and people were rushing from all direction to have his darshan. However, he made his way towards the temple and asked the people to follow him. At the temple the priests and temple authorities, who seemed to know him well, received him cordially and respectfully. He came out after the darshan and sat on the verandah of the temple which was big enough to accommodate any number of persons. People came in batches for his darshan and he had a word of kindness for everyone of them. He enquired about them and their family affairs in such a way as if he knew them intimately. Almost everyone of them had something to ask and he listened to them patiently. I was surprised to hear him speaking various south Indian languages fluently. It was about two o'clock in the afternoon that he was able to leave the temple and accompany us to the place where we were staying. On our way home, I asked him whether he was tired; he only smiled but did not reply. Our host with his family was ready to receive Gurudeo as he entered the house. I could see that he considered himself a privileged person because Gurudeo decided to stay with him. Arrangements were made for Gurudeo's bath. He was bathed with ceremony which was a novel sight for me and I treated it merely as an interesting spectacle. After bath, Gurudeo looked fresh and I could see his long black curly hair which was then properly done. Immediately after bath, food was served. Gurudeo took very little of it while myself and Swamiji did good justice to the food. After dinner Gurudeo retired to the room to relax. Swamiji told me to rest and he himself went in the room of Gurudeo to wait on him.

I was hardly in my room for half an hour when I heard Swamiji calling me. In his room I found Gurudeo resting and Swamiji sitting at his feet. Gurudeo looked at me and asked me to sit by his side. He enquired about my health and also about the health of my parents. He talked about us in a way as if he knew all of us intimately and that made me completely at ease. He had a sweet voice with a ring in it. His eyes otherwise shining with abundant energy, were sometimes completely vacant as if he was engrossed in thought, looking towards a very distant object. He asked me whether I was in a hurry to go to Madras and whether I had any particular appointment with anybody there. I told him that I was only on a pleasure trip and wanted to meet a friend of mine who was a professor in one of the colleges there, as I happened to be in the South. With me he spoke in Marathi, which happened to be my mother-tongue. He wielded the language so fluently that it was difficult even for me to say that he did not belong to my province. Since morning I saw him speaking number of languages so that it was as difficult to say to what province he belonged as also to judge his age. He casually asked me my decision about marriage and how I was feeling about Malati, the daughter of Mr. Gokhale. Though casual, the question was so sudden that I was nonplussed for a moment. He could read that from my face and without waiting for my answer he asked Swamiji some other information. I was more puzzled to see that he was not at all keen about my answers to his questions. It was really difficult to form any opinion about him from his talk and the questions which, from my point of view, had no relevance. He told me to rest for some time and that I should be ready to go out with him after about an hour. With this he seemed to have dismissed me and I went to my room. Gurudeo greatly disturbed my mind as I was not able to form any opinion about him. I had never come across a stranger personality than Gurudeo. Swamiji had told me many stories about his mystic powers, knowledge and attainments. I did not accept them all as true then and even now I was hardly in a position to say anything about him. To me he did not look a mysterious or powerful person or a great saint. At the moment he was definitely a puzzling personality and hence I postponed my opinion to a later period.

Thoughts were rushing into my head and it was difficult to rest. I tried to read a book but could not concentrate. I was restless and I wanted to be in the company of Gurudeo to see more of him, not out of any reverence or respect but I considered his puzzling personality a challenge to my intellect. I definitely wanted to find out who he was and what were real attainments to his credit. I was not prepared to accept him as a superintelligent or a supernatural man.

It was about past four when I heard Swamiji asking me if I was ready. I went to his room and found tea waiting for us. We hardly finished our tea when people who were waiting outside the house started coming in for the darshan of Gurudeo. Gurudeo said that he was going to the temple of Rameshwaram and those who want to meet him may go there. At the temple Gurudeo sat on the verandah and allowed the people to touch his feet. He was blessing everybody. I did not understand what attracted the people to this unassuming figure and what he was capable of giving them. I was watching his movements closely with curiosity. People asked him many questions as well as told him their difficulties. Surprisingly enough he had an answer for everybody and his simple explanations seemed to satisfy them. There was neither any superiority consciousness in him nor did he treat the people with inferiority consideration. One thing, however, did not escape me – that he was being highly respected by people and nobody dared take any liberty with him. He was, moreover, treating them as children and seemed to take interest in a parental way in their complaints as well as difficulties which from my points of view were trifle as well as silly. He told everybody a different thing either to follow or practise and added, if followed correctly, it would give them the relief required. I did not believe a single word that he said and thought that he was putting people off that way.

It was about seven, he said to me: "You look bored, this is a novel experience to you. Let us go out for a walk on the sands." We had a good walk and we sat on the sands. He asked me whether I was in a hurry to return home. I did not understand the significance of his question; so I asked him whether he wanted me to stay. He said that Swamiji was to go next morning to Punjab and he wanted to know whether I would be able to accompany him to Madras, where he said I would be able to see the city as well as my friends. Not only I but Swamiji was also surprised to hear this, but he kept silence. I said to

Gurudeo that I would consider it a great pleasure to go with him but I was doubtful whether he would find my company congenial and helpful as I had no experience of travelling with Saints. I further added that I did not know how to serve, much less a sadhu. He laughed heartily and assured me that I should have no misgivings on that account. He casually asked me what I read on philosophy and how I had understood the various Eastern as well as Western philosophers. He discussed with me the point of view advocated by English, German and French philosophers, which surprised me. I thought, from such a versatile knowledge that he must have read a lot. We returned home late at night and after meals I went to bed.

When I got up in the morning, I learnt that Swamiji had already left and I was to take care of Gurudeo in his absence. I hurriedly finished my bath and accompanied Gurudeo who was ready and waiting for me. Instead of going to the temple, we went to the house of a local merchant who had invited Gurudeo at his residence. When we reached the place, I found that everything was ready for our reception and people had gathered there for the darshan of Gurudeo. I felt shy and rather disturbed, when people tried to treat me with respect because I was with Gurudeo. They would not listen when I tried to explain to them that I was an ordinary being as anyone of them and was not in any way greater than what they were. Gurudeo seemed amused and enjoyed the situation. The mother of our host was too ill to come out and was lying in the bed. Gurudeo enquired of her and we went to her room. She was about eighty years old and seemed to have come to the end of her journey. She tried to get up to pay him her respects, but he very sweetly told her to lie down and sat near her on the bed, stroking her white hair. The old lady was in tears. She was looking at his face as if he was her God. I could see that she was feeling very happy and peaceful by his presence. She asked him who I was and he said that I was a friend of his. I left Gurudeo in the room and came out with the host. I asked him how long he knew Gurudeo. Shockingly enough he said Gurudeo was known to his family long before his birth. I asked him what he thought of Gurudeo's age. He said it should be definitely more than hundred years. To me he looked hardly fifty years and I thought Gurudeo was a problem difficult to be solved. In the afternoon we left for Madras. There was a big gathering at the station to see him off and everybody was disappointed at Gurudeo's short stay. The train was detained for some time as the rush for darshan was very great. Even the railway authorities accepted this as a matter of fact and did not raise any objection. I thought Gurudeo was a challenge to my intellect, education, culture and understanding. Our journey was uneventful. At some stations on the way, people had come to garland Gurudeo. Early morning when our train steamed in Madras station, I found quite a good number of people had come to receive Gurudeo with basketful of garlands. There were some ladies belonging to south-Indian community amidst them. When he stepped out of the compartment there was a rush to touch his feet and he was most profusely garlanded. Mr. Chettiar, one of the multi-millionaires of Madras, was there to receive us; and we were going to stay at his place. My luggage was taken care of by the servants and I accompanied Gurudeo to the waiting car.

CHAPTER VII

MR. CHETTIAR was a well-known businessman of Madras. His family since the time of his father were devotees of Gurudeo. Mr. Chettiar was nearing fifty, was heavily built and of cheerful disposition. Mrs Chettiar was a lady of good reputation, past middle age and was a known social worker. They had one son and a daughter. His son was in business with his father and the daughter was married to a son of a Landlord. His son too was married only a year before. Mr. Chettiar had a big bungalow in a decent locality outside the town which was nicely and tastefully furnished with a beautiful well-laid-out garden. Number of servants were there to look after us and I found myself completely at ease with this jolly good family. I was shown my room immediately on my arrival, opposite to the one given to Gurudeo. After a shave and a bath, I joined Gurudeo in the hall. A lot of people had come to have his darshan. Mr. Chettiar's son and the daughter met me in the hall and took me around their bungalow. Money seemed to have been lavishly spent over this palatial building in furnishing and decorating it. Both the brother and the sister were highly educated and possessed charming manners. In the course of conversation they told me many stories of Gurudeo as well as a number of miracles he had done. They also admitted that Gurudeo possessed powers that baffled intellect. Personally they had experienced various superhuman phenomena in his presence which proved that he had powers which may be said to be supernatural. Some people from the town who had come for his darshan joined us in the conversation. Everybody had some say in the matter relating to powers possessed by Gurudeo. They asked me how I came into his contact and considered me lucky for having received Gurudeo's favour in so short a time and to have the privilege of accompanying him.

People were streaming in for darshan and it was about one when Gurudeo could free himself for meals. We went to the dining hall and took our seats. Number of dishes were prepared and I joined the meals. After meals Gurudeo told me that I was free upto six in the evening and that I could go to meet my friends if I wanted. Mr. Chettiar very kindly said that one of his cars was kept at my disposal and I should use it whenever needed. One of my friends who was with me in the college at Poona was a professor in Madras college. Soon after the meals I went to see him. He was extremely pleased to see me and as soon as his lecture was over, we decided to go to his place. He with his wife was staying in the quarters provided for by the College. His wife was a graduate and was a teacher in a school. She too came by the time we reached the quarters. They were surprised to learn that I had come in the company of Gurudeo about whom they had heard but whom they had no occasion to meet. They were rather eager to see the man, who was being highly talked about by his admirers. They had no faith in any supernatural things nor did they consider any human being as supernatural. Even then the curiosity to see him was there. They asked me number of questions about the life of Gurudeo, his behaviour, particularly about the miracles he was supposed to be capable of doing. They were rather disappointed when I told them that my acquaintance with Gurudeo was hardly a week old and I knew nothing about his life as well as miracles, adding that he had not performed a single miracle during the time I had been with him. I, however, said that Gurudeo seemed to be a good man, though enveloped in great mystery. Our topic changed from subject to subject and my friend asked me what I had decided about my future. I frankly told him that I had not taken any decision and was in a way idling away my time.

My friend and his wife very sincerely advised me that it was time I should settle in life. I should either proceed to England for further studies or take up a job. They also suggested that I should get married at the first opportunity. Tea and refreshments were brought in. It was past six when we finished our tea and I felt that I was getting late. My friend and his wife wanted to see Gurudeo; so I took them with me to the house of Mr. Chettiar. When we reached the bungalow, I found the big hall packed to capacity and people were standing in lobbies and the passage. I cursed myself for having come late. I pushed myself in with my companions. The hall was so much crowded that any progress further was difficult.

Gurudeo was sitting on richly embroidered silken seat with cushions at his back. He was dressed in white robe and was commanding reverence. His large eyes were beaming with lustre as well as a charming smile adorned his lips. As soon as he saw me standing near the door, he asked the people to make way for me and my friends. I went near him, and he asked me to change and join him. I went to my room, changed myself into pyjamas and a long shirt and joined him; my friend and his wife were sitting in front of him. He aksed me to sit by his side, which everybody considered to be a great honour. Naturally all the eyes in the hall turned towards me with curiosity.

People of all classes were in the hall, while majority of them belonged to higher middle class. They looked fairly educated and I could not understand why they had assembled to see him. I could not reconcile myself into thinking that they had come there to ask for his favours or to see the miracles. I looked at Gurudeo; he was calm, self-possessed and looked as if he was unaware of the audience. There was pin-drop silence in the hall and everybody was expectant to see what would happen next. A well educated gentleman from the audience stood up and said: "Gurudeo, we are all eager to hear some precious advice from you." Gurudeo said: "Instead of general talk, you ask me your specific difficulties so that my telling would be of guidance and help to you as well as to other listeners." The gentleman asked what is the easiest way of attaining peace and happiness. Every ear in the hall was strained to hear the reply. Gurudeo said: "We are all trying to attain happiness and peace in the world in various ways, but the difficulty is that you do not apply serious thought to understand what is meant by peace and happiness. If that were our objectives they should be thoroughly understood, not by mere words or on verbal level but by serious application of mind. If we examine this problem in a right earnest spirit of understanding, we find that what we mean by attaining peace and happiness is a desire to overcome those factors, which disturb our happiness and consequent peace. If these factors could be eliminated, avoided or solved, the happiness and peace would be there. It is now for you to find out the factors which disturb or come in the way of your happiness and peace. You will find when you examine this, that your desires, ambitions, greed, infatuation, jealousies and so on are the factors which have made your lives unhappy and miserable. You will also find that the disturbing factors are of your own creations. They may be due to your living in particular society, particular setup of life, religions you follow, creed that you identify with or your own dogmas. This means that you are covering your body with so many woollen blankets on; and then desire fresh air. The solution you yourself will find is simple. Throw off the coverings and you will be able to get free and fresh air. You can throw off the coverings you have put on yourself by owning, identifying, monopolising, with ambition to become something which you are not or to retain something which is not yours. Barring biological needs, you pursue various objectives in life created by your mind, intellect and fanned by ego which mainly are responsible for the major disturbances in your life. An absurd argument is sometimes advanced that a person living in the world has to follow the worldly ways. When we examine this, we find that the world of today is composed of various societies, religions, creeds, castes and different Isms. Everybody wants to convince others of what he is following, trying thereby to establish that his ways of life are correct and should be followed by all. There is, therefore, continuous struggle in the world to lead, to follow, to identify, to attain power, to gain monopoly etc. etc. How could you attain happiness in the midst of such a great struggle and conflict that is going round about you? If you desire calm and quiet you cannot have it in market place, where all noises and activities are going on. If all of you assembled here, start shouting to have a peaceful hearing, obviously you will not get it. The only thing that will have to be done is to observe silence by each individual so that in a moment there would be perfect calm in the hall. Similarly the factors that create disturbances in your life if stopped or avoided then automatically your life will be peaceful and happy, not otherwise. You will thus see that it is you yourself who come in the way of your happiness as well as peace and you will be able to attain the same if you would seriously try to understand the problem. Your search to find out solutions with outside help is waste of time and energy. You are searching a thing from where you cannot get it. Reading books, following a religion will only help to increase your ego or your fund of information, beyond that they are not capable of giving you a thing which already exists in you and for which you search outside. You have moulded your life in such a way that it has become difficult for you to think correctly and freely. You may not like if I say that you do not know even how to listen. You will say that you are listening to me attentively but observe the activity going on in your mind simultaneously. In your mind you are comparing as well as contrasting what I am telling you with the knowledge you have already acquired and at the same time, you are trying to remember what you have read in the books or what you have learnt from others. You are also thinking various things in relation to the talk I am giving you as well as other things which have nothing to do with the talk. Such a big mental process and struggle to remember etc is going on in your mind. It is, therefore, obvious that you will have left very little capacity to hear me and still less to understand the significance of what I am telling you. The right way, therefore, would be to hear me with concentration i.e. with still or blank mind so that you will understand me. Don't be in a hurry to pass any judgment immediately on the spot. That would not only come in the way of your proper hearing but would muddle your power of understanding. You also will be wasting your time as well as the time of others who have assembled here. I have to request you all to understand that I am trying to answer your questions and solve your difficulties. I am trying to explain things and they should be understood in the right spirit of understanding to arrive at the truth. Please do not try to be logical nor you should try to cross-examine me like a lawyer. You have to forget all that if you have to understand the truth. Do not also try to impress me or those assembled here, with your knowledge or intellectual gifts; that would be sheer waste of time." Somebody from the audience asked: "What is the process, Gurudeo, to make mind still or to be without any thought?" Gurudeo said: "If you mean by process, a mantra, worship or a certain practice to follow, then I would say that you have not followed what I have told you. All that which is called a process is nothing but an escape or an excuse, because what is required of you is that you have to observe and be aware of things actually going on within yourself. It is obvious that your problems of peace and satisfaction are the problems pertaining to your psychology or I may say belonging to somebody within and not without. Therefore the solutions also could be found within and not without where they do not exist. You are, therefore, to watch your inward process, that is to say, how the mind works, how the thought arises, what activity actually goes within that creates ambition, greed etc. When you are aware of this activity and watch it carefully without identifying yourself with it, you will find the solution to your problems. You will in short find a solution to the problem by clear earnest thinking and watching your psychological process. The idea of process being taught by somebody else, Guru, or guide, guidance, worship or prayer have at their back the idea of escape."

Somebody said: "Excuse me, Gurudeo, do you mean to say that Guru or guide, his advice or guidance do not lead men to realisation? Do you mean to say that it has no meaning and what is being said about them is sheer nonsense?" Gurudeo smiled and said: "You have raised so many issues in one question. Now please listen to me with attention. In this world values are changing rapidly and they have undergone a drastic change. In the old times the word Guru might have a different value as well as significance but it has long ago lost the same. It has deteriorated and is deteriorating day by day so far as its moral, social and ethical aspects are concerned. Materialism which had no significance and importance in the past has gained predominance over everything. All values today are considered in terms of materialism. The main trouble with the world is that it is advancing towards materialism at the cost of other valuable things which would have made the life peaceful. By following materialistic tendencies you have lost sight of factors essential for your own good. The words of advice, prayers, scriptures, religious books etc. had significant relationship to that side of life which has definitely nothing to do with the economic values. Economics has been made a sort of religion or I may say it has gained superiority over everything in life while things conducive to happiness have completely lost their meaning, value and importance. What is being understood of them today is in pieces here and there without reference to its reality and totally on verbal level. Unfortunately today nobody understands what is faith, what is love, what is truth, what is morality and much less what is God. These words are used or pronounced without understanding. How can you, therefore, understand what is Guru (and what is process)? Today Guru is being sought for, as an escape or for relief from worries of daily life and if he fails to give the relief wanted you try to find out or go in search of another Guru. Thus Guru has become a marketable commodity or a business house. It has become a regular business of give and take. If you hear that one Guru is capable of giving more economic or physical relief than the one you had, then you definitely leave your own Guru and go to the other for improving your future. Thus people go from Guru to Guru to get relief. This obviously can never be the meaning of Guru and the people who think of Guru in this way definitely need no Guru. Guru is not a means of escape or a bank or a power that would solve your economic and worldly problems. Guru cannot be either a profession or a vocation in life. You would not understand the meaning of words truth, faith, love, joy etc. Guru cannot be an institution or a fad or a creed. The moment he identifies himself with any of these forms he himself has not understood the truth and one ignorant person cannot teach or educate another. I want you to observe very clearly and find out why you need a Guru. I am sure you all think of Guru only because you desire an outside help for relief without troubling yourself to understand your own problems. As a matter of fact one can become one's own Guru if at all he has a fascination for the word Guru; and find out the truth. Books will not serve you in any way except as a reference and any process you follow will be an impediment to your own progress. It is, therefore, obvious that you are to be blamed for creating various obstacles in your own way of becoming happy as well as peaceful and therefore you only are competent to remove them. Please do not bother about Guru or try to follow others." Gurudeo stopped speaking, his clear and sweet voice was ringing in the ears. The audience was spellbound and for a few minutes there was complete silence.

Somebody from the audience said: "Excuse me Sir, if the books are not able to give guidance why they are at all written and with what object we are being asked by every preacher as well as great men to read them?" Gurudeo said: "I am not here to criticize or praise the preachers or great men, as you say, who have written the books. But I have again to say that the books have no powers to guide anybody. They serve only as reference. Every saint or philosopher has tried to put his own experiences and findings in his words but they would be only useful to those who are plodding their way and may get similar experiences. Peace and happiness is a condition experienced by a person. It, therefore, can't be attained by reading books or by hearing sermons. It is a condition within and any efforts outside will not help to attain it. Words fall too short to express correctly the condition experienced by a subject. Various efforts have been made to express experiences but they have not been able to bring about the condition of experience only because the experience cannot be verbal and words can never help to attain it. Books could be read for information, factual knowledge and scholarship. They may help to attain certain status in life and society. They are necessary for professional attainments to gain proficiency in various subjects, scientific or otherwise."

Gurudeo waited for a few minutes; nobody asked any question. There was complete silence in the hall. He got up and folded his hands which was a signal that he had finished the talk for the day. People tried to rush for his darshan but he told them not to leave their seats. Most leisurely he walked through them so that verybody could have his darshan without trouble. It was eight at night when he came out of the hall. I followed him out when he said to me: "Madhav, we are going out for fresh air." I put on my slippers and a servant brought his sandals. We came down the stairs to the waiting car while Mr. Chettiar joined us.

We left the house and made for the famous beach.

CHAPTER VIII

GURUDEO was slowly but surely unfolding himself to me. His voice, heard only a few minutes before, was still ringing in my ears. It wasn't oration nor was there any show of scholarship or parading of knowledge. It was a simple talk given more out of experience than scholarship. To me he seemed narrating his own findings and not theories. I felt that there was something dynamic in him and I was being conscious of a pull towards him. I realised that it was not an easy thing to know Gurudeo but I thought by long association I may understand him to a certain extent. The secret of his influence over a large number of people as well as their love, whatever we may call it, was also revealing itself to me. We walked on the beach and sat on the soft sands. I was still thinking about the talk of the evening and decided to jot it down fully so that it may be of use as reference in future. Gurudeo was talking to Mr. Chettiar and I was only a listener. Suddenly he asked me what I was thinking about. I promptly said: "Your talk sir." He said: "There is nothing to think about it now as it is a thing of the past and stale as ever." He had only answered the questions put to him in a simple way. He said: "Madhav, you have only to think of your problems yourself and you will not find it difficult to solve them. Only your being sincere and honest about them would help you to arrive at the correct findings." I said: "Gurudeo, you have in a way denounced Guru and a process, calling them as escapes which I neither understood nor liked." Gurudeo said: "You are trying to understand me or what I said in reference to what you have read or heard and that is why you are in a confused state of mind. If you only knew, as I already said, how to listen, you would not have said this; the word Guru and his teachings have long lost their real meaning. Today both these things are being used as means of escape. The terms are more or less commercialized and valued in terms of material gains or relief. Naturally they are nothing but escapes. Guru, as a matter of fact, is not required to be searched or chosen. It is he who choses his disciples or whatever you may call, imparts to them the knowledge or rather dispels their ignorance. The so fortunate disciples consider their Guru above everything in life and consider any sacrifice too small to please him. The disciples in their turn do not care to judge knowledge, capacity or calibre of Guru as their confidence in him is implicit, unshakeable and they consider him even above God. The Guru fully knows how to handle his disciples; he could have no expectations whatsoever from them; there cannot be any fixed course or curriculum for all but he treats every case separately fully understanding their calibre and mettle. Now tell me how many Gurus and disciples of such nature you have come across." I pleaded my ignorance and said: "You may be right. I have no personal experience either of Guru or a disciple." We returned home late and after meals

Gurudeo said: "Madhav, you can now retire." I went to my room and wrote down whatever Gurudeo had said that evening. I thought Gurudeo had shown to me a new angle of vision to look at whatever I had heard and read. I was getting new insight and old fixed ideas as well as notions were falling off. This was giving me enough shaking to cause mental uneasiness. I thought here was a perfect clarity, and whatever he said were his convictions based on personal experience. It must have been very late at night when I went to sleep.

When I opened my eyes the sun had hardly risen. I was feeling fresh and light as if a load had been taken off from my head. Fully dressed I left my room at 7 to join Gurudeo. Master Chettiar met me in the hall. He informed me that Gurudeo was already in the garden with his father. He led me to the table where his wife, mother and sister had assembled for tea. Gurudeo had his cup of milk and Mr. Chettiar his tea. After tea I joined Gurudeo in the garden where I found him in an earnest conversation with Mr. Chettiar about the arrangements of various flower beds and growth of flower plants. He was talking with confidence as if he was an expert in gardening and knew everything about the plants. By this time visitors started coming in to have his darshan. Mr. Chettiar suggested that we should go upstairs in the hall but Gurudeo said that he would like to stay in the garden and sit under a tree. Mr. Chettiar issued necessary instructions; carpets were rushed to the garden and Gurudeo sat under a leafy Ashoka tree and asked the people to sit on the carpets. It being Sunday, people were free from occupation and soon the part of the garden where we were sitting was full. I could see that barring very few people, majority of them had come to see Gurudeo with some expectations. Everybody wanted something to get or seek relief at his hands. I doubted whether he was capable of giving any relief but whatever may be my views, those assembled looked to him as a great man who possessed supernatural powers and was capable of giving relief to them if approached. For a moment, I thought that Gurudeo, though nearer to us physically, was far away either in thoughts or in communion with somebody at a distance. He was talking to everybody, cutting jokes in jolly good mood but even then I could sense his detachment all the while.

While Gurudeo was blessing and talking to those who were touching his feet one after another, one of those assembled said: "Gurudeo, do you mean to say that faith in God or worship of a particular deity would not lead a subject to realisation?" Immediately there was silence and everybody seemed keen to hear what he said. Gurudeo said: "Unfortunately the words God and faith are being loosely used without understanding. Due to environment, family traditions, upbringing, education and so on, you have formed a habit or fallen into a pattern of thinking and behaving in a way influenced by all these elements. You have, therefore, not been able to understand the correct meaning and significance of these terms used so loosely. This mainly is due to the fact that you never felt a necessity to think of it otherwise than what you have understood, having all the time taken for granted that your uderstanding was correct. You have never been unfortunately observant of your process of thinking and action, with the result that you have been deceiving yourself into thinking that you are right and do not require correction. Let me know how you have understood God? What you mean by a deity and whether you have understood what is faith?" Without waiting for an answer Gurudeo said: "I do not want to waste time in showing that you are wrong. But you can examine yourself in the light of what I have to say. The faith is that which is unshaken, has no expectations, no ideas of gratification and which never changes. Now tell me if you claim that you have faith in God who I suppose you believe is omnipotent and omnipresent, is capable of giving justice, upholding the righteous, punishing the wicked and fulfilling your desires, ambitions etc., etc., then you cannot have faith in any of the deities or demi-gods. It is very simple that a person having faith in Almighty need not approach anyone else for relief, physical or otherwise. When you approach others, it means that you have not understood what is faith. There is no point in losing faith because faith is never lost. If you have understood what is God, you would find that there is nothing like displeasure in Him. He is not required to be flattered, bribed, offered presents, worshipped in a particular way, prayed or to be met at a particular place. It is, therefore, very clear that you have been doing all this and talking about it without proper thinking and with no understanding. I have, therefore, to tell you not to bother about these things but to be a keen observer of your mental or psychological process and I am sure you will find the truth. Even my answer to your questions will not lead you any further than where you are or even may cause confusion. Because that would be only information received from me but not an experience. The important thing in life that leads to realisation or truth, whatever you may call it, is an experience."

I was expecting somebody to ask another question when our attention was drawn towards the commotion in the garden. Servants were running in the direction of a great tree shouting. Myself and Mr. Chettiar rose immediately to see what was the matter. Gurudeo was calm and quiet and he told the people not to leave their seats. All eyes were turned towards the place where the servants had gathered. On enquiry we learnt that a big serpent was sighted and pursued by the servants. The reptile had found its lodgement at the base in the hollow of a big palm tree. The servants and the gardeners had encircled the tree and were trying to find out means to destroy it. A word was sent to Master Chettiar asking him to come with his gun. We saw him coming with a gun in his hands. Just then we heard Gurudeo's firm voice asking hin to stop and not to shoot the poor reptile. Gurudeo got up and came towards the palm tree. He asked the servants to stand aside and not to harm the serpent when it comes out. The servants pointed out the place where the serpent was supposed to have hidden. Gurudeo went quite close to the tree and softly whistled. Out came a very big reptile with spread-out hood, measuring about seven feet. It was really a fearful reptile and everybody moved back with a sort of fear. In a moment I realised that Gurudeo was in danger of being stung and without thinking of myself, I rushed to him and caught hold of his hand. Surprisingly enough, he was smiling and the hand I had held seemed to have great strength. He said: "Madhav, do not be afraid. Just stand where you are and see what happens." The serpent spread his hood, for a moment stood still, looked at Gurudeo and came slowly towards him. It encircled his feet. Gurudeo bent down and lifted it as if it was his pet. It looked so harmless in Gurudeo's arms that I forgot it was a deadly reptile. Gurudeo patted it gently and told the people that they need not be afraid of the snake. He added it was harmless and would not bite anybody. He asked the servants to attend to their work and came back under the tree with that large cobra in his hands. In spite of the assurances, nobody would go near Gurudeo while the serpent was there. Ladies from the house had come there to see the serpent. At the instance of Gurudeo, milk was brought and Gurudeo fed it with it. The ease with which the deadly serpent was playing with Gurudeo was really a sight to see. Gurudeo said: "It is innocent as well as harmless. It bites only in self defence, when given pain or ill-treated, which is natural not only in animals but even in human beings who claim rationality. If convinced of love, no animal can harm anyone." It was rather difficult to accept what Gurudeo said but it was equally difficult to contradict him when we had seen what he had done. Gurudeo got up and moved towards the house with the snake round about his neck. Mr. Chettiar rather in an anxious voice asked him what he was going to do with the reptile. Gurudeo said: "You may keep this in your house and let me assure you that it will harm nobody." Mr. & Mrs. Chettiar said: "Gurudeo, excuse us. It is not a pleasant sight and we are afraid of having it in the house." It was, therefore, decided that it should be allowed to go unharmed to the place of safety. A car was brought. Gurudeo and Mr. Chettiar went out with the snake. People dispersed and I returned to the house with Master Chettiar and ladies.

CHAPTER IX

We were hardly in the room when Miss Chettiar suddenly turned round and said to her brother: "Ravindra, was it not a wonder that such a fearful reptile played in the hands of Gurudeo as if it was an innocent creature? I personally consider it to be a feat of superhuman power." I could see in her large eyes and in her tone nothing but reverence and respect for Gurudeo. She looked at her brother and myself in a way as to carry her convictions to us. We moved towards the big window of the drawing room to talk. Ravin plaintively said: "When Gurudeo is a human being I cannot say that this was a superhuman feat. I do not know how these things could be done but I can say that Gurudeo may be knowing some trick or may be having some powers that snake-charmers generally possess." Mrudula and his wife did not like this remark, much less his comparison of Gurudeo with snake-charmers. They asked me my opinion about the incident. I said : "I have little faith in what is called superhuman. But being quite near to Gurudeo at the moment I am convinced that it was not a trick. Let me assure you that the snake was unknown to both of us and believe me that we did not bring it from Rameshwaram. I did not hear Gurudeo reciting any mantra nor did he do any action that is generally being done by hypnotists and snake-charmers. I only heard his soft whistle and the snake came out as if he understood the language. To be candid, there is no intellectual explanation to the whole episode. We should, therefore, better ask Gurudeo about it than form opinion." Mrudula thought that I was avoiding the question, so she said: "You are not telling us the truth or it may be you are afraid to hazard any opinion." Ravin said: "Whatever may be the case we must find out how this could be done and we should ask Gurudeo about it. I am sure he will not be offended as he knows us so well." Mrudula's stand was that Gurudeo definitely possessed superhuman powers and that he could easily control animate as well as inanimate objects. Ravin's wife as well as Mrs. Chettiar who had joined us in the conversation ably supported this point. Ravin said: "Women are credulous and could be easily influenced; so they accept superhuman as an explanation for things they don't understand." His wife retorted: "Men are proud of their intelligence and knowledge, so their ego as well as pride does not allow them to accept the superiority of any other person who baffles their understanding as well as intellect." I thought that discussion was unnecessarily creating heat and we were drifting into a totally different subject.

I was, therefore, thinking to change the subject when a lady known to the family, entered the room and asked Mrs. Chettiar what we were discussing about. The interruption was most welcome from my point of view. I said: "Let us sit down and talk." Discussion again started. The lady section did not like Ravin calling Gurudeo a human being. Mrs. Chettiar said: "It was ungodlike to discuss or talk about Gurudeo." Ravin persisted and said: "There is always an explanation to everything that happens, it may be done by Gurudeo or somebody even greater." I said:

"I partially agree to what Ravin's wife has said. We must leave aside our ego and admit the limitations of our intellect as well as of the knowledge we have acquired so far. We are wrong in thinking that we know everything or rather the education that we have received has given us enough capacity to understand everything. So far as this particular incident goes there is no intellectual explanation to what we have seen. The ego in us is really coming in our way of understanding." We stopped talking as we heard the car returning. We all stood up as Gurudeo and Mr. Chettiar entered the hall. Gurudeo smiled for a moment and went straight to his room. Mr. Chettiar, however, occupied a seat. Mrudula rather impatiently asked what happened to the snake. He said: "We went out of the city limits and Gurudeo got down with the snake near a small hillock. We just walked where the growth was thick. Gurudeo very gently put the snake down and told the reptile in a very plain language not to bite any innocent man." To his great surprise Mr. Chettiar said: "The snake seemed to have understood what Gurudeo said because when left loose, it crept a few yards, suddenly turned back, returned where Gurudeo and I were standing, spread its hood, swagged to and fro to show that it had understood the command, touched both the feet of Gurudeo as if paying its respects before parting and made for the hillock. We were watching the progress of the reptile who went to a big bush and disappeared. Gurudeo was still standing as if waiting for something; just then I could perceive a movement in the bush and suddenly there appeared the head of the snake. The snake sent forth a most melodious whistle which still rings in my ears. I think that was to convey us that it was safe in the bush and out of danger. Gurudeo turned back and we are here." Mrs Chettiar folded her hands in reverence and said: "There is no doubt that Gurudeo is God. She said to her son "Ravin, if you could please Gurudeo, you will be happy throughout your life. You must shed away all false notions and ungodlike ideas. We should consider ourselves most fortunate to have Gurudeo in our house as well as his love for us." Mr. Chettiar endorsed her remarks.

Dinner was announced. I went to the room of Gurudeo to see if he was ready. We all met at the dining hall. As soon as dinner was served Mrudula who had suppressed her curiosity opened the subject. She said: "Gurudeo, would you tell us something about the morning incident?" Gurudeo looked at her for a minute, and said: "There is nothing to explain as all of you have witnessed what has happened. The snake was in danger of losing its life for having done nothing. I, therefore, had to save the innocent creature from being killed." Ravindra said: "How do you call the dangerous reptile innocent? He would kill anybody with his bite. I don't think anybody should have mercy for the creatures that cause death, many have lost their lives from snake bite. With due respect I might say whatever may be the reasons that tempted you to save the life of the snake, I still maintain that your kindness was misplaced. Dangerous creatures like that do not deserve any pity and should be killed wherever found." Gurudeo said: "You are talking out of sentiments and hence not correct. The talk or action done out of impulse or sentiment has neither correct thinking nor reason at its back, hence it is more often wrong and accidentally right. Have you ever thought what is life, what is death, why birth takes place and why beings die? If you think you can kill or save, give birth or stop taking birth, then I must say that you are totally wrong. It is not possible for anybody to kill or to save or do any such thing. It is only your ego and ignorance that make you talk in this way." Mrudula thought that the topic was getting philosophical; she was more anxious to understand the incident of the snake than philosophy. She interrupted the talk and said: "Gurudeo could teach philosophy of life to Ravindra at some other time but here I am trying to understand how the snake came out of his hiding immediately you whistled, and whether he did understand your language." The lady section supported the question as they wanted to make the atmosphere light, which was from their point of view made hot by Ravindra's unwarranted remarks. Mr. Chettiar also did not like the way in which his son talked to Gurudeo. Gurudeo smiled and said: "I do not know the language of the snake but I could make it understand that I had plain and simple love for it and that I meant it no harm. This is not with the reptile alone but with every being in the world. It is the only language which is understood without being spoken. If you could only know what is love, you will have no fear and nobody will be afraid of you. From ferocious lions down to the worms, from standing mountains down to the sands of the waters of the seas, the language of love is understood. It is only ego, love for possession, desire to acquire, zest for power, wealth, etc., that comes in the way of understanding love." Mrudula said: "Excuse me, Gurudeo, if the snake did not understand your language, why it fell at your feet when it came out and you lifted it?" Gurudeo said: "It is very simple. When the reptile knew that its life was saved, it was grateful and it was the only way it could express its gratitude." Mrudula persisted further and added that she thought Gurudeo possessed supernatural powers as well as what is called SIDDHI. Gurudeo laughed loudly and said: "Not only you, my child, but almost everybody might have thought that way. By circumstances, environments, education you have received, you look at such incidents in a way you have decided or rather you interpret them in your own way. If you do not find a suitable explanation, you call them supernatural. What is supernatural to you now, may look natural only when you know what it is. It is therefore, the knowledge and ignorance that makes the difference." I do not think that Gurudeo's explanation satisfied everybody but Ravin and Mrudula kept silence. We finished our meals and I returned to my room.

I wanted to write letters to my father and brothers informing them about my whereabouts. In the afternoon my friend and his wife called on me and all of us had tea together. They had come to invite me for dinner but I could not accept the invitation. I explained to them that I was supposed to be attending to Gurudeo and personally I wanted to spend as much time as possible in his company. They could see my point of view and did not press any further. They told me that both of them were highly impressed by the talk Gurudeo had given last evening; moreover they had heard about the serpent incident in the morning. I had to relate to them what had actually happened and also about the subsequent talk Gurudeo gave us on the subject. My friends said that the explanation given by Gurudeo was not convincing and I asked: "What other scientific explanation could be for such incidents?" I further said: "To me the explanation given by Gurudeo seems feasible and if one could attain that pitch of love it might become possible to control animate as well as inanimate objects. Of course, how to attain that love remains a problem. It may be possible to learn how to love, from masters like Gurudeo." We were discussing the subject for a long time when a servant came in to tell me that people had already assembled in the hall and I was wanted by Gurudeo. We all went to the hall which already was full and sat in front of Gurudeo. The same gentleman who had asked questions last evening, stood up and said: "Would Gurudeo favour us with a similar talk today?"

Gurudeo said: "Everybody is at liberty to ask questions. But they should be of general interest and not pertaining to any individual case, only because the explanation given by me should solve the problems of many and not one." The gentleman said: "Yesterday you told us that we were responsible for the miseries of life and if we could properly understand how the life is made miserable by our sentiments, passions, etc., we would get the required happiness and consequent peace. You also said that Guru and process are mere escapes. I thought over what you said but still I am not satisfied. I think without process, sentiments, grief, anger, passions and greed could not be understood and expelled. Therefore there should be a process to attain peace as well as happiness. A man showing the way is called Guru, if you have no objection to the word." Gurudeo said: "You have not properly thought of what I said yesterday. It is not your fault but because of traditions, environments, education, upbringing, social circumstances, etc., you do not know how to think and much less how to tackle your own problems, without the help of past memories and the hope of future attainments. When you think of a problem with preconceived notions, prejudices, bias or with the memory of the past, I must say that you cannot understand the problem and your solutions would be faulty as well as defective. Clear perspective of the problem can be had only when your approach is fresh and unaffected by anything whatsoever. When you talk of process, you think that it must have been a path trodden by somebody, clear of obstacles, and the goal must have been attained by the person who teaches you the process. You also think that merely by following his instructions, you will attain the goal definitely. All your life you have been trained into thinking that a particular ideal could be achieved by following somebody. This idea of fixed objective and the process inevitably leads to frustration and disappointment, because the ambition, desire for acquisition of wealth etc., have no satiation point and moreover the objectives or ideals go on changing as you progress towards them. That is how the world is going on and you all are complaining of unhappiness and misery. It is a pity that you do not become wise by experience when you find that your present pursuits do not lead you anywhere near happiness as well as peace. It is really a wonder that with the experience you have gathered so far, you have no convictions to your credit. As a matter of fact, you do not require a process if you only could look or rather observe your own life, actions, etc. May I know what process and teachings have taught you not to take poison when you learn that a particular thing is poisonous? Similarly, tell me what process has taught you not to touch a serpent, jump into a burning fire or set a match to your clothes or jump into sea? Who was your Guru that taught you all this? You have learnt a number of things in life without a Guru or a process. Today you are a respectable citizen of the city without any process or Guru. You have attained this position, I may say, by mere observations and thinking. You have moulded your life that way because you thought it most important. You have spent years to attain position, wealth, etc., as you thought that such attainments would give you happiness as well as peace. You have wasted enough time and money to satisfy your ego. Now you are disillusioned to a certain extent; so you complain that with all that you have done, you are still miserable and unhappy. Is it not clear that all your efforts were in wrong direction? It should have convinced you long ago, had you but honestly thought that peace and happiness do not lie that way. When we search for a thing where it does not exist, do we not stop in our search and seriously think of the mistakes we have committed and correct ourselves? For this, we do not require a Guru or process; but our own observation, honest thinking and experience lead us in right direction.

"All of you have searched for happiness as well as peace by exerting yourselves on things without. Now it is high time that you should think, understand, observe, be aware of what is going within. The moment you are convinced that greed, desire, ambition, etc., are harming your interests, rather come in your way of happiness as well as peace, you will without any effort keep away from them as you do from serpents, fire, poison, etc. In other words, they will drop away or you will be free from them without any effort only as a result of your convictions; and for this, I am sure, you do not require a Guru or process. There is no time-space between conviction and experience. The moment you are convinced, you are free. Therefore there cannot be any process between conviction and experience as the very idea of process connotes (implies time-space or period) – a length of time. In the process, expectation and gratification are implied factors and, therefore, it may result into frustration and disappointment."

An intelligent question was heard: "Excuse me sir, even the observation of psychological working or the serious thinking you have been telling us could be called process and you could be called Guru because you have shown us the correct way of thinking. We, therefore, do not understand why you condemn process."

Gurudeo said: "You are playing intelligently with the idea and you may be deceiving yourself into thinking that you are right. I do not condemn anything much less the process, but I want you to understand that it does not lead you to the experience of truth or realisation. The idea behind the words process and Guru is not as simple and straight as you put it. While talking, I am thinking of people in general and do not take into consideration the few exceptions. When faced with a problem, confronted with difficulty or when you want to attain your goal or ambition, you talk of process. You fully know the objective or the motive with which you have taken to process. It is neither a leap in the dark nor an aimless wandering. You have formed a definite idea in your mind as to solution of your problems, or the result of your process. You also know that if somebody shows you the way you will reach the destination definitely. You, therefore, go in search of a Guru who gives you the process. This you do because you have a knowledge or information that somebody has attained his ambition by following a process which is required to be given or imparted by a Guru. You might have formed this opinion by reading books, religious or otherwise, or from persons following that line. You, therefore, come to a conclusion that what you need is a process and Guru and once that is done, you will attain your ambition or goal whatever it may be. In a way you think that it is something like taking a train or a conveyance to reach a particular place. When you take a train, you are satisfied that you have done your best under the circumstances to attain your objective or reach your destination. After following the process and doing as per the teachings of Guru, if the results are not gratifying as per your expectations, you are confused and feel at times deceived or cheated. What you do then is to drop the process altogether or change it radically, take another Guru and fresh process. At times, you change your goal or make compromise with your ambition. It is, therefore, obvious that your whole struggle is to avoid facing the realities, understanding of the problem and therefore you seek Guru and process, which is nothing but a simple escape.

"Truth, joy, realisation, God, etc., etc., are experiences beyond the power of conception, expression, indefinable and can never be definite. You cannot, therefore, set it as an ideal to attain or as a solution to your problems. It is an experience and not education or a definite pattern of culture. Being an experience it is immediate, that is to say in the present and not in future. It has, therefore, no relation whatsoever with any process, which is gradual, step by step, stage by stage, and has element of time in it. Experience cannot be given like a gift, imparted like knowledge or information and cannot be expressed in words. Without experience any claim to the undestanding of God, truth, joy, realisation, etc., intellectual or otherwise, is nothing but an ignorance, expression of ego, parading of education or knowledge from books. You will thus see that in life, process has a definite place to attain factual knowledge or to achieve that which is concrete. It will never lead you to experience or to that which is abstract. For attaining proficiency in singing, you need a teacher; there is process, also a progress stage by stage, there is time factor and your progress, too, can be ascertained from time to time. So is the case with all factual attainments. Yoga in any form is a factual attainment, it may give you proficiency in yogic feats but is not capable of giving you any experience or realisation. A person having attained all yogic powers may not have realised while a man without even an idea of yoga might have attained realisation. You will thus see that it is an experience that is needed and not an achievement through process. Thinking of the activity going within, observation and the convictions have an immediate effect of transformation. It is such a tremendous activity that you live only in the present and have neither past nor future. In it there does not exist either a tradition or planning.

"You have, therefore, to be fully observant, and be aware of activity going within. Throughout your life, you have tried, laboured, exerted yourself to become something, to attain some objective, of course with an idea of becoming happy and peaceful. You should now realise that all your labours have gone waste so far as happiness is concerned. On the contrary, you have developed an "I" and more the achievements, the stronger and the bigger becomes the "I". It has completely taken possession of your body, senses, mind, etc., etc. It has completely blinded your vision and comes in your way of correct thinking and honest understanding. You should observe for yourself how much damage it has done to you and how it stands as barrier between you and true happiness. As you start honest thinking, observation of internal activity, you will be conscious of the causes and the effects. Your "I" would start to melt and you will feel relief as the consciousness of the "I" reduces. Your problems will be solved, difficulties overcome without external aid or process with the vanishing "I". You will have no problem or difficulty left.

"When you want quiet, you expel the noisy elements from your room or sit in a quiet place away from the noise. Similarly when you want to have internal peace, you find out the elements or the factors that disturb your peace and drive them out; you can do this only by understanding and not otherwise. Without serious and honest thinking, nothing could be achieved in this world. When you are honest and serious in your quest for happiness as well as peace and start a search within, you will find for yourself the cause or elements that have been responsible for all your troubles. The moment you have found out this, you will get what you want. You will then not ask for a process or Guru. I think I have explained to the best of my abilities and you should have understood what I meant."

There was complete silence in the room. The talk had set everybody thinking seriously. No more questions were asked. Gurudeo waited for a few minutes and then rose. We all stood up and made way for him to go. Soon the hall was empty. I joined my friend and his wife, who were waiting for me outside the hall. Both of them talked about Gurudeo as if they were hypnotized. They said he was really a saint and undoubtedly a master. They wanted to invite him at their place and asked me if I could help them. I had to admit that I was unacquainted with the habits of Gurudeo and did not know whether he would accept any invitation. However, I told them to call on him next morning when I would request him on their behalf.

❖❖❖

CHAPTER X

THAT night we were invited at the house of one Mr. Mudaliar, a friend of Mr. Chettiar. Mr. Mudaliar was also a wealthy businessman. We were very nicely entertained at his residence. Besides refreshments, there was musical entertainment and Gurudeo greatly enjoyed the same. We returned home late at night. Next morning my friend and his wife came to see Gurudeo. I took them to his room. When he saw us he said: "I know why you have come. Heavy food does not agree with my health as I am not used to rich diet. I do not want to disappoint you; but I will one day come to your house for a cup of milk, the only thing I relish most." My friend's wife, however, persisted and to my great relief, Gurudeo consented to visit the place in the afternoon. Just then Mr. Chettiar entered the room with his friend Mr. Mudaliar. Tea and refreshments were served in Gurudeo's room. Over the tea Mr. Mudaliar said: "Gurudeo, I have been listening attentively to what you have been telling us for the last few days. But I do not agree when you say that our life is motivated by expectations and gratification. To be more plain, do you mean to say that we are maintaining our families, helping our friends, doing charities, social work, etc., only out of expectations and with the idea of gratification?"

Gurudeo said: "When you think honestly you will find that all your efforts as well as labours are done with the only idea of gratification and expectations. From your wife as well as children you have certain expectations and you always desire to be gratified by them. If they fall short of your expectations you are disturbed, disappointed, angry and you feel that you have been let down. From the very beginning you have had a plan or pattern for your family; you want all the members to follow the same because it is your ambition to become somebody that you are not or to get that which you have not. Do you mean to say that you rear up family without any expectations? When you have an ambition you obviously admit that you have expectations and gratification. These very things deny you the pleasure of love. Love is sublime, pure and simple. It is not based on expectations and gratification. What you talk of love is an attachment of convenience based on ambition, expectation and gratification. In helping your friends, doing charities and social work, you expect returns by way of gratitude, fame, name, social position or recognition of your good deeds. You feel badly treated and sometimes disappointed if you do not get these returns for your good work. You are pleased when those whom you have helped show their gratitude to you either by words or deeds. You feel elated when you are praised for your charitable deeds and when your donations get recognition from the people. Your visiting the temples, prayers offered to God are not without the idea of gratification. Search all your actions, sentiments, feelings, and mental attitude; you will find the same thing. I, therefore, want you to honestly think of all this and find out for yourself the truth of what I have told you. With age, experience, success, wealth, position, etc., etc., the ego is developed in every human being and it comes in the way of his or her real understanding, pleasure, happiness, peace, love and all that is sublime."

Mrudula entered the room in her own noisy way with Ravindra. Gurudeo had stopped speaking. Everybody looked at her. She sat near Gurudeo and said: "Gurudeo, I have a complaint against you. You are a Saint and a Master. You always say that you love us. I know you from my childhood. But you have not given or taught us anything. Our friends and acquaintances ask us what we have received or learnt from you. We have to admit shamefacedly that we have received nothing. We consider ourselves fortunate or privileged persons for having your love and blessings; but beyond that what tangible achievements we have to our credit? Is it that you do not consider us worthy of receiving anything or is it that you do not want to give or teach us?" Gurudeo laughed loudly while all of us were rudely shaken by so blunt a question, though we appreciated her courage and frankness.

Gurudeo said: "You are a very nice little baby. You have grown up in years but not in wisdom. May I know what is it that I have not given you when asked? When you were a small baby, I have fondled you, played with you and given you and Ravin whatever you wanted. I do not know who has prejudiced or put this new thought in your mind." Mr. Chettiar tried to intervene, but Gurudeo said: "Please allow her to talk. I like it so much." Mrudula said: "In a way you have deceived me and Ravin. You have not given us anything that could be called tangible or of permanent nature. You will treat us as if we are children and you do not think that we have grown up." Gurudeo said: "Let me now treat you as a grown up baby. I think you have all that one should desire in life for your age. You have rich parents; you are happily married to a wealthy, educated, young, handsome boy, who loves you. You have excellent health. You will soon have an excellent healthy son if you have come to ask me about it." We all laughed. Colour rose to Mrudula's cheeks. She said: "Please do not make fun of me. I am really serious. I have a genuine grievance against you and I would not be satisfied unless you give me something."

Gurudeo said: "Now tell me what is it that you desire? What is it that makes you feel unhappy or miserable? What could it be that you are not satisfied with? Let me tell you that the greed for possession, acquisition, monopoly, power, status, position in life, etc., etc., has no end, no satiation point. When you are in a ship you cannot avoid its rolling. Similarly when you are in the world you cannot avoid worldly troubles. So long as you hold the physical body, you cannot avoid physical ailments. When you marry and desire to have a child, you cannot avoid the troubles of pregnancy and pangs of delivery."

Mrudula said: "I understand what you say and I am confident that you, as in the past, shall ever help us in our difficulties, troubles and misfortunes." The expression on her face did show that she was speaking the truth. Gurudeo said: "If you are so confident, and have so much faith in me then I do not understand why you complain." Ravin said: "Gurudeo, Mrudula is right when she says that you treat us as children and put us off by arguments. To be frank, you have not given us anything worth mentioning and her complaint is right." Gurudeo said: "You both are in a confused state of mind. Both of you have come to ask for something but you do not know how to put it in words.

This is not only the case with you but with so many. Everybody is confused if the objective is not clear.

"Now let us take your case. You have come to ask for something, that is to say you want to have something that you have not or you want to become somebody that you are not. It is, therefore, clear that you are not contented with what you have at present. Tell me exactly what is it that does not give you satisfaction or why you desire a change in your present life. It may be that due to long association, affluence has lost its powers to give you any thrill or kick. It is for you to find out why and how you are dissatisfied with your present circumstances and you are in need of something. If you think that I should give you lesson in mysticism, let me tell you that it is altogether a different thing and would neither suit your temperament nor your age."

Mr. Chettiar said: "Gurudeo, is it too much to request you to teach us mysticism?"

Gurudeo said: "There is nothing like too much or too little. Generally speaking, when people talk about mysticism, they do not think about it as a science but they think about it only in terms of supernatural powers. What attracts them is only the spectacular or stage effects of powers. They have no idea with what troubles, sacrifice, and years of study, these powers might have been acquired. Believe me, those who possess what you call powers, have lost interest in them even before they are acquired.

"As to desire to have, to possess or acquire there is no end. They go on increasing in dimension as well as intensity as they are being fulfilled. It is just like adding fuel to the fire. You have, therefore, to fathom the root cause of your desires. Your efforts to satisfy your longings have increased your ego at a great cost and you are still unsatisfied. When you think honestly you will find that you have wasted your time as well as energy on worthless things so far as your happiness and peace is concerned." Gurudeo looked at Mrudula and Ravin and said: "Now tell me what you exactly want."

Mrudula and Ravin did not speak anything. They were confused by Gurudeo's simple but clear talk. I could see that Gurudeo was earnest when he asked the question and there was nothing like putting off the children. At the same time, I could realise that it was very difficult to decide what one wants when asked by a master like Gurudeo. It would be ridiculous to ask of so great a man, a paltry or trifle thing. They had ample money and everything that money could bring them. I thought that had Gurudeo asked that question to me, I would not have been able to decide on the spot what I really wanted. Wealth would not give permanent physical fitness or satisfaction or peace of mind. It was, therefore, a problem that needed serious thought.

Mr. Chettiar said: "Excuse me Gurudeo, could you show me any person who has no wants, desires and one who is fully satisfied and happy?"

Gurudeo said: "There are so many whom I know. They are less known because they have no wants and desires. They are not after wealth and acquisition. They flatter nobody and do not go out of their way to please anybody, that is why they are not known to you.

"Personally I have no wants and desires. I never know what is it to be miserable and unhappy. My peace has never been disturbed. You may call me a saint or a hoax but I am as simple a human being as all of you are. I have no possessions to lose nor objectives to gain. I have no caste, creed or religion or dogmas to follow or to propagate. I do not observe or rather feel any barriers between me and the creation of God.

"I have no fear only because I have nothing to be afraid of. You all know that a thing which is perishable is not worth much worrying about. The time and period required for a thing to perish may vary according to its nature. Everything that is composed of matter is to perish one day or the other. As for example, vegetables may perish within a few hours but a solid thing may take a long time. The same law applies to human body. If one could understand this, it does not require a long time to know that a body is perishable and not worth much worrying about. Personally I believe in taking care of physical existence so long as my physique gives me service and nothing beyond that. You keep your clothes clean so long as they are giving you service and discard them the moment they are unserviceable. I, therefore, as you will understand, have no fear and that has brought me satisfaction as well as peace. I am happy and nothing disturbs me because there is nothing in me that could be disturbed. If you can understand this or a part of it, I think you have understood a great deal."

Over the meals all of a sudden Gurudeo told me that I should be ready to leave Madras that very evening for Bombay and that I should take leave of my friends and do marketing if any. Not only I but everybody was surprised to hear Gurudeo's instructions. I could not understand whether he was displeased with me or that he did not need my services any more. He must have read my thoughts and said: "Please do not misunderstand me. I am neither annoyed with you nor I am tired of your company. But your presence is more urgently required by your parents. You have therefore to go." After meals I went to my room and packed my things for the journey home. Mrudula and Ravin both seemed disappointed. They followed me to my room and asked whether I was really packing off. I said: "Look here, I have developed faith in Gurudeo and I have decided to follow his instructions which I am convinced would always be in my interests. I am in Madras as his attendant. If he says I should go, I have got to go and I can't ask him why I am being sent away. I am sorry I am leaving your sweet company. I shall ever remember the hospitality shown to me by all the members of your family." Mr. and Mrs. Chettiar also came to my room to see me and expressed their sorrow at my leaving them so early. I assured them all that next time when in south, I would definitely visit Madras and would stay with them. I went to the town and made some purchases, took leave of my friends and returned home in the evening. I met Gurudeo in his room and he told me that he was staying in Madras for some time more. He said that he was highly pleased with me and the way I conducted myself. He, however, assured me that whenever in difficulties or in needs, he would be with me at my slightest desire and I should not think that he was away from me on any account. He further assured me that he was deeply interested in my future and he would ever take care of me. I was greatly moved by his assurances and I fell at his feet. I also felt happy at the assurances of so great a man. In the meanwhile Mr. Chettiar entered the room and enquired of me whether I needed any money to proceed to

Bombay. He handed over to me my ticket to Bombay with berth reservation slip. I thanked him profusely for his offer which I declined and paid him the price of the ticket which he would not accept. With great difficulty I could convince him that I was in a position to pay my fare to Bombay, as I was happily placed in life and had enough money to spend for my needs. While we were talking, a servant entered the room with a telegram for me. I hastily opened it and found that it was from my brother asking me to return to Bombay immediately as my father was unwell. We all could now understand Gurudeo's instructions to proceed to Bombay that very evening. I looked at Gurudeo and he said: "I know that you have received instructions from your brother to come home to meet your ailing father." He further said that I need not worry as father would be alright in a short time. I felt greatly relieved at his assurance. I touched his feet; and he blessed me. Immediately I took leave of all and left for the station. The whole Chettiar family was there to see me off.

PART II

CHAPTER I

I was ill at ease during my journey to Bombay and found it rather tedious. In spite of Gurudeo's assurances the anxiety regarding my father's health was there. I arrived at Bombay after about twenty-four hours' journey, feeling completely tired. To my great relief my brother had come to the station to receive me. He informed me that father had a heart attack but now he was improving. I went home and met my parents. Our entire family had gathered there and I was much relieved to learn that father was out of danger. He looked much pulled down but was pleased to see me. He enquired about Gurudeo and the time I spent with him. I gave my parents the account of the tour and the days I spent in the company of Gurudeo.

We were in Bombay for about a fortnight and decided to return to Ahmednagar as father's health was greatly improved. The day we were to leave for Ahmednagar, I received a letter from the Government of Bombay enquiring whether I was free to accept an assignment in the Government secretariat, the post for which I had applied a year ago. I was also called for an interview. I was not much inclined to accept any job as I had not decided about my future. My mother and brother, however, desired that I should accept the post if offered, as a temporary change. They also thought that it would give me enough time and scope to decide the future course. My mother said that I should accept the assignment so that it would create interest in my life. My tour to south India and the association of Gurudeo made me indecisive as to my future. As a matter of fact I was doing nothing and there was no justification in my remaining idle. Therefore I accepted the suggestion and decided to try the Government job. My father and mother left that day for Ahmednagar and I stayed in Bombay. They, however, were pleased at my decision and wished me all success.

I presented myself for the interview as desired and was selected for the provincial service by the Government of Bombay. I joined my duties in Bombay and was under training as well as on probation and after about a year I was confirmed and transferred to Poona. At Poona I stayed with Uncle Gokhale, who was happy to have me at his place and so were the members of his family. His son Shrikant by now had returned from England as a full-fledged barrister and had joined his father in his practice. Malati graduated herself recently and had now grown up into a beautiful lady. Uncle Gokhale and his wife had grown old. He had almost retired from the profession which he had handed over to his son. He had accumulated enough and was placed in life beyond needs. He and his wife now were anxious to see their children settled in life. Negotiations were going on for the marriage of their son and as to their daughter's marriage, I was looked upon as one of their favourite selections. I learnt uncle Gokhale had written to my father about the proposal and father had informed him that it all rested with me. Now as I had accepted service, they decided to push the matter further, thinking that I was moving towards settlement in life. As regards my own views,

I was not feeling like getting married so early; and though I knew and liked Malati, I could not look upon her as my life-long partner. I could also feel that she was not eager to marry me for reasons unknown. Of course, there was no positive denial from me or Malati to the proposal but it should be admitted that there was not any active love between us that would lead to matrimony. If at all we marry, I thought it would be a marriage of tolerance on both sides. How much that would make us happy was a problem and sort of a gamble. As per the traditions and customs we both had reached a marriageable age and personally I had no plausible excuse to refuse matrimony. I was thus in a great fix and a confused state of mind. I tried to assess Malati's opinion but I found her rather reserved on the subject though free in other respects. My friend Ramesh, now a professor in Deccan College, Poona, was a constant visitor at the house of Uncle Gokhale. He was pleased to hear when I told him about Gurudeo and my short association with him. I, however, felt that Uncle Gokhale, his wife and Malati did not approve of my taking interest in Gurudeo. I thought they suspected I was highly impressed by Swamiji as well as Gurudeo and they harboured a sort of fear that I may follow their path. Various means were tried to convince me that I should marry early and settle in life. I do not know why, but I felt greatly relieved when I was given a bungalow in Poona Cantonment by the Government, which was vacated by an Officer of my rank. The bungalow was fully furnished and I had a number of servants at my disposal. My father and mother came down to Poona to stay with me or rather to set my house in order. Strangely enough I thought that Malati felt a sort of relief when I left their house. It might be that the proposal of marriage might have unnecessarily strained her nerves. I was extremely busy with my office work as well as with the preparation of some departmental examination that was considered necessary for my further rise in the service. Even then, I was finding ample time to think about Gurudeo and his teachings. The so-called process of honest thinking and observation that Gurudeo had given to us at Madras was being followed by me, without understanding where and to what it would lead. I was also realizing the truth of what Gurudeo had said and taught, that thinking and observation would definitely lead to the solution of various problems in life, if not to the happiness and peace. The honest thinking and observation would, I was sure, solve half the problems of the world and avoid unnecessary complications in life. We create unnecessary confusion and make our life a drudgery, mainly because we are not truthful and honest to ourselves, let apart the world outside. There is no reason why one should tell a lie unless one is a coward or afraid of consequences; this may have some meaning so far as one's outside activities are concerned, but there is no justification whatsoever to be dishonest and untruthful to oneself. Though I was in this sort of psychological condition I was undisturbed; this may also be due to the fact that I had no responsibilities whatsoever and nothing to worry about.

One day after the meals I was in the drawing room, discussing with my parents some household matters of no particular importance, when my mother suddenly asked me what I had decided about my marriage. I was all along trying to avoid the subject but now I had to face it. I, however, tried to make light of it by asking her whether I had annoyed her in any way or she was finding me troublesome enough to put me into the bond of marriage. My father, however, without giving me any opportunity, with a serious face added that he too wanted to ask me the same question. He further said that unless I had decided to lead life in a different way, it was high time for me to settle in life. From his point of view, I had everything that I should desire. Moreover I was in Government service with bright future prospects, excellent health, personality and education and he had enough to give me that would last for the rest of my life. He said that we had big property enough to give me decent living at any stage if I decided to leave my service and look after the property alone. He further added that my mother and himself were not keeping good health; so both of them would feel happy if I got married early. My mother pressed the subject further and asked me what was my opinion about Malati from the point of view of matrimony. My father and mother liked the girl and we all knew her from her very childhood. She was educated, beautiful and healthy. My mother said that I should accept the proposal which already was placed before them by Mr. Gokhale and that I should not lose any time in unnecessary foolish thinking. I told her that I had not thought seriously of marriage and that they should not rush me into it without giving me time to think about it. Both of them laughed at this childlike answer and said: "We shall give you time but not long enough to postpone the matter." My mother asked me whether I had any objection to accept Malati as partner in life and whether I was in love with some other girl not known to them. I found my father anxiously looking at my face to hear my answer. I said: "Look here, mother, to be truthful, I have not been in love with any girl and have very high opinion of Malati; I know her and we have spent days together; but I had no idea of making any love nor did I look upon her as my future partner in life." I, however, assured them that I would seriously think of what they had said and would also consult Malati to find out what she had to say about it. Mother said that the proposal had recently come from Mr. and Mrs. Gokhale and they must have consulted their daughter before. My father, however, said to my mother that it would be really in the interest of all, if the parties to the marriage discuss the subject among themselves and inform them of their decision. I then changed the subject and we all went to the Officers' Club for the evening. I was all the while thinking about the talk and I decided to take the first opportunity to meet Malati.

The next day even in the office this problem was troubling me and I was unable to find a way out of the tangle. To be frank, I did not want to saddle myself with the responsibilities of marriage, partly because I wanted to probe deeply into metaphysics and partly I thought that my present psychological condition was not conducive to marriage. Moreover, by following masters like Gurudeo, I wanted to find out the truth and solve the ever difficult problem of life. I thought that peace and happiness could be found by honest efforts. By marrying I thought I would not only create a problem for myself but even for those like Gurudeo who desired to help me. I, therefore, wanted to postpone if not avoid my marriage but did not know how to do it. Under the circumstances, I had no excuse for refusing to marry and I could not persuade myself to offend the feelings of my parents in their old age. My refusal, I thought, would greatly disappoint my mother who loved me so much. My ideas about my future were hazy and were not convincing enough even to me and much less to my parents. While in such a psychologically confused state, I remembered the assurances given to me by Gurudeo that he would help me whenever in difficulty. I, therefore, prayed for his help and felt confident that prayer would reach Gurudeo and that he would help me. That night my father and mother had gone to Uncle Gokhale and they were to stay there for the night. I was all alone in the bungalow and was feeling lonely. I was going through office files and must have slept late at night. In the early hours of the morning I had a dream. I saw Gurudeo standing in my room. I hastily got up and touched his feet. He lifted me up and said: "Madhav, I received your message and here I am to help you. You need not worry about anything. Your problem will be solved to your satisfaction. Everything will be as you desire." With great reverence I fell at his feet. He looked cheerful and happy. He told me that he was in Bengal and was going towards Himalayas. I opened my eyes and found it was five o'clock. I felt that my worries had vanished and I again went to bed. My parents returned in the morning and we were having tea; just then I received instructions from the Collector that I should immediately go out in the district for some urgent enquiry work that would keep me engaged for about a month. Anyway, I felt great relief by the diversion and thought that the change would do me good. It was, therefore, decided that my parents should leave for Ahmednagar by the afternoon train and I left Poona by night train for the district. The whole thing was so sudden and as I was busy making arrangements for my tour, my mother had hardly any time to talk about marriage.

CHAPTER II

I was thus away from Poona for about a month. I returned from my tour on one Saturday evening. Next day being holiday, I decided to take complete rest as I had not to attend office. I had a good sleep at night and woke up quite fresh on Sunday morning. I was having my tea and was going through papers, when I heard the familiar horn of Uncle Gokhale's car entering the compound. I got up to receive Malati who came smiling and I could not help looking at her exquisite, beautiful figure with appreciating gaze. She was in excellent health and full of energy. Colour rose to her cheeks when she saw me looking at her rather intently. She laughed and asked me whether I had my tea. I said: "How on earth did you know that I was at home today as I was due here on Monday?" She said: "I have also developed intuition and I knew you would be found at home and so I am here to invite you for lunch." I asked her what was all this humbug about intuition and whence she had acquired that. Instead of replying to my questions, she said: "Madhav, you are not even asking me to have a seat, let alone offering a chair. You have acquired bad manners by staying all alone and moving in villages." I told her that she was only a child and thought of teaching me manners which I possessed long before. My servant in the meanwhile brought tea for her. She asked the servant how did he know that she wanted tea and who gave him the orders. The servant said that they had standing orders from his master and that he knew she would welcome tea. I pushed aside the papers and started talking over the tea. I found myself once again looking intently at her. She raised her eyes and looked at me. She blushed and I again found colour rising to her rosy cheeks. She was bit uneasy, avoided my eyes and looked down. We were silent for few minutes. She took the newspapers lying on the table and pretended to read. From behind the papers she asked me what was the matter with me and why I was behaving in a funny way that morning. I did not reply to her questions; so she said: "Look here Madhav, if you have finished your tea and are ready, we would go together." I asked her where was the hurry and whether she was asked to come home early. I asked her also whether she was finding the atmosphere of the bungalow too hot to sit a little longer. She looked at me straight and asked me what was exactly in my mind and why I was asking her that way. She also observed that something was going on in my mind and that I was not my normal self. I asked her whether she was afraid of me, at which she laughed and said: "You are the last person in the world of whom I could ever be afraid of." I said: "Malati, listen, I want to talk to you something which concerns you and me both." She blushed a little and said: "I well guess what you are going to talk to me about; but I do not wish that we should spoil such a fine morning. Let us postpone that serious talk to some day convenient to both of us." I asked her how could she guess what I was going to talk to her. She said: " I have already told you that I have developed a sixth sense and I have full idea of what you are going to consult me about." I wanted to press the subject further and know her mind; just then my servant came to clear the table and said that I had a caller. Malati took advantage of this and said that she would be going home as she had to look after the arrangements for the lunch. She warned me that I should not be late. She left me so abruptly that I could not detain her any longer. I, therefore, thought of discussing the problem of our marriage at the next earliest opportunity.

I saw a stranger waiting for me in the hall and learnt from him that he had come to see me in connection with Government work. He left me after about an hour and I went to have my bath and be ready to go to the house of Uncle Gokhale. After bath while I was thinking of dressing, I thought it was too early to go for lunch and, therefore, decided to relax for some time. Naturally my thoughts turned towards the problems of my marriage. I could not understand why Malati postponed the subject for which girls are supposed to be so eager. Was it that she was in love with somebody or had I offended her in any way? I also thought that she may not be considering me a man of enough status to desire her hand or she might have developed a sort of superiority consciousness. Thoughts of this nature were rushing through my mind with great speed. I honestly believed that with the education she had received, she was at liberty to choose her husband and she must have decided upon a type of person who would make her life happy. It was no use forcing marriage on her against her will nor she would tolerate any such coercion in view of her independent nature and the education she had received. Taking stock of my own feelings I found that with the tendencies which were developing in me, I would be a misfit to lead an ideal married life. Of what little I had seen of the world, I had formed an opinion that the people whom we call respectable with all affluence, social status and prestige were not really happy as they outwardly looked. Whatever may be the reasons, the fact remains that none of them was happy in his lot. On the contrary, I found that with almost nothing to claim in this world, Swamiji and Gurudeo looked more happy and peaceful. I was, therefore, curious to know whether I was right in my findings. If the objective of human life could be happiness and peace, then I would try to follow the lines followed by Swamiji and Gurudeo and not follow the much-trodden path of married life which hardly led anybody to happiness. From any point of view, it would be foolish to gamble with life like that. How to convince my parents of this and whether my experiment with life would lead me to success was also a problem. In following Swamiji and Gurudeo I would have to sacrifice my career, ruin my prospects and destroy all aspirations. I would also be disappointing my parents, my brothers, my friends, in short, all my well wishers, who had seen a great promise in me. I was confident that I was capable of fulfilling my ambitions, whatever they may be. I could rise to any position of eminence in life, if I seriously exerted myself. It was not only in Government service but whatever I would undertake I would succeed without a shadow of doubt. I was roused from my thought by ringing of the phone. I looked at the watch and found that that I had spent a long time in thinking. When I went to the telephone to find out who was there at the other end, I heard Malati's voice, reminding me that I was already late. I, therefore, dressed myself in hurry and made for Uncle Gokhale's house in my car.

At the house of Uncle Gokhale I found that I was really late and they were waiting for me. To my pleasant surprise, I found that my old friend Ramesh was also invited. By now Ramesh had gathered a sort of fame as a Professor and as he happened to be a friend of Shrikant, I thought he must have been there. I could not, however, understand the occasion for inviting all of us for lunch. Soon I learnt that it happened to be the birthday of Uncle Gokhale. We all congratulated the old man and wished him a long life. Uncle Gokhale was in good mood but particularly Mrs. Gokhale was more lively and energetic as ever. Usually so talkative, Malati was unusually silent and her silence was felt by everybody. The lunch was excellent and various nice dishes were prepared. After lunch I asked Malati whether she was indisposed and whether she would like to come out in the evening for a picture. She, however, pleaded headache but I was not convinced. I asked her whether I had disturbed her in any way. She said: "Madhav, it is not that: I am not feeling well and I have a headache." With this she left us and went to her room. After tea in the afternoon, I left for my club and Ramesh went to his place. At the club I had good games of billiards and as I did not feel like taking meals, I went to a show with an office friend of mine. It was really a good picture and relieved me of my worries for some time. I returned home late at night and went to bed.

CHAPTER III

The whole week I was busy with my office work and some complicated case did not give me leisure even at home. I had to appear for my departmental examination which was due next month and I had to prepare myself for the same. With this in view, I had arranged for leave from the office and instead of going home, I had decided to stay in Poona and prepare for the examination. My father wanted me to go home and read but I thought by staying in Poona I would be able to get necessary books and records from my office which would help me a lot. Exactly a week after my meeting Malati, Mr. & Mrs. Gokhale came to my bungalow to see me and enquire how I was getting on with my studies for my departmetal examination. I could guess what was the purpose behind their visit. Tea was brought in and Mr. Gokhale opened the subject of my marriage and asked me whether my parents had said anything about it. Mrs. Gokhale said that I was already due for marriage and I should decide about it early. Mr. Gokhale said that I should not be formal and that he expected me to be frank with him. He further added that he had talked to my father about Malati, and enquired whether I had decided anything. I told them both that settling of marriages by parents was now a thing of the past. The world has progressed and it is natural that these things should be left to the parties to the marriage. Malati was fairly educated and so was I. Taken for granted that all other circumstances are favourable to the settlement of marriage, the important factor is that Malati and myself should have a complete understanding on the subject. Both Mr. & Mrs. Gokhale laughed and said: "You and Malati know each other almost from childhood: we do not understand what is it that should come in your way to accept each other as partners." He further added: "Unless, of course, either or both of you have decided otherwise." I told them that I had a talk about the matter with my parents but until I discussed this subject fully with Malati, I could not say anything definitely. It is not only the question of my consent but also Malati's choice which should be considered final from my point of view. I am sure you would not like that the marriage of Malati or mine should be a matter of adjustment, convenience or tolerance that would not make any of us happy. The object of marriage should be perfect understanding and happiness. I assured them that I had no other girl in view nor I was in love with any other girl. However, I was not in a position to give any definite reply to them until I get time and opportunity to exchange my views with Malati and she accepts me. So far as I was concerned, I would be willing to accept Malati as my wife. I said to them: "As you have come to ask my opinion, I would like to know whether you have ascertained Malati's views on the subject." Mrs. Gokhale hastily added "Malati is not that type of girl who would go against our decision." Mr. Gokhale, however, understood my point of view and said: "Whatever may be the case, it is in the interest of all that we should discuss this with Malati first so that the matter would be easy for both the parties concerned." He also said that after ascertaining Malati's views on the subject, he would inform me so that I may talk to her about it. They left me soon after the talk and strangely enough I felt greatly relieved. Next week I received a letter from my father enquiring about my health and preparation of the ensuing examination. He also asked whether I had discussed the subject of marriage with Malati. He seemed confident that there would be no opposition from her. He had admitted before leaving Poona that he and my mother had discussed the subject thoroughly with Mr. & Mrs. Gokhale. As a matter of fact, he wrote that the proposal had come from Gokhale family and was accepted by him and my mother with the only reservation of my final consent. As I did not raise any objection when he asked me about it, he had taken for granted that the matter was almost settled. I wrote back to him in detail the talk I had with Mr. & Mrs. Gokhale on the subject. I also wrote to him that the consent of Malati was as important as that of mine. She was highly educated, fully grown up and was competent enough to decide this important issue herself. She must have formed her own ideas about marriage and about the type and nature of the person whom she would like to have as her husband. It would be neither reasonable nor just under the circumstances to enforce upon her the views of her parents or anybody. In all fairness, she had a right to think freely and was at liberty to arrive at her own decision. I also wrote to him that I was now awaiting information from Mr. Gokhale on the subject; till then I was not going to take any initiative in the matter. I concluded my letter with the information that I was in excellent health and had decided to stay in Poona to prepare for the examination.

My examination was over. I had done my best. I was confident not only of success but hoped to top the list of candidates. I did not meet Malati during the whole month. I did not want to press the subject because I was not eager to get married nor I had come to any decision about the future course of my life. Somehow or other I felt the suspense relieving rather than worrying me in any way. Of course, it looked rather strange why Mr. Gokhale was silent on the point. Perhaps Malati might have thought that it was early to get married and settled. She might be thinking of prosecuting her studies further. These were all my conjectures but I did not try to find out the truth because it did suit my psychological condition at the moment.

CHAPTER IV

I RECEIVED orders that I was transferred to Dharwar and during the period of leave before joining duties at Dharwar, I went to Ahmednagar to stay with my parents. On my arrival there, my mother asked me whether I had received any intimation from Mr. Gokhale and if I met Malati. When I told them that I had no message from Mr. Gokhale and Malati did not meet me till I left Poona, my father and mother were surprised but did not say anything. I also told them that it was now left to Mr. Gokhale and I could proceed in the matter only after I learnt from him Malati's definite views on the subject. I stayed with my parents for a couple of days and left for Dharwar. It was over three months that I had joined my duties and I was going on nicely. One early morning I was hardly out of bed when I heard my telephone ringing. I found that it was the Collector of Dharwar who was at the other end of the wire. I was surprised to hear his voice so early in the morning and he gave me a pleasant news that I had topped the list of successful candidates in the examination. He further informed me that I was selected for the post of an Assistant Collector. He heartily congratulated me and asked me to see him immediately. His wife also congratulated me and said that I was welcome for tea in the morning. I was naturally pleased with the result of my labour and sent a telegram to my parents informing them of my selection. In the afternoon, telegrams started coming in. My telephone was also ringing congratulations from various people. I received congratulations from my parents, brothers, Uncle Gokhale and my friend Ramesh. It seemed that almost all people interested in me one way or other had not only known the result of my examination but of my selection as an Assistant Collector.

Next two days I was busy acknowledging telegrams and letters. During the week, I received orders from the Government to relieve the Assistant Collector of Dharwar who was proceeding on leave and to take his charge until further instructions.

I was well acquainted with the work and found no difficulty in taking over the charge. Amongst other correspondence, I received letters from people known to me and to my father enquiring about my views on matrimony. Instead of replying their letters directly I wrote to them to approach my father and also sent their letters to him for his consideration and disposal. My father wrote back to me that he had already written to Uncle Gokhale about the proposal and now he was awaiting the reply which from his point of view was overdue. I was rather puzzled as I failed to understand why Mr. Gokhale was silent. I thought perhaps Malati might have refused her parents' proposal or else she must have asked for time to think over the matter. Even then, in all fairness, Uncle Gokhale should have frankly written to my father as well as myself as to how the matter stood. A fortnight later, when I returned to Dharwar from my routine tour of the district, I found amongst letters awaiting my arrival, a letter from Malati. I opened her letter last as I wanted to read it carefully. For a long time I looked at the letter before opening, trying to guess what it would contain. Supposing Malati had agreed to the proposal the course of my life would entirely change. It would be a problem for me to steer myself out of the family tangle if I were to accept the life of a married man. In that case I may be required to sacrifice my aim and ambition to fathom the mysteries of metaphysics. Of course, I could only imagine the seriousness of family life and how it entangles a person. I knew many of my friends and acquaintances had lost sight of their ideals, had given up their objectives and had entirely changed their course of life, once they had accepted married life. It was certainly doubtful whether I would be strong enough to withstand all that which engulfs a person in married life and pursue my objective with or without the co-operation of Malati. A thought passed through my mind that I should not have staked my objective, just to please my parents. I thus wasted a long time in thinking and speculating over the content of the letter before I opened it. I read the letter twice over, it ran as under:

Poona,

My dear Madhav,

After repeated unsuccessful attempts I have been able to write this letter to you, which, I am sure, you will read and understand in the spirit in which it is written. If I am not able to express myself properly, instead of misunderstanding you will please attribute it to my poor power of expression. It is probably for the first time that I am writing to you and you should not treat it as unmaidenlike. As a matter of fact, I was expecting a letter from you asking me my views about the proposal of marriage that was being discussed between our parents. As I did not receive any communication on the subject from you for a long time, I decided to write to you leaving aside all formalities in consideration of our long acquaintance and friendship, so as to clear the matter once for all and end the suspense.

Some months back when you were in Poona I called at your bungalow on one Sunday morning; you were anxious to open some topic with me, which, you said, was important as well as serious. I put you off lightly but I knew well what you were going to talk to me about. The negotiations of our marriage were going on between our parents for a long time; perhaps you may not have been aware of it but I knew. Our parents had decided our marriage while we were in teens. Fortunately for me, our families, being educated, cultured as well as highly progressive, wanted to give me education to my fullest capacity before taking any hasty step and I think they have achieved their object. So far as we are concerned, we know each other from our childhood and I was under the impression that our union would be an ideal one. You were looked upon almost as a hero by me and your success in various games, your scholarships in schools as well as in colleges and your excellent character was a matter of pride to me. When I came to know myself I found to my disappointment that you were more given to your games as well as studies and did not much care for me and on no occasion you showed any interest in me. It might have been that I was not able to kindle a fire of love in you but I learnt that even in the college you were considered a dry person though possessing charming manners. You were thus found rather dry and I could not help noticing that you were developing into a person that would not satisfy a woman's heart. I do not know the reasons but there might have been some incidents in your life or reasons beyond my knowledge that made you dry so far as women are concerned. Your leaning towards the life of a philosopher rather than a worldly man greatly upset my calculations. Strangely enough if I am right, you have formed a habit of calculating things, balancing values of life as well as giving priority to the intellect over the heart. This was shocking from my sentimental outlook of life. I cursed the moment you met Swamiji at our house, which I think was responsible for radical change in you.

On your return from Madras I found that you were entirely changed; you completely lost sight of the values of those things which dominate youth and which are most essential to make married life successful. I have a great respect for your ability, admiration for your personality and high opinion for your personal achievements.

To come to the point, I am convinced that if I marry you, our married life would not be a successful one. Unfortunately, I am not finding in you anything that would make you my successful husband. Our ways of looking at life are poles apart and I am sure that, if married, I would be a sort of drag on you and would not be able to give any harmonious blending to your life. Our married life, I am sure, would be a failure and would not make either of us happy. I have my ambitions as well as aspirations in life, and I am sure that they would not be fulfilled by marrying you. Our nature differs fundamentally, if you minutely observe. Please do not treat me as a child but I have thought over this problem very seriously for the last two years and I have come to a definite conclusion.

I am sentimental, light and have desires to enjoy pleasures of life. You are dry, calculating and, I may say, have developed ascetic tendencies. You are a man of dominating nature and, I am afraid, would hardly submit to anything in family life. On my part, I am not submissive and naturally have ambitions to dominate. I would not like to lead the life of a tag to an apron. I would never permit to consider myself a load or a burden to anybody. All these considerations have helped me to come to a definite conclusion that we cannot join in wedlock. By remaining friends we might be able to help each other but even if that does not happen, we should not at least be stumbling blocks to one another in our individual progress. Fortunately, I have been brought up as happily as you are and I am placed beyond needs in life because of sound financial position of my father. I have also received enough education to enable me to maintain myself independently and fulfil my ambitions in life.

I know what my refusal to marry you means to my parents. They would be greatly disappointed and may even misinterpret my action. Their life is practically exhausted and I have yet to start my life. I, therefore, cannot sacrifice my life and career to please them. You always say that truth is fearless and solves all problems. I am, therefore, solving my problem by truth and I should admit that it has been able to take a great load off me. Suppressing the truth, because of other considerations, would, I am sure, ruin our individual lives. Let me assure you that I am not in love with anybody and have not decided my future course of life.

Somehow or other I am under the impression that our parents have forced this proposal of marriage on you; but whatever may be the case, I am absolving you from any proposal of that sort so far as I am concerned. You are thus free to choose any partner in life whenever you so desire. It would give me a great pleasure to see you married and settled in life, though I do not think that you would ever marry. Marriage can never be your idea of life or you have, it seems to me, formed an opinion that a married life would be an impediment to your progress towards your cherished objective. I have already intimated my decision to my parents and I hope you will please write to yours accordingly. Please excuse me for this very frank letter and consider me always your friend or disciple if you ever happen to attain the position of a Guru. Convey my respects to your father and mother and request them on my behalf not to misunderstand me in any way.

Hope this finds you in excellent health and good spirits,

Your sincere friend,
Malati

Malati's letter did upset me to a certain extent. Currents and cross-currents were passing through my mind and I was not able to think properly. I had a feeling of admiration for Malati's capacity to think and understand things. I never credited her with so great an ability to tackle her problem by herself and a sense of keen observation. I thought she was rather harsh while analyzing my actions and rude in passing judgment. It did hurt my pride and I felt slighted. I, however, felt that she was not wrong in her surmise. I did not make love to her was a fact; but I think that it was due to my being totally engrossed in my own affairs. Now I realised that women had no place in my life and I never cared for them in a way they are required to be cared for. Malati naturally expected that I should have paid attention to her and I should have made love to her before accepting the proposal of marriage by her parents. Love which a woman expects is something like a harmonious blending of senses, passion, youth and energy. It is required to be genuine and inspired. My trying to please my parents by consenting to marry Malati without love for her was not only wrong but unpardonable. I was trying to drag Malati into a loveless union which would definitely have made her life miserable. I had no right to do it. I only considered, rather thought, about myself and did not think anything about Malati and her feelings, whom I wanted to tie down as my life-long companion. I was definitely selfish and self-centred. Her letter was an eye–opener to me though it did hurt me to a certain extent. I could now understand my ignorance about psychology of a woman's mind. Her letter reminded me that the old days of settlement of marriages by parents were gone and marriage without love would no more be tolerated, least of all, by educated and cultured girls like Malati.

Next day I wrote to Malati as under:

My dear Malati,

I have received your letter which I have read carefully and have to thank you for the same.

I am much obliged to you for the frank analysis of my character. I do not want to defend myself nor do I want to point out where you are wrong. I tried to ascertain your views when we met last in Poona but, for some reasons of your own, you did not give me an opportunity to do so and to explain myself. I had put my views very clearly before your parents on the subject of our marriage when they met me last. I do not know how far they had taken you in their confidence. You are to a certain extent right about my leanings towards philosophy and metaphysics but I cannot at this stage say how they would affect my life in future. Swamiji and Gurudeo have not only made an impression on me but they have a definite place in my life, which I can't deny. Today I am leading an ordinary Government servant's life but I cannot say what turn my life would take in future. Being fond of sports and having indifferent temperament towards finer qualities of life, I could not pay attention to fair sex. Love was never a sport with me and I am sorry that you found me dry. Being ignorant of feminine nature I could not understand your psychology for which I am sorry. You have very clearly stated your views and I have understood them rightly.

I have always been interested in your good and I wish that you should be happy in your life. You are capable of choosing your companion and chalk out your future career. I wish you all success and everything best in the world.

Please remember that I would be ever ready to help you.

Hope this finds you in excellent health.

Yours sincerely,
Madhav

I wrote a letter to my father informing him of Malati's decision. I also intimated to him that he should entertain no more marriage proposals for me as I had decided to remain a bachelor.

After I wrote to my father and Malati, I had a feeling of great relief as if I was free from a great responsibility. I could see that Gurudeo had helped me greatly to solve this problem in the way I desired. I was now free to mould my life as per my inclinations.

CHAPTER V

IN about a week's time I received a letter from my father acknowledging receipt of my letter. He wrote to me that Malati's refusal should in no way disappoint me and that I should not take it seriously to heart. He suggested that if possible I should secure leave and return home to stay with him. He further informed me that my mother was not keeping good health and she would be happy if I stayed with them for a few days.

Though I was busy with my office work, I was feeling lonely when at home. I did not know where I was drifting to. I was constantly thinking of Gurudeo during this period and had a great desire to meet him. Getting in touch with Gurudeo and Swamiji seemed difficult as I did not know their whereabouts. I, therefore, thought of writing a letter to Master Ravindra Chettiar and enquire about Gurudeo's whereabouts. I had not written to him for a long time and I thought a letter to him was overdue. I, therefore, wrote to him about my whereabouts and my present activities. Ravin was very prompt in replying my letter. He congratulated me as well as conveyed congratulations from his parents, wife and his sister

Mrudula. He wrote that they were all pleased to know that I was doing nice and as to Gurudeo he was not aware where he possibly could be. I was thus, in a disturbed frame of mind and in depressed psychological mood. Just then I received a letter from my friend Ramesh intimating me that he was proceeding to Oxford for further studies and that he desired to meet me. I welcomed this as a diversion and thought that his visit would help me to cheer up my spirits. I, therefore, informed him by telegram that I was at Dharwar and he should start at the first opportunity.

It was Saturday morning and I went to the station to receive Ramesh. I was happy at the prospect of spending the whole Sunday with him without any botheration of office work. The train was in time and Ramesh got down from his compartment. He looked healthy and in excellent mood though a bit tired by the tedious journey. He remarked that I looked pulled down and asked me what were my worries. I laughed and told him that I was in harness and had to work a lot. When at home I felt my mood changing for the better. Ramesh was not only my friend but a jolly old companion. We had spent years together and we had so many things of common interest to talk about. He was looking forward to his trip to England and considered it as a great stepping stone to his future career. I fully knew that he would succeed with distinction so far as examinations were concerned as he was not only brilliant but painstaking too. I asked him to rest and went to office. It was Saturday afternoon and I was at home early. Ramesh was still resting when I reached home. He had a good rest and looked quite fresh. Over the tea he opened the subject of my marriage with Malati. He said: "Madhav, if you don't mind and if it is not a secret, please tell me what is it that exactly came in the way of your marriage with Malati, which was talked of as almost a certainty. All of us who knew you and Malati were in a way shocked to learn of your broken engagement." I told him that there wasn't any engagement, nor settlement of marriage. I was also not aware that it was a talk of the town and that those acquainted with us one way or the other took so much interest in it. It was a fact that parents of both mine and Malati desired that we should join in wedlock; but mere desires do not serve any purpose. It is not only that our natures fundamentally differ but we have different tastes and outlook in life. Our aims, ideals and objectives have nothing in common and you understand that marriages cannot be arranged by parents. You also know that I have developed a sort of taste which is not in any way conducive to married life. Perhaps married life may even prove a hindrance to my progress in the line I have decided for myself. I am not prepared, at this stage, to saddle myself with any responsibility and if I succeed in my undertaking, there would not be anything like marriage in my life. So I have decided not to marry and to remain a bachelor. I, therefore, did not want to make Malati's life miserable." Ramesh was a bit serious when I told him this and said that in spite of his long friendship he had completely failed to understand me. He said that I was changing so rapidly that it was difficult to imagine what would happen next. He said that he was a student of philosophy and that it was he who created a sort of interest in me for the subject. He had gained scholarship or proficiency, whatever it may be called, in the subject and was satisfied with his academical success; while in me he was not only finding the practical side of it but said that he was not sure whether I was gambling with very high stakes. I told him that there was nothing remarkable, but I was pursuing an objective and I did not want to create complications that would come in the way of realising my ambitions. In an effort to change the subject, I asked him when he met Malati last. He said that he was at their place a day before he left for Dharwar. He further informed me that Malati was likely to get a scholarship to prosecute her studies in social science in England. Ramesh stayed with me for two or three days and we had jolly good time together. His visit restored me fully to my normal mood and when he left for Bangalore I was able to fully concentrate on my work. I wrote a letter to Malati intimating her about the visit of Ramesh of which she was fully aware and took the opportunity to congratulate her upon the prospects of her visit to England. I wished her all success in advance. I also wrote to her to inform me sufficiently in advance before she sailed for England, so that I may be present to wish her *bon voyage*.

CHAPTER VI

SOME tedious inquiry and lengthy proceedings of the criminal cases detained me in the district for a longer time than I had anticipated. In spite of the precautions taken, I contracted malaria for which this district is notorious. When I returned to the headquarters after completing my work, I was ill and the Civil Surgeon asked me to take complete rest. My leave was sanctioned and I decided to visit Bangalore and then stay at Ooty for a change. The day I was to leave Dharwar I received a telegram from my father informing me that he had learnt that Gurudeo was in Bombay at the house of one of our acquaintances. I, therefore, changed my plan and instead of proceeding to Bangalore, I went to Bombay.

My brother examined me and said I had contracted malaria. He prescribed medicine for me and advised complete rest. In the afternoon I made enquiry about Gurudeo and learnt that he had already left Bombay. He, however, had kept a word for me that I should proceed to Ahmednagar, where he will definitely meet me. The same night in consultation with my brother I left for Ahmednagar. My mother was extremely pleased to see me and so was my father. My mother, however, remarked that I had lost weight and looked thin. My father said that it must have been due to malarial fever. Both of them were extremely pleased when I told them that Gurudeo promised to come to our place and he could be expected any day. My mother was in high ecstasy at the news and she said: "We must not lose time in getting the house in order for the reception of Gurudeo." She called all the servants, issued instructions and set herself working earnestly. My father was also pleased and he told me that he had met Gurudeo years back and did not then consider him to be so great a man. He also admitted that he had not taken any serious interest in this aspect of life. For two days mother was extremely busy; turned the whole house upside down in arranging things in her own way. She asked me times over number what were Gurudeo's likings and the way in which he could be pleased. I told her that I was with Gurudeo at Rameshwaram and Madras. At Rameshwaram we were staying with an ordinary Brahmin family at their humble residence. Gurudeo was quite comfortable and at ease with them. At Madras we were staying in the house of a multi-millionaire but even there Gurudeo did not show any more interest because of wealthy surroundings. I, therefore, told her that the financial circumstances, luxurious atmosphere or otherwise, do not produce any impression upon Gurudeo. This did not satisfy my mother and she was all the while taking pains to make his stay comfortable. The servants also were at a loss to understand who was this personality that was to come to our place for whom such laborious arrangements were being made. The arrangements at last were completed from the point of view of my mother.

We had hardly finished our morning tea, when we heard a cab stopping in front of our bungalow. I jumped up from my seat and ran out when I saw Swamiji getting down and Gurudeo following him. I shouted aloud and hurriedly came down the steps to meet him. Servants rushed to take the luggage; but there was nothing for them to pick up. Swamiji carried two bundles of clothes, while swung on the shoulders of Gurudeo was a bag of cloth, a bowl of water in his left hand and a robust wooden staff in his right. I could not express my feelings of joy at the sight of Gurudeo, whom I met after a long time. Tears were racing down my cheeks. I was not aware that he had produced such a great influence on me. My mother and father received him at the door with great reverence. The presence of Gurudeo relieved all of us in different ways; it seemed we were all in a psychological tension and his presence brought us relief. Gurudeo was in normal mood and Swamiji, a silent obedient disciple as ever. I embraced Swamiji and was also pleased to see him after years. We had not met each other after he left me at Madras.

Gurudeo as expected was completely at home and at ease. He said he wanted to see me and my parents and so he was there. He asked me how I was doing and why I was looking thin. I told him about my illness and that I was under treatment for malaria. Gurudeo and Swamiji were conducted to their rooms and my mother went to the kitchen to supervise arrangement of food. I left my father in the hall and went to see if Gurudeo wanted anything. After bath, Swamiji came to my room and asked me how I was getting on. He said that he wanted to meet me but as he was away travelling in Bengal, he did not come this side. He asked me how I spent my time with Gurudeo at Madras and added that he was pleased seeing my attachment to Gurudeo. He congratulated me over my good fortune that Gurudeo had taken interest in me. He also said that he was glad to know that I was happily placed in service. We had so much to talk as we had met after a long time. While we were talking, my mother came and told me that lunch was ready. Gurudeo enjoyed the lunch much and thanked my mother for having taken the pains. Gurudeo asked my father about various persons whom he knew in the town and the talk at the table was general. He told my father that he should take particular care of my mother's health as she did not look well and also remarked that he, too, looked emaciated and not in good health. My father said that they both were getting old and that it was now Madhav who should look after them. Gurudeo smiled and did not say anything. My father said that he had almost retired from his practice and was living a retired life. He said: "Gurudeo, you should stay with us and teach us something that will be helpful to us in life beyond if there be anything like it." Gurudeo did not reply but added that he was going to stay some days as he wanted to visit various places round about Ahmednagar. He knew the geography of the Nagar district so well that he described each and every place minutely which surprissed even my mother. I asked Gurudeo how long he was in the district. He said: "I have rambled over this particular part many times so that I know by heart every stone and tree if it has not been removed, let alone other things. I am a globetrotter and there is not a single place in India which I have not visited." Lunch was over; Gurudeo and Swamiji went to their rooms for rest.

In the afternoon we were in the hall and some of my father's friends who had learnt about Gurudeo's arrival, had come to meet him. Gurudeo had expressed to my father that his visit should not be given publicity and he wanted to be alone if possible. It was, therefore, almost a family gathering as no outsider not intimately known to us was allowed to come. There was, therefore, no rush for darshan and unwanted gathering. We were all comfortably seated and were having a cordial talk.

My mother said: "Gurudeo, Madhav is our youngest child. We both are naturally anxious to see him settled in life. He is well placed in service and it is high time that he should get married. He says that he has decided to remain a bachelor. You have great influence over him and I am sure, if you tell him, he would not disobey you. Don't you think that he should now be settled?" Gurudeo smiled, looked at me and asked my father whether they desired the welfare of their son or they wanted him to follow their chalked programme. My father said: "What else remains for Madhav excepting to settle in life? He has completed his education, has secured a permanent job, has everything he desires, and we would be satisfied if he gets married and settles in life as everybody of us has done. I do not know what particular purpose is going to be served by his remaining a bachelor. He can marry any girl of his choice which, we are sure, will be always good and we won't come in his way if he marries outside caste and community. He is capable of looking after his own interests but what we desire in our declining years is his happiness." Gurudeo looked a bit serious. He said: "With all his education and upbringing, do you think that he is not capable to choose his own mode of living? Do you maintain that he is a child and has no capacity to think freely? Do you desire honestly the welfare of your son or whether you are anxious that he should follow your pattern of life? Are you very sure that yours is the only good pattern of life on earth, and everybody should follow it? Have you ever thought with what ideal you chose married life, saddled your two sons with the same and whether you or they have realised the ideal?" My father said: "What other ideal there would be excepting peace, happiness and satisfaction?" Gurudeo said: "I would like your true confession, honest statement whether you have been all along your life and even at this age happy, peaceful and satisfied. Please do not answer me," he said, "without proper thinking, close observation of your past and present. I want you both to think of this and give me your reply at your convenience. If you think that you are peaceful, happy, satisfied, having no cravings, desires and aspirations and if you also think that you have no worries, cares or anxieties left, then you can ask your son to follow your path, which is so foolproof and leads definitely to happiness. Otherwise, it would not only be foolish but in a way criminal to ask him to follow the pattern which would lead him to sorrows, miseries, pains, ever-increasing desires, as well as cravings and would not lead him to complete satisfaction. I, therefore, should know whether you have interests of your son at heart or you deliberately want to harm him, which, of course, cannot be conceived of. The object of life of all of you naturally has been happiness, peace and satisfaction. Have you attained this by your so many years of labour and hard work? If all of you haven't, then it is obvious that yours was not a right course. I can understand that it is difficult to change the course and think otherwise, when you are caught in the midstream and being dragged by the force of the current. It is an uphill task to change the course and swim against the current. Hardly very few have succeeded in that attempt. Is it, therefore, not wise to avoid going deliberately into the midstream which naturally would avoid danger, disappointment, frustration, etc? If you are really interested in the well-being of your son, you should honestly tell him your experiences and try to keep him away from the dangers of disappointment, frustration and the rest of the miseries of life which have been the lot of almost all the persons who have followed that set pattern of life. You have to value things in relation to your experiences and not in relation with your society, status, position, standing in life, social laws, family traditions and your paternal aspirations. It is no use thinking superficially and from the worldly point of view, of a problem which affects the vital interest of your son. What is material as well as important is the inward thinking, your intimate experiences and findings based on both. I have, therefore, to impress upon you both to think very seriously and observe what have been your experiences, jointly as well as severally and then tell me what you would advise your beloved son to do. Reluctance to think honestly, fear of keen observation, lest the finding would be unpleasant, has resulted in making most of you miserable. It is not only you and your wife but this has been the case with everybody that constitutes what is called society, faith, religion, dogmas, principles, nation and the world. In what you call society or social order, people have been miserable and strangely enough they are eager to force their pattern or their planning in life on their children by one way or the other. This has added to the misery in the world. This may be due partly to ignorance and partly to the absence of honest thinking and observation. I am sure when you honestly think and observe you will not force your pattern upon your children, which has failed to give you happiness and added to your misery. I, therefore, would like you to honestly think and observe your own past and present before forming your opinion. You should find out ways and means that would make the life of your son without frustration and disappointment, less complicated, more free and what would be called sublime. I give you enough time to think and would like to hear your views tomorrow, when we continue understanding the problem. Let me tell you that I am here to help you and your son, without any expectation from you and no gratification from your son either." Gurudeo finished his talk and all of us were silent for some time. He said that he would like to go out for a walk. Myself and Swamiji left the hall to go out with him. We had a long walk and returned home late. Gurudeo did not take meals and took only a cup of milk. Over the dinner my father asked Swamiji how long he was associated with Gurudeo. Swamiji said that it was more than thirty years that he was with him. My mother said: "You must have learnt a lot." Swamiji said: "There is nothing to learn but I must have unlearnt many things which had made my life egoistic and miserable." My father asked him: "Tell us frankly, Swamiji, whether you have attained realisation." Swamiji said: "Excuse me, I cannot answer your question either in affirmative or negative. To be more plain, realisation is an experience and not an attainment. You cannot, therefore, be definite about a thing which is primarily indefinite. You cannot know or be said to know what is unknown. When unknown become known, it does not remain unknown. Realisation is such where ignorance is dispelled or the factors that have covered the knowledge have been removed. It is, therefore, not possible for anybody to say that he has realised. In realisation, the "I" completely vanishes or rather merges into the vast ocean of knowledge. A river has a separate identity all along the course but not at the point where it merges itself into the vast ocean. Many rivers merge into the ocean at various points and from various directions. But once they merge into the ocean, they so completely lose their identity in the water of the ocean that not only others but they themselves would not be able to distinguish themselves as separate. Before merging into the ocean, each river had its separate identity and so the ocean had its separate existence: but when once merged, not only the rivers lose their identity but even the ocean loses its separate existence so far as the rivers are concerned. It is, therefore, that one whose ignorance is dispelled or has convincingly understood what is nonduality or duality, has nothing but an experience where "I" has no separate existence or identity. You have to excuse me for my poor vocabulary or power of expression which is unable to carry me further." Mother said: "Will you tell me whether by renouncing the world and by remaining a bachelor you have been happy as well as free from worries? Do you mean to say that your pattern of life is without any blemish and foolproof?" Swamiji said: "Mother, you have asked me a question without proper understanding only because you are looking at it with preconceived angle of vision. To be explicit, I have neither renounced the world nor I am out of it. The only thing that I have done is to avoid the complications of life. By world, if you mean the worldly pleasures and social life, I may tell you that I have not followed any set pattern; by observation I found that any pattern, when followed, would create unnecessary complications and lead to misery as well as worries. I did not marry for the same reasons, that is to avoid complications. From my point of view, marriage as well as married life was too great a price to be paid for biological needs. The result today is I am without problems, no expectations and consequently no disappointments and frustrations. To all intents and purposes, I am really happy and peaceful. To your second question, the answer is very simple. I have no pattern of life at all and hence the question and its being foolproof does not arise. Unfortunately, we are being interpreted in a wrong way and consequently misunderstood. We do not identify ourselves with any school of thought, any cult, any religion, have no principles or dogmas to teach, have no traditions to follow nor rules to observe and hence no pattern. We have nothing to preach and have no ambition to collect followers or to pride over our following. Honest as well as free thinking, observation with one's own inward process, without any expectation or gratification if it could ever be called a pattern, then I have no objection to the word which is itself meaningless." My father said: "If you do not take it ill, I would like to know what is the objective behind your aimless wanderings throughout the length and breadth of India and what purpose does it serve?" Swamiji said: "I take no ill and never feel insulted. As I have already told you that, ills as well as insults are felt by "I" and I do not find where that "I" is which was so prominent in me. As to the wanderings, surely it is aimless as I have no objective to gain; but I pass my time visiting various places, meeting acquaintances and helping the humanity if possible." Dinner was over. Swamiji went to his room. My father and mother were in thoughtful mood. However, they expressed great satisfaction at Gurudeo's visit to our house. Mother said: "Madhav, it is very difficult to understand Gurudeo and that is why I have not been able to understand what possibly could be his tastes." I told her not to worry about the tastes of Gurudeo as he is quite indifferent as to his pleasures. My father said: "Let us hope that he stays with us a few days more. I am sure, we would be much benefited by his association."

CHAPTER VII

NEXT morning Gurudeo was up early and we three went to the town. To my surprise he visited temples as well as mosques where he was received with a sort of affinity. Wherever he went people knew him and he was free with everybody. At every place we were offered tea as well as refreshments. Gurudeo took little of everything. To me it seemed that barriers of religion did not exist for him. He was acquainted with various scriptures, books, religious rites as well as practices. Instead of giving the people we met sermons on honest as well as free thinking, he told them to follow their own religious practices. I did not understand when Gurudeo was against religion, etc., why he should ask people to follow the principles laid down by different religions. I couldn't ask him about it then and there, but decided to open the subject at the proper time. The people of the town were rather surprised to see me in company with Gurudeo as we were all considered atheists as well as reformists.

We returned home for meals. Gurudeo was in his usual mood and while dinner was in progress, he asked my mother: "Have you thought over the problem of your son's marriage?" She said: "Whatever may be the experiences of our life but marriage would definitely make the life of my son happy. There is no stability in life without marriage. There cannot be a home for him if he does not marry. Home implies wife and children. Without home there are no comforts and no satisfaction. His relations and friends cannot go and stay with him if he has no home. He loses his place in society and has no standing whatsoever. I am sure, with blessings from saints like you he will be happy as well as peaceful and free from misfortunes and worries even when enjoying married life." Gurudeo laughed heartily as if he had enjoyed my mother's findings. He looked at my father who said slowly, as if he was talking after a long thinking that what my mother said was not true. He said: "I was born with a silver spoon in mouth, was highly educated and piled up a great fortune. From my very childhood I remember that there has been struggle to become something, to get something, to achieve some position, to acquire wealth and so on. My life, therefore, with all education, affluence, position has been throughout full of struggle even to this day." He added that in my mother he had fortunately found an excellent companion and nothing was left to be desired in that direction. His two sons were also highly educated, well placed in life and well provided for; but even then there was no peace, no happiness, no satisfaction for both of them. He further said: "The desire that Madhav should marry, rather should follow our pattern is out of fear that he may not go astray if he remains unmarried. As an unmarried man, he may be induced or tempted to do that or follow that life which has wrecked the careers of many a brilliant person. We also think that the fetters of marriage would chain him to a particular pattern, which he would not be able to discard or toss off easily. You will thus see that in asking him to marry, we are choosing a lesser evil to catastrophe."

Gurudeo looked at my mother who said that she endorsed every word father said. Gurudeo said: "Once you accept a pattern as bad, you should not advise anybody to follow it even if it were your son. You have thought about your life and you admit that you are not happy and peaceful. You should now think and find out what were the factors that came in your way of happiness and peaceful life. Once that is found out, I am sure, your problem will be solved. If you think that your son should marry to satisfy his biological needs or to avoid the danger of falling into immoral ways, then the price he has to pay is so great that he has to remain in bondage for the whole of life. Even then at the fag-end of his life he will have to admit that he did not attain happiness and peace. I would call it too great a sacrifice for too paltry a thing. I have nothing to say against marriage as an institution. We are at the moment handling the problem of your son and hence my remarks should not be twisted or misunderstood in any other way. To lead an unhealthy life and then to search for remedies to cure the various ailments cannot be called wisdom. Once the cause of the ailment is found out, one has to remove the cause rather than devise ways to minimise the effects. So long as the cause is not removed, no treatment could produce ever-lasting effects. The wise thing would always be to root out the cause of illness to avoid its relapses. You have already admitted that cravings and desires to be somebody which you were not, to achieve something which you had not, to possess something which you had not, made you struggle throughout your life and in spite of struggle, you could not get happiness, satisfaction as well as peace. You will thus find that if a person could eliminate cravings and desires from his life he has a chance to be satisfied, happy and peaceful."

All of a sudden Gurudeo stopped speaking and we all looked at him with great surprise. My father almost rose from his seat to enquire what was the matter. Gurudeo smiled and said: "Everything is alright. But we will continue this discussion in the afternoon when somebody equally interested in Madhav will be present to hear the talk." None of us could understand what he meant by this and we all looked at him for explanation. Just then we heard the sound of a car stopping at our door. Who could that be was a question on the lip of everyone of us, when Gurudeo said to my father: "That is your eldest son who has come." He had hardly completed the sentence when I saw my eldest brother enter the dining hall. He was surprised to see Gurudeo and Swamiji. He bowed down to them in respect and said: "Please finish your dinner. It will take some time for me to be ready. Please carry on." My mother asked him how it was that he did not intimate about his coming. He said that he had been to Poona to conduct a case but as it was postponed to next day, he took a chance to come to Ahmednagar. He left Poona early morning so as to be at home for dinner. He said: "All are well at Bombay," and we found him to be in good health. We all were really pleased to have him amongst us when the problem of my marriage was under serious consideration. We finished our meals and Gurudeo went to his room. After his meals my brother joined us in the drawing room and my mother told him about the talk they were having with Gurudeo in respect of my marriage. She asked my brother his opinion about the subject under discussion and quite frankly he said that it is Madhav who should finally decide the course of his life. "Whatever may be our wishes," he said, "it is for Madhav to know what would suit him. Our individual opinion need not put him into an awkward position. He has to take decision that affects his entire life and Madhav is fully competent to know his own interests. I can only say that this is the right moment when Madhav should arrive at a decision. It is no use wasting time if he wants to get married. He has now reached an age when he should get married unless he has decided to remain a bachelor." My father said: "What you say is correct, but let us hear what Gurudeo has to say in the matter. He is the person in whom Madhav has great faith and who is supposed to be guarding his interests in life. Fortunately you are here and we will find out a solution to the problem."

CHAPTER VIII

IN the afternoon my father's friends and relations who were present at yesterday's meeting, came to hear Gurudeo. Tea was served in the drawing room and Gurudeo started speaking. He said: "To continue the talk we had, while at the dinner, I would say now the problem is:

"Is it possible to eliminate cravings and desires from life? Before we do this, we shall have to examine what is meant by desires and cravings. That is to say, we have to understand what is desire and what is a craving. How they are created, who creates them? If you could understand this, I am sure, you shall get rid of them early.

"We have to eliminate physical and biological needs. The desires that spring out of them are natural and could be understood immediately and early. The solution of them is also simple because they are temporary and have no permanent or lasting effects. What we are concerned with, is the problem of desires which could be called abstract which are due to the projection of the mind, heart, intellect, ego, etc. In a child, all these desires and cravings are absent. This shows that they are not natural but are the creations of developed heart, intellect, ego, mind, etc. When they are traced to the development of inner senses, we find that they are the outcome of following certain patterns, religion, principles, cult, social, economical and political ideal.

We identify ourselves with them in one way or other and in doing so we seek either protection or security, affluence or wealth, possession or monopoly, position or leadership or the gratification of our ego. It is, therefore, obvious that if you could avoid following a pattern that has elements already stated, we should have solved our problem. If you are interested in the real well-being of your son, you would not enforce any pattern on him which would make his life unhappy. You have, therefore, to think again of this problem with free mind and you may tell me tomorrow what you have decided. Please understand that I have nothing to do with the marriage of your son, as well as I am least concerned whether he accepts or rejects your pattern." One of my father's friends said: "Excuse me, Gurudeo, do you mean to say that all patterns are bad and can life be worth living without a pattern? I personally think that life without a pattern would be without any interest and consequently meaningless." Gurudeo said: "In each and every pattern of whatever motive and significance it may be, there is ambition, gratification of ego, idea of security, etc. All the patterns have been evolved like that and new ones are being set on almost similar lines with little variations. They might have been created by persons of genius or experience but the followers will have to struggle, strive and make efforts throughout their lives, without attaining happiness and peace. The reason being that when happiness is a goal it cannot be attained, only because it is an experience and not an attainment. Goal is always moving, ambition always increases and the subject can never reach a satiation point.

"You will also find that you have completely subjected or enslaved your mind to follow a particular pattern, either of your choice or choice forced upon you by somebody. In such a condition your mind is not free, your intellect has a projection towards a definite objective, your ego moves in an orbit so to say defined for it, and your mind has to follow dictations of your heart, intellect and ego. Yours, therefore, is a most confused state and pitiable condition. What else could you expect from such a confused state of mind but dissatisfaction, want of peace and misery? When your mind and intellect are free from any bondage, then only you will be able to see or rather enjoy every effort that you make.

Every action of yours will give you immense joy as well as peace. You will understand this only by experience and not by intellectual conception. It is definitely beyond the powers of intellectual understanding and hence cannot be understood by logical arguments. When the mind is free, intellect is not burdened by any pattern, memory of the past, family traditions, ideas of prestige, fear of losing anything, either concrete or abstract; then mind and intellect both remain free to act, observe, think and find out for itself the working of the inner self. A completely free mind is in a position to hear, see, observe and get most important experience, the manifestations of the inner self which may be called God. The mind is then in tune and harmony with the nature as well as the power that pervades the entire creation. Being completely free, it always moves with the present, from moment to moment, and has no burden of the past, whether historical, social, religious, dogmatic, political, economical and so on. It is not concerned with the future as there is no ideal before it to attain or any pattern to follow. It is happy and peaceful so long as it is free and unburdened. What I want you to understand is that free mind not burdened with any past or future, or prejudice, without identification with or without reference to anything, is capable of observation and correct thinking. Do you not think therefore, that a young man of intelligence, education and promise like Madhav should be given a free chance to decide what is good for him?" My brother said: "I thoroughly agree with you and I have to thank you for the way in which you have solved the problem." Gurudeo did not say anything. My father, mother as well as those assembled there seemed highly impressed. I personally thought that Gurudeo was perfectly right in accusing us that we have stunted our natural growth and have made our life miserable by following several patterns. It is our cowardice that we are afraid to admit truth as well as weakness that we fall prey to various sentiments. Gurudeo's plain talk was an eye-opener to all of us in various ways. Swamiji was silent but he seemed pleased with the talk. Gurudeo and Swamiji went into the town as they wanted to meet some of their acquaintances. I went out for a walk alone as my brother was explaining to my father legal points in the case which he was conducting in Poona court. Gurudeo returned home late and immediately retired. My brother was anxious to know what Gurudeo had said before his arrival and how he happened to be in Ahmednagar. I told him all about it and he said: "Gurudeo is really a great man." The way in which Gurudeo had talked impressed my brother. My mother was in a thinking mood, so I went to my room immediately after the meals. My brother left early morning for Poona and when we assembled for tea, my mother said: "Gurudeo, we have thought over what you said yesterday and I admit you are right. I would, however, like to know the alternative you suggest, or the way that would make Madhav happy. If you could convince me and my husband that Madhav would be happy by following the path you show, we would not press him to marry." My father, while endorsing the opinion of my mother, added; "To be frank, Gurudeo, we are really ignorant of real happiness, joy and genuine pleasure. It may be due to our not meeting saints like you. Personally I am convinced of the truth of what you said. I would, therefore, willingly leave my son in your able hands and under your masterly guidance with a request to help him to attain that happiness and peace which have been denied to us." Gurudeo said: "I am glad that you have developed confidence in me but I should like you to understand again that I have no designs for your son nor planning for his future. Any planning or design would create problems for him as well as conflicts and contradictions. There would also be various projections of mind as I have already explained. His mind and intellect would not be free which is a keynote to peace and happiness. I, therefore, have to say that not only your son but whosoever desires peace, satisfaction and happiness in life should liberate his mind and intellect completely from any bondage of whatsoever nature it may be. This will lead him to correct thinking and understanding which obviously should solve his problems. All his actions and activities will be natural, free from past and future considerations and obviously free from conflict and contradictions. He will then experience joy, perfect peace and happiness. This is the experience which cannot be understood on verbal level. I, therefore, want your son to honestly think, observe and lead life in a way that he thinks natural. I do not either want to influence his present mode of life or career in any way." He looked to my mother and said: "Mother, you should harbour no fears that I am going to convert your son into a Sanyasi or that I desire to keep him a bachelor throughout his life. It is none of my business. He is free to marry at any stage in life if he thinks that it will be in his interests. I have, therefore, to say that instead of leaving his interests in my hands, let us all leave his future in his own hands and I am sure that it will lead him to happiness. He has heard whatever I had to say on the subject and that is enough for him to understand and solve his own problem. I have nothing more to add to what I have said." Gurudeo stopped speaking. Swamiji said: "We want to go to Vriddeshwar and stay there for a couple of days. We also desire that Madhav should accompany us if possible." My father said: "I would be pleased to keep my car at your disposal as there is no other conveyance to go there except a bullock-cart. I, therefore, request that Gurudeo should use my car so that it would make the journey comfortable and speedy as well as it would give me immense pleasure for being of some service to you." Gurudeo said: : "We are used to walking on foot miles together. As Madhav is accompanying us, we are pleased to accept the offer of your car. We are leaving immediately after meals and return after a few days." My father immediately issued instructions to keep the car ready.

During meals my mother said: "Gurudeo, excuse me, what particular significance Vriddeshwar has from your point of view? Are you visiting the place with any particular motive?" Gurudeo said: "Mother, we have no motives in any of our actions. Our actions, as I have already told you, are natural and are not activated by any motive. As to the significance and importance of Vriddeshwar I may tell you that it is a place where the most liberated minds have stayed and the place by their association has developed a sort of atmosphere which is conducive to free thinking. There is a temple of Shiva, amidst the hills, which were centuries back big mountains. The natural beauty of the spot is enchanting and exhilarating. It is away from human habitations in the jungle and one can find undisturbed peace there. Whenever I am in this part of India, I visit Vriddeshwar almost as a rule."

❖❖❖

CHAPTER IX

AFTER the meals I put some provisions in the car and other requisites to make our stay comfortable. In addition to the motor driver, I took one more servant to be of help if need be. I wanted to take my rifle but Swamiji said: "Madhav, you would not need it and Gurudeo would not like harming anybody." I at once remembered what Gurudeo had said at Madras about the power of love and the incident of the serpent in the gardens of Messrs Chettiar. We left for Vriddeshwar at about 2 p.m. The road to Vriddeshwar was not properly built and though the journey was short, was not comfortable. Gurudeo was silent and so was Swamiji. I was thinking of the past two days' stay with Gurudeo and the talks he had given to us. I did not know where I was drifting to and what turn my life would take for the future. I was as well indifferent towards the future for which I least cared. In spite of all this I was in high spirits, I think, due to the nearness of Gurudeo. His presence somehow or other infused a sort of energy in me and I felt that I was not alone so far as my future was concerned. Of course, there was not any fear nor I had any problem that required courage. As we approached Vriddeshwar I became conscious that the atmosphere was pervaded with a sort of sweet smell and faint sound of bells as well as notes of music reached my ears. I tried to listen and looked about to locate the direction of the sound in that desolate spot. Gurudeo looked at me and smilingly said: "We are in the vicinity of Vriddeshwar which as I told you has preserved its sanctity and celestial atmosphere for centuries." I did not say anything because I had been to Vriddeshwar so many times when I was a student and even thereafter with my friends for picnic and shooting parties. But never did I experience the atmosphere like this, which must have been definitely due to the presence of Gurudeo. In about half an hour's time, our car stopped at the door of the temple. We got down from the car; I asked the driver to keep the car at a safe place. Vriddeshwar is an old temple of Lord Shiva, situated in the midst of a number of hills round about. It is a sort of a valley between the hills where the temple stands. A square wall runs round about the temple. The priest of the temple who knew Gurudeo and Swamiji received us cordially. He knew my father well and was equally pleased to see me. He offered us refreshments but Gurudeo said: "We should have our bath first." Our luggage was brought in, in the meanwhile, by my servant and we left the temple for taking bath. Swamiji led us to a big well called the well of knowledge. Gurudeo said: "I will tell you the history and importance of this particular spot at night. It is so interesting and I am sure you will like it." The water in the well was crystal clear and cool. The bath really refreshed us. After bath, we went into the temple. The temple, though built centuries ago, has retained its old form even to this day. The building itself is not very big and has no grandeur from any point of view. At the entrance there is a big hall where people congregate for prayers and bhajans, that is to say, singing songs in praise of God. In the inner chamber, there is an image of Lord Shiva and from some source underneath water continuously oozes through the image. Owing to the proximity of hills round about, I think a current of water underneath the image may be the reason for continuous oozing of the water. The inner chamber being dark, the visibility is poor in spite of the four big oil lamps burning day and night. When I looked, the image was fully covered with flowers and leaves, I think by the persons who might have come earlier to worship God. The chamber was full of incense burnt there. Gurudeo led the way in and most reverently bowed down. Swamiji and myself did the same. After darshan, we came to the place given to us by the priest to stay.

The priest offered us some refreshments. My servant had prepared tea. Gurudeo and Swamiji took milk and some fruits, I took tea, biscuits, etc. After tea, Gurudeo said: "Madhav, let us go out for a walk in the hills and I will show you the places of importance." He led the way and we followed. On the top of the hill we ascended, there is a sort of structure that looks like a tomb, which is said to be the samadhi or a place where a great saint or rather originator of the sect called Nath-Panth, known as Machhindranath used to stay. Gurudeo most respectfully knelt down before the Samadhi and I thought I saw tears in his eyes. Swamiji and myself also knelt. I do not know what were the feelings of Swamiji but on my part personally I felt nothing. I paid respects only out of formality. On another hill, a little shorter than the one which is called the hill of Machhindranath, there is a samadhi of his great disciple Gorakshanath. Here also Gurudeo and Swamiji most reverentially paid their respects. I followed suit. We returned to the temple late in the evening. After meals, we sat in the compound of the temple. The full moon was shining and the sky was clear. I requested Gurudeo to tell me the history of the temple as well as of the sect that is called the Nath-Panth.

Gurudeo said: "There are different versions as to the birth of Machhindranath. We are, however, least concerned with it. We are only concerned with his greatness as a man who fully realised. He had undertaken penance for number of years to attain mastery over entire yogic science in all its branches, obviously he had attained the powers which are called supernatural to their maximum capacity. In spite of all that attainment he was completely unattached and free in every conceivable respect. Very few persons of that eminence could ever be found. Those who were attached to Machhindranath called themselves as his followers and thus the sect called the Nath-Panth came into the being. The main teachings of this particular cult was to completely liberate mind and intellect. No attachment of whatsoever sort even with the body, let alone other things, no consideration of future, nor reference to the past, naturally made it possible for the subject to live in the present alone. Detachment from everything including the physique made the subject completely fearless. The free thinking, observation, liberation of the mind and intellect created stalwarts in this particular cult, which was not, as you will see, a religion or anything of that sort for the so-called followers to identify with or to preach or to be followed by. It was, therefore, not the cult in the sense in which the word is understood or interpreted by the people at large. Gorakshanath was the first so to say, the disciple whom Machhindranath trained in his own way and who subsequently experienced what is called realisation. The persons belonging to the particular cult led bachelor's life and used to stay in this particular part of India which was a huge forest inhabited then by wild beasts. Big rivers were flowing here and this part had a most beautiful scenery. They used to stay here in perfect peace and calm without any disturbance from outside world. They occasionally used to visit various places. Once, for some reason or other, Machhindranath was requested by his so-called disciples to perform a Yagnya. Invitations were sent to all big persons, kings and even to those celestial beings called demi-gods. It is said that it was the biggest congregation ever seen on earth. Lord Shiva was requested to preside over the ceremony of the Yagnya. This great historical function was celebrated at this very place and Lord Shiva who presided over the function took his seat where now stands his image, round about which the temple is built. It is called Vriddeshwar which in fact is the name of Lord Shiva. The fire of the Yagnya which was kindled by Machhindranath is still kept burning for centuries by the people and it is just at the entrance of the temple. For generations the sanctity and divine atmosphere of the place has been maintained by the so-called followers of the Nath-Panth and even to this day you can experience the greatness of it if you know how to think, to listen and observe with free mind and intellect." I said: "Gurudeo, I heard what you have said at Madras and even at my place. I have been trying my best to understand and follow what you have said. I have understood the meaning but I must say that I have not been able to observe or listen as you say. I, therefore, request you to explain to me or rather make me understand how to listen, observe and think." Gurudeo said: "We all know how to listen but lack of observation is the root cause why we do not understand things which we do. At the dead of the night or rather when there is quiet all round, we hear the slightest sound either near us or away from us. When such sound is heard you have no thought in mind. You alert all your senses to locate the direction and the origin of the sound. As soon as you do this, you try to interpret the sound or to understand it with reference to your past memory or what may be called acquired or accumulated knowledge, then you understand whether it is a sound of footsteps of a human or animal or if it is some other sound. You will thus see that you understand all about the sound after you listen to it. That is to say, first you listen with no thought in your mind, all the senses tuned to hear the sound, that is to say, at the moment when you listen you concentrate or rather centre all your energies into the power of hearing without any past or future consideration, without reference to anything or I may say without any memory. This act itself is called listening. What takes place afterwards is the interpretation of what you have listened and action that follows. The whole process is so quick that you understand it by observation and not otherwise. Understanding of a thing follows listening. I, therefore, want you to understand the difference between listening and hearing. In hearing the process of understanding, interpretation. comparing and contrasting with the knowledge already acquired, consequences or considerations of future simultaneously take place which is not the case with listening. When you pass through a forest or a desolate dangerous spot, you are very keen to listen because you are afraid of a danger from unknown quarters. At the slightest noise, you strain your ears to listen. You thus see that you all know the art of listening. You may not be aware of it only because you might not have observed it in the way you should have. You will thus see that nobody requires to be taught how to listen.

"Similarly when you observe, you concentrate your energy and power in the act of observation. You are at the time so much engrossed in it that you are not aware of what goes on round about you. If you are really observing anything keenly you will not be able to hear the noise made round about you or even if somebody talks to you. You would be totally forgetting yourself only because your entire energy is concentrated in the act of observation and, I am sure, this state has been experienced by all of you many a time in your life. When you observe a thing you try to understand it as I told you by your memory. The same is the case with honest thinking which takes place without the past memory, future consideration and with no reference to anything. When you think of any problem or any incident, you should not think how it affects you; how it will be interpreted by others; whether the solution will be accepted or rejected by those who are connected with it; how such problems were solved by the people in the past; what will be the reaction of the solution to the posterity, all such and other considerations should not at all arise while thinking. It must be traced as to how the thought has arisen, whether it has any idea of satisfaction, expectations or gratifications in its origin or whether it is the outcome of an ego. If our action or thought undergoes honest analysis, I an sure, you will understand honest thinking." Gurudeo said: "Madhav, you will thus see that listening and observation are most important things in the life of a human being. In both these, you are more or less in a thoughtless condition, that is why you are able to understand what you listen and see. We thus come to a state of mind that could be called a thoughtless condition or in other words a still mind. A state in which mind does not work, no thought arises, nothing is seen or heard, or interpreted, functions of the senses do not stir or create any activity in the mind. When the mind is so still, then the subject gets an experience, which is neither translated nor understood with reference to anything. That is an experience which gives immense joy and creates unparalleled state of pleasure which cannot be expressed in words. This state is not an attainment but an experience which is followed by understanding. This is not an outcome of any process as I have already explained to you."

I said: "Gurudeo, I now understand what is listening and observation. As to the stillness of the mind I have to admit that I have still to experience that state. In listening and observation, we are, for a very short time, in what may be called thoughtless condition but that is for so short a period that it passes our observation and hardly we are aware of it. If this state – that is the stillness of the mind – could be extended over a longer period, that is to say, if one could remain in thoughtless condition for a long time, he may, I am sure, get the experience of that tremendous joy and happiness you have said. Now the problem is how to remain in thoughtless condition for a considerable time." Gurudeo said: "You have now understood what is required. From time immemorial, various ways and means have been tried to attain the thoughtless condition and they are called various Yogas. They all have been devised to attain an harmonious condition of mind and sense. If there is any discord between the two, there won't be any harmony and the subject who has not experienced the stillness of the mind will feel disturbed. As I have already explained to you, while listening or observing all other senses are in perfect harmony with your power of listening and observation, or to put it in other words, the power or energy of other senses is concentrated in your power of observation or listening. If this is not done, then you will not be able to observe or listen. Similarly your body, mind and senses must be in perfect harmony and tuned together in such a way as to create a condition or atmosphere helpful in all respects to create a thoughtless state of mind. However great a singer you may be, you will not be able to give best performance if you are in bad health, not in good mood or the instruments over which you sing are out of tune or the atmosphere round about you is not conducive or helpful to create the desired effects. You will thus see that everything must be in perfect harmony or in tune to have the desired results. Similarly, the physical, psychological and mental harmony is necessary or, I may say, helpful for thoughtless condition. When once this is attained and if the subject gets experience, then the experience is by itself so rich, complete and absolute that the stillness of the mind remains a permanent state, not dependent upon anything and undisturbed by any of the factors stated above. It has, therefore, been found necessary that a subject who desires thoughtless condition, stillness of mind, has got to create an harmonious atmosphere round about him conducive to the thoughtless condition if and when that takes place. In the absence of any other suitable alternative, yogic methods, samadhi, concentration, devotion have been found to be the best methods to create such an atmosphere. It will take a long time and it is unnecessary also to explain to you the pros and cons of these various methods. What I want to tell you is that it has been found by experience that a Yoga, particularly the Samadhi and more particularly the Nirvikalpa Samadhi, leads the subject to the thoughtless condition and definitely to the atmosphere wherein he may get the experience I have already told you." I said: "Gurudeo, will it be too much if I request you to teach me some of the things you have said now? Shall I have to change my present course of life, mode of living, and my present activity? Am I required to renounce the world, that is to say, to leave my parents and lead a life of an ascetic to learn Yoga, Samadhi, etc..?" Gurudeo laughed and said: "Madhav, you will not have to do anything like that. I will be pleased to teach you what you desire. The yogic practices, instead of being obstacles in your present life, will be definitely helpful to you. They will help you to maintain excellent health, peaceful psychological condition, to create immense physical and mental energy and, I am sure, will help you in your progress. I will give you guidance where necessary and warn you against pitfalls, where others have not only failed but suffered disaster." I was overwhelmed by the kind assurances given by Gurudeo and his willingess to teach me. I rose from my seat and fell at his feet. Gurudeo said: "Madhav, tomorrow is the most auspicious day and I will initiate you into Yoga."

Next day I got up at four and found Swamiji and

Gurudeo were already up as if waiting for me. We all had bath at the Well of Knowledge and in the inner chamber of the temple, Gurudeo gave me the first lesson in Yoga. I was free at about 8 o'clock and had my cup of tea; Gurudeo and Swamiji their milk. I asked my driver to take the car home with a message to my father that we will be returning to Ahmednagar after about a week. My servant also went with him to bring some provisions and to return by evening. We were thus at Vriddeshwar for about a week. The atmosphere of the place, the bath at the Well of Knowledge, where every disciple of Nath-sect was bathed before initiation, was found by me very conducive to the study of Yoga. When we returned home my parents were pleased to see me restored to my previous health and in excellent spirits. It may be due to the excellent climate and open air at Vriddeshwar, or even due to the nearness of Gurudeo or to the study of Yoga. Whatever may be the reasons, I was feeling perfectly healthy and full of energy. Gurudeo and Swamiji stayed with us for a couple of days more and left for Pandharpur. We all felt lonely when they left. Gurudeo had produced a singular effect on my mother, who was all the while talking about him and tried to think of what he had said. My father was also in a deep thinking mood. I was acutely feeling the absence of Gurudeo. I, therefore, decided to take maximum advantage of my leave and practise what Gurudeo had taught me. That night after dinner, when we assembled in the hall, my mother said: "It is rather difficult to attain a state of mind or intellect where no problems remain." My father said: "If you are referring to the problem of Madhav's marriage, I think we have done wisely to leave his fate in the able hands of Gurudeo and Gurudeo has rightly left everything to Madhav to decide for himself. Madhav may be our son and we may consider him to be a child. But, undoubtedly, he is sufficiently grown up, has developed intellect and is capable of deciding what is good for him. It is really absurd that we should decide his course of life. I, therefore, think that the best thing would be for both of us to let him alone and see how he progresses. What Gurudeo has said affects both of us, although we are at the fag-end of our life. We have been carrying unnecessary loads and burdens throughout our life and that is why, I think, we have not enjoyed life as it should; not being able to understand the purpose of life as it should, we have not been able to attain peace which was our legitimate due. It is not too late even now if we both think together and try to attain that which we have missed throughout our life. I think it is not impossible to have peace if we are honest in our intentions to rectify the mistakes we have committed. Even now we are utilising our energies in wrong directions." My mother said: "Let us now work together or rather leave off those things with proper understanding, which have marred our happiness. We have been together, led the life so far with perfect understanding, let us now walk together hand in hand to the end. I am confident that with the blessings of Gurudeo we shall definitely succeed." It was getting late and we dispersed in a pleasant thinking mood. I went to my room and tried to sleep. I could not sleep for a long time. I tried to read but couldn't concentrate. I was in a thinking mood and was subjecting myself to a sort of self-introspection. I started remembering things from my childhood, how I grew up and what I was now. It was a fact that I had followed a pattern given to me by my parents as well as in a way forced upon me by the society or the social atmosphere in which I was brought up. I had followed it with great vigour and energy and I thought I achieved success to a great extent, thereby justifying the confidence reposed in me by my parents, maintaining the tradition of family and rising to a position of honour. The way I succeeded so far was commendable from the point of view of my family members and friends. So far I had no regrets for my doings.

The education that I received was the knowledge of various subjects, the necessary training of intellect to grasp and understand, and to accumulate information on various subjects as much as possible. The value or importance of all this was to keep me free from necessities of life, that is to say, the education I received was capable of giving me my requirements in life. To that extent I must admit that it had served its purpose. I, therefore, maintain that I had no regrets for my past. Now the problem was: What were my real wants and whether I had been using my education, attainment and success for the purposes of accumulation of wealth, satisfaction of my ego and gratification of my desire? I had to admit that I had used all my achievements for the above-mentioned purposes. One has to provide for his personal and biological needs as well as for the bare necessities of life, but the aim and object that I was following, the ideal on which I was concentrating my efforts, the centre of all my activities was the one which defied any justification of the life I was leading at present. As Gurudeo had explained I was pursuing an illusory object, that is to say, I was wasting my time and energy over things which were of no use if I were to attain peace in life. I was not a sentimental being, and had formed a sort of habit to understand realities as well as weigh the values of everything in terms of benefit and experience. It was, therefore, necessary from my point of view to continue my present activities without any change, at the same time follow the teachings of Gurudeo and then decide what would be beneficial to me. I, therefore, decided to let the life take its own course in the light of experience and not to disturb it by weight of sentiments. I also came to a conclusion that upbringing and academic education is not so important a factor in life as free thinking and the action it generates. It is the thought that generates action. Actions make up the life of an individual, that is to say, the life of an individual is full of actions which are the outcome of various thoughts. If we could honestly watch our thoughts, the actions are automatically watched. If one is self-centred, his action would be towards the satisfaction of his desires, ego, etc., irrespective of their effects and consequences. It is, therefore, obvious that the desires and sentiments generate actions from moment to moment to satisfy that particular desire or sentiment. I, therefore, decided to watch my thoughts and consequent actions from moment to moment that were meant to satisfy the particular desire or sentiment. Thus I thought that the entire activity of my life could be observed and rightly guided if I could succeed in watching as well as understanding my thoughts. It was late at night when I slept but with all that, I got up early in the morning quite normal and fresh. I went to the club to play tennis as usual. On my way back home, I thought I should go to Bangalore to spend a few days with a friend there and the change will do me good.

When at home I thought over the idea of my going to Bangalore; I tried to understand how the thought of going to Bangalore arose in my mind. As a matter of fact, I was quite at ease at my home and in the most congenial atmosphere. Was it then the fear of tackling various problems in life that desired me to go to a far away place? Was it that I was overworked and needed rest? I found on examination that this was not true. The climate at Nagar was excellent, I had no worries of whatsoever nature, I was afraid of nobody, was in good health, and there was nothing to disturb peace of my mind excepting my own mental condition. What was it then that I was trying to get at Bangalore which was not available at Nagar? It was obvious that it was my present mental attitude and wrong conception that was disturbing my peace and, therefore, I wanted to go to Bangalore. I heartily laughed over this as soon as I understood that my mental disturbances and faulty thinking would follow me not only to Bangalore but to whatever place I may go. It was, therefore, obvious that no change of place was capable of giving me rest or peace except correct mental attitude and right thinking. Soon, as I understood this, the desire of going to Bangalore melted away and I was completely at ease at my home. I thought this was the correct way of solving the problem and it should help me in future.

PART – III

CHAPTER I

I SPENT my leave in Nagar and rejoined my duties at Dharwar quite hale and hearty. One day, we received a communication from the Government that persons of abilities were being selected for important posts under the Government of India. The provincial Governments were asked to recommend the persons from their provinces who would be required to undergo an examination and test for the purpose at Delhi. The Collector of Dharwar strongly recommended my name and I was called at Delhi for personal interview, for the necessary test and examination. I, therefore, left for Delhi to appear before the selection committee. On my way to Delhi, I tried to examine my action as to why I was proceeding to Delhi at all. Was it greed of money or attainment of position that was taking me to Delhi? Placed as I was in life, I had no worries and as I decided to remain a bachelor, attainment of position or accumulation of wealth was not the attraction that was inducing me to go to Delhi. It was, therefore, obvious that the selection was a challenge to my intellectual abilities, to my ego of having attained a certain superiority in academic field, and I was going to Delhi to accept the challenge. The problem, therefore, was whether it was right to accept the challenge. I thought it would be a sheer cowardice which I had never known in my life, not to accept the challenge. My refusal to go to Delhi would mean that I was afraid of competition and I had no confidence in my abilities. By accepting a higher position, if I succeed, I was not barring anybody's prospects, nor I was doing any dishonest thing. If I fail, that would also show me what I was wanting in and the reasons of my failure. That would in a way add to my knowledge about myself. I, therefore, thought that there was nothing wrong in going to Delhi. I did not worry about my future in any way, mainly because there was nothing to worry about and I had decided to allow life to take its own course. I was more interested in the present, the activities from moment to moment than future.

Action without thought did not seem to me a reality. I did not think it possible that thoughtless condition of mind would ever generate action. Since last meeting with Gurudeo, I was feeling a change in me. I was much less worried, was getting less annoyed or upset and had formed a sort of habit of watching the mental process and the resultant action. I was thus getting interested in watching my own mental process. I was also becoming watchful so that I may not be taken unawares at any moment, that is to say, I was getting alert day by day and aware of activity within. I did not much bother to think whether this would be helpful to me in life or otherwise. But I was certain of one thing, that it was helping me to avoid complications as well as confusion, mental and physical. I thought I was getting more peaceful and more energetic within than before. During this period, I was enjoying excellent health, was doing my yogic practices and physical exercises regularly as per my habit. I was finding pleasure in all that I was doing and during this period I never felt lonely or out of spirits. Now and then I had a desire to have more association with Gurudeo, to leave everything including my present activities and spend the rest of my life in his company. But this desire of mine had no logical conviction behind it. I could not understand nor reason out why this desire was there and how I would benefit myself by leaving the present position in life and staying with Gurudeo. I, therefore, postponed giving any serious consideration to this desire of mine and allowed the life to proceed in its own way.

It was now over two weeks I was in Delhi. Candidates from all over India had come to appear for the examination. We had a cosmopolitan jolly company. Our written examination was over and turn by turn we were appearing for oral tests. I was awaiting my turn and, therefore, I had nothing particular to do. I was meeting my friends as well as acquaintances mostly in the Officers' Club where I was putting up. At last the day came when I presented myself to the committee for oral examination. The committee was composed of officials and persons holding very high positions in Government. Much did depend upon this oral examination and I was asked various questions which I thought I answered satisfactorily. Almost all the candidates had decided to stay in Delhi till the result of the selection was announced. I, therefore, got my leave extended for a fortnight more by which time the selection was expected to be announced. We had jolly good time in Delhi. We spent days in sight-seeing, and evenings in the Officers' Club. I was fond of tennis and badminton in which I had acquired proficiency while in college. I had maintained my standard in games as I was fortunate enough to have the opportunities to play regularly. In Delhi, not only that I found good scope to play but met a number of good players. Delhi was the seat of Central Government and as such was full of highly placed Officers with their families. Many rich and aristocratic people, Nawabs, as well as Maharajas stayed there in great style and pomp.

Here I came across Miss Vinodini Gupta, a girl belonging to a famous aristocratic, wealthy family, extremely beautiful and a good tennis as well as badminton player. In a friendly match, she happened to be my partner. We won the match and I congratulated her upon her good performance. Her father, too, was a good tennis player and was on friendly terms with me. We met every morning on the tennis court and my acquaintance with Vinodini deepened. She had extensively travelled with her father and was educated in England. She was unmarried as Mr. Gupta could not find a suitable boy in his community and the marriage outside community was an affair left to Vinodini. Mr. & Mrs. Gupta, being fairly educated and widely travelled, had no strong views on the point of marriage in community and they never insisted that Vinodini should marry somebody belonging to their caste and creed. Day by day my association with Vinodini grew and for some reason or other I was finding her company interesting.

CHAPTER II

THE result of the selection Committee was announced. I was one of those who were selected. I had to stay in Delhi for six months under training before I was assigned any post. I received orders to that effect from the Government of India and the same were conveyed to the Collector of Dharwar for relieving me from duty.

Apart from my parents and brothers I received congratulations from various quarters as well as numerous friends. Mr. & Mrs. Gupta were highly pleased and Vinodini was very happy. For reasons unknown, I was pleased at the prospect of staying in Delhi for some time more. The work at the office was not so strenuous as at Dharwar, particularly because I was required to move from Department to Department to get myself acquainted with various duties and manifold work. There was no specific responsibility on my head and I was to work only during office hours which were, as a matter of routine, fixed. I thus found my mornings as well as evenings free to follow my other pursuits.

I was able to spend a good deal of my time in the sweet company of Vinodini. In the morning as well as in the evening we were to be found at the tennis or badminton court of the club. I found Vinodini to be highly cultured, intelligent, as well as possessing charming manners with attractive smile. One day while at the Club, when we were resting after a game of tennis, we overheard a remark passed by one of our acquaintances in respect of our friendship. Vinodini greatly blushed and looked at me. I did not like the remark but tried to laugh to make the matter light. Delhi was a city of gossips and I found everybody taking more interest in the affairs of others than his own. I wanted to meet the gentleman who passed the remark and give him a bit of my mind, but I thought I should see Vinodini home first and then handle the unmannerly fellow. I, therefore, got up and Vinodini followed me. I saw her home. She did not speak anything on the way. I returned to the club immediately and saw the gentleman and asked him what he meant by passing the remark. To my surprise he immediately apologised and said he never meant anything serious. He also said that he would apologise to Vinodini and that he meant no harm. I, however, warned him that he should take more care when dealing with people of my type. It might a fun to the people of his own class but I strongly resent anybody taking interest in my personal affair and the consequences may be serious as I did not believe in tolerance.

Next day when I went to the house of Mr. Gupta, I found Vinodini was not ready to come to the club. I enquired whether she was sick or had any other appointment. She did not give any definite reply but said I could alone go to play tennis if I wanted to. I asked her the reason why she did not want to come. She said that she did not like people passing remarks on our being together. She thought that the talk of that nature may adversely affect my prestige as she considered me to be a promising young man who would rise to a great position. She said that she had extensively travelled in India as well as in foreign countries, and come in contact with many young persons: but she had hardly met anybody of my type for whom she had high regards. I stopped her speaking any further and said: "Vinodini, thank you for the compliments. I am not so great as you think. I am even more ordinary than what you are. I had already taken the gentleman who passed the remarks to task; and, if you desire, I will see that he tenders his apology to you. If we do not appear together in the club we would be encouraging the gossipers to talk about us. It is, therefore necessary that we should continue going to the club together to show that we are not afraid of their talk and their inferences, whatever they may be." She could see the truth of my argument and accompanied me to the Club. At the Club the gentleman who talked about us last evening came to meet us immediately he saw us entering. He straight went to Vinodini and said: "Vinodini, I think you know me, I am very sorry if my remark yesterday offended you in any way. I never meant anything and I am sure you would not take it seriously either. However, if you desire, I am prepared to make amends whatever you suggest. You will please accept this as my apology." Vinodini smiled and said to him: "I have to thank you for whatever you have said. Those of us who live in Delhi are used to irresponsible talk and unwanted remark, but people like Mr. Madhav who come from outside would resent any such talk or liberty taken with them. You may, therefore, explain the matter to him rather than to me." He said: "I talked to him yesterday and expressed regrets."

That evening we finished our play early and left the Club for a long walk. We both did not talk on any particular subject as both of us were occupied with our own thoughts. Suddenly I became aware that we were walking only in silence. I, therefore, said: "Vinodini, you have still not regained your usual mood. If you are not feeling well, let us go home."

Vinodini said: "I am quite alright, but I think I need rest." I, therefore, saw her home and went to my quarters. Days passed and though we were meeting almost everyday, something had come between our free relations which was weighing on the minds of both of us. It seemed that both of us were seeking an opportunity to give vent to our feelings and express what was really going on in our minds.

One Sunday morning Mr. & Mrs. Gupta arranged a picnic and we left Delhi in their car. Vinodini heaved a sigh of relief as soon as we were out of Delhi limits and I found her mood changing. It was a pleasant party and we had engaged a dak bungalow for the day. After breakfast, Mr. & Mrs. Gupta made themselves comfortable in the bungalow while myself and Vinodini strolled out. We walked in the direction of a hillock. The way over there was crude, and a climb was not easy. I had to help Vinodini from time to time on the ascent. There was a big banyan tree and we decided to sit under its inviting shade. I got over the rock with difficulty; but it was difficult for Vinodini to climb up. I, therefore, gripped her hands firmly and pulled her up. I had never taken liberty with a lady in my life and the way Vinodini yielded her person to me when I pulled her up was a novel experience. It set a sort of electric current through my entire person; and I could not understand what was happening. Vinodini was flushed with the exertion of climbing and she looked charming. I found her eyes sparkling with pleasure. When she found me staring at her, she blushed and avoided my eyes. Without looking at me she asked me when did I form the habit of looking at girls intently. I replied that she looked so charming at the moment that I could not help staring at her. It was a tense moment and both of us were silent for some time. In that silence we not only understood each other but knew what was going on in our hearts. It was for the first time in my life that sentiments were gaining superiority over reason, heart over intellect. I even felt that I would not know how I would behave next moment. Something unknown was taking possession of me and I was slowly losing control over myself. With a woman's instinct Vinodini could perceive this and she became serious. To change the subject she said: "Madhav if we sit like this without talking, somebody might suspect that we have quarrelled." She moved a little further away from me and asked me whether I had become normal. I laughed and said that it was impossible for anyone to behave normally in her sweet company placed alone at so charming a spot. She said: "Madhav, you are still talking to me as a raw youth and you should think seriously what you are talking about. I should not remind you that you are highly educated and a man of position and that you should behave in a proper way." This remark from her brought me to my senses. I felt ashamed of myself and thought I did not behave in a way befitting a gentleman. I also felt that I had taken advantage of her being alone at that lonely spot and in a way abused the confidence her parents reposed in me. I said: "Vinodini, kindly excuse me. I am very sorry, if I offended you in any way." She said: "There is no question either of offending or annoyance, but I think that you were behaving in a strange way not seen by me ever since we met. I can understand what may be going on in your mind; but both of us have reached a certain age when we are capable of thinking rationally and clearly understand the consequences of our behaviour. It is not that you have behaved in a wrong way, but I have to think a lot before I could encourage you any further. You have also to think seriously before you lead me on. There should not be anything between us that would give a cause for remorse or repentance. I know very little of your past, your habits as well as your ambitions in life. You are totally ignorant about myself and my life so far, as well as my ideas about the future. We are not small children to allow passions to rule us. We are sufficiently grown up to consider or rather to understand the various aspects of life in their true perspective. Let us, therefore, remain friends for some time till we mutually decide to change the friendship into some other close relationship. You have gained my admiration from whatever little I have seen of you and that feeling has transformed our acquaintance into genuine friendship. For further transformation of the friendship into something, you will appreciate that a still longer period is required. I do not know what exactly you feel for me, but it is apparent that you have accepted me as your friend. Let us, therefore, not mar the mutual feelings of friendship by any hasty action." By now I had regained my self-control, and I said: "Vinodini, you are right. It is probably the first occasion when I allowed my heart to rule my head. I now understand what you say and we have to think twice before we rush into any hasty action. Please forget whatever I might have said in the impulsive mood. I have to thank you for reminding me of my behaviour." Just then we saw Mr. & Mrs. Gupta coming towards us. We got up and in a few minutes joined them at the foot of the hillock. We went to the dak bungalow and had our lunch. After tea, we left for Delhi and Mr. Gupta dropped me at my place on their way home.

Immediately after meals, I retired with the idea of going to sleep. I could not get sleep for a long time. I started thinking not only of the incident of the afternoon, but of my life since I came to Delhi. I recollected how I came in contact with Vinodini and how our casual acquaintance developed into friendship. As time went, the aspect of friendship, too, changed into something which could be called infatuation, if not love. It was a fact that I was feeling something more than a pleasure in her company and a sense of loneliness was there in her absence. I was away from my family and friends. I was seeking a sort of comfort in her company. I could now observe the various incidents that took place during this period and how greatly I was influenced by her charms. It was, of course, no fault of Vinodini nor she had any idea of leading me on. It might have been that she, too, may have found comfort in my company. It might have been purely accidental too, without any intention; whatever may be the reasons, I could now see that I was behaving in a rather foolish way. I could not think what would have happened had not the incident of the afternoon brought me to my senses. I owed a great deal to the incident and much more to Vinodini who timely warned me. It was not the fear of any moral lapse as I had not any great respect for the fixed standard of morality. But even then I did feel that my individuality was in danger and I should not have exposed myself so easily. I thought: what was it that had brought so great a change in me that I abandoned my process of thinking and observation? Was it love? Was it a passion? Was it a desire? Or was it merely an idea of pleasure? What exactly could genuine love be?

In love, the only idea would be to love a thing, animate or inanimate, and derive pleasure, satisfaction and joy, only in the process of love itself. There can't be any idea of desire for possession or monopoly in love, because possession or monopoly means satisfaction of one's ego. There can never be also an idea of gratification which implies that one expects returns for his love from the object he loves, and there can't be love in any bargain at all. If it were a passion, that is to say, an idea of meeting biological needs then to make Vinodini a victim of it was not only absurd but mean and too low for a man of my education and standard. If it were a desire, what I was expecting from her and what I was prepared to give her in return was also a problem. I had no right, as a matter of fact, to play with the life of Vinodini for so frail a consideration as satisfying my desire. I would definitely consider it criminal. As to the idea of pleasure, it was my duty to consider what harm I was doing to Vinodini in various ways. Had I a right to behave like that with a girl of her type? It would definitely be indecent for anybody, least of all for a man like me, to behave with a girl of education and culture only with the idea of seeking pleasure without any consideration of the consequences. I could not deceive myself into thinking that I had neither passions nor biological cravings. But even then, I should not have allowed myself to forget my culture and education. I should not have behaved in a way not befitting myself. Was there any idea behind all this of getting united with Vinodini so that I may lead the rest of my life in harmony as well as in peace? But how absurd was it? Could there be any harmony and peace in the corporate married life? Would not marriage and the family that would grow from the union create various problems that would make life miserable? Was I not more happy, more free to take care of myself, when I had no problems than a family man who creates never-ending problems for himself and makes his life miserable? Would I ever be earnest in married life? Could I ever be a man of society and shoulder the responsibility of a family life when I had leanings towards philosophical side? Had I not decided to follow Swamiji and Gurudeo to attain that peace and joy as well as to fathom the mysteries of metaphysics and spiritualism?

If I were to give myself away to passing pleasures, sentiments, biological needs and like that I would definitely mar my prospects and make it difficult for my well-wishers to help me. I should, therefore, understand these things in their right perspective and decide my course of action. It was almost morning and I did not know how the time flew. I was now completely exhausted and did not know when my eyes closed. It was past 8 o'clock when my servant woke me up, and I had a headache and I did not feel like going to office. I arranged to send a note to office and stayed at home. I also informed Vinodini that I was not going to the Club to play tennis as usual as I was a bit indisposed. I spent the whole morning resting and had a good nap after lunch. In the afternoon, I felt normal with the rest and the nap I had. I was sitting in the verandah having my tea when I saw Vinodini entering my compound. She looked fresh and normal and was smiling. She looked at me and asked whether I was ill. She said that I looked tired or had no sleep at all. I asked her to sit down and offered her tea. I said: "I am alright now and have no complaints. I had no sleep last night, that is why I did not go to office." Vinodini said: "Madhav, have I offended you in any way or am I the cause of your indisposition? As a matter of fact, I sincerely voiced my opinion yesterday and I wish you should understand the spirit in which I told you the truth. What I meant was that before we commit ourselves to any relationship of whatever nature it may be, it is necessary that we should know and understand each other completely. It is no use saying like inexperienced sentimental youths that we love each other and desire to live a united life. I have decided my way of life and I know what I should have and what would please me. I have no knowledge of your ideas about life. We are friends and I found your company comfortable and desirable. If we decided to change this relationship into something closer, don't you think that we should understand each other thoroughly so that we avoid disappointment, frustration as well as misery throughout the rest of our life? Let us cast aside all formalities and think honestly. If I were to take you as my husband and you were to accept me as your wife, we both must know the likes and dislikes, ambitions and aspirations, shortcomings and faults, desires and expectations, gratifications and satisfactions of each other without which there would not be peace and happiness in our union. I am the only child of my parents who have more money than they could ordinarily spend. I am brought up in luxury and fondled to the degree of being spoiled. I possess a strong will and have developed a taste for free luxurious life. I would not like to leave my parents or their home for anything on earth. I am not capable of any sacrifice nor do I desire to make it even for the sake of love or married life. Even when married, I would not like to have subordinate position or to play a second fiddle even to my husband. I have no inferiority complex in me nor would I accept anybody's domination in my life. I may not be knowing much of you but from whatever little I have seen, I think you are of quite a different nature. With all your culture, education, your excellent manners, you are a person of independent nature. You seem to have a strong will-power, consciousness of your merits as well as your abilities. You are a man of independent thinking, aggressive as well as adventurous. You have a sort of pride in your abilities and consciousness of your manhood. Sometimes I am afraid that you will be doing anything to satisfy your intellectual cravings and ambitions. You won't care for anybody or anything, however great they may be while pursuing your aims and objectives. This is my reading of your character. I have told you about myself and also what I think of you. It is now for you to think of what I have said and decide whether it would be in the interest of both of us to change the present relationship into something else. Let me assure you that I have a genuine friendship and admiration for you as a friend."

I liked the way Vinodini explained herself. I did admire the way she analysed herself and the candid admission of what she thought. I thought if everybody would be so candid and truthful, there would be little of misunderstanding, confusion and subsequent disappointment in life. Lack of honest thinking and admission of truth are the reasons that cause misery in the world. I said: "Vinodini, last night I thought deeply over the matter and have come to the conclusion that I am not in a position to undertake family responsibility, as I have decided to unravel the mystery of peace and happiness being enjoyed by some persons who may be called saints or sadhus. I have also decided to understand what could be said to be the realities of life. You may not understand the significance of what I have said, but in pursuing my objectives marriage or family life would definitely be an obstacle instead of being of any help. I have, therefore, decided to lead a bachelor's life so as to make my way easy." I told her in short my contact with Gurudeo and Swamiji, also various incidents I had witnessed in company with Gurudeo. I told her that wealth, affluence and position have not been able to bring peace and happiness to my numerous friends, relations as well as acquaintances. I definitely know that happiness and peace do not lie that way. To my great disappointment and dismay I have found out that everywhere there is struggle, frustration, dearth of happiness and want of peace; I have, therefore, decided not to follow any set pattern but to lead life in a natural way without creating any complications. I do not know what would be the consequences, but as it seems today my life would be quite different from the one led by my father, brother and rest of my relations. I am more interested in understanding the secret of peace as well as happiness than passing pleasures of senses, ego, mind, etc. I am carrying on with my present occupation only as a *mere passing phase* till I get hold of something tangible to pursue and find out a convincing way to go ahead. I believe in rational thinking as well as intellectual solutions. To be honest, I know that marriage and family happiness could never be my aims and objectives. Your charms and sweet manners got the better of my intellect and rational thinking. I was taken up by a storm, if I could say so, and no time was given to me for thinking. I had almost lost my balance but luckily like a God-sent good friend, you came to my rescue and saved me from possible disaster. In you I have found a great friend and I owe you unrepayable debt. I, therefore, have to request you to forgive me and forget the last afternoon's incident. Let us remain as friends for the rest of our life if it could be possible."

Vinodini smiled and extended her hands. I gripped her tender hands and pressed them like a friend. She was with me till late in the evening and left me when I promised that next morning I would be at her place to take her to our Club.

CHAPTER III

DAYS passed; I was in Delhi for over two years. Myself and Vinodini were now good old friends. I was spending most of my leisure in doing or, say, rather practising what Gurudeo had told me. The process of thinking as well as observation was giving good results and I was feeling quiet and peaceful. The observation of thought and the consequent action had not only become my habit but almost a second nature. It was most interesting and gave me pleasure as well as joy. During this period, I could find a great change in me, not of physical nature, but something psychological.

I lost desire to read, which was so prominent in me, to talk and to mix in company. With excellent health as well as ample energy I wanted to be alone during my long walks and also at the residence. I felt that my whole body was also undergoing a sort of transformation. My inner senses were developing rather rapidly. To be more explicit, the power of sight, hearing, smell as well as feeling had greatly developed. When alone, I was getting visions which were not daydreams, I was sure. I used to see various phenomena, some celestial beings and personalities not belonging to earth. I used to hear various sounds, sounds of bells, music, singing and various instruments.

I used to smell various fragrances and sweet smell not from various objects in the room or nearby. In the beginning I thought it was a hallucination and it puzzled me. After some time I became used to it. All these things gave me a sort of peace and pleasure. Nothing of it disturbed me and whenever I was alone, I used to get this sort of experience. There was no explanation for this, nor could I think of any. I thought this was due to the yogic practices and the process that I was following given by Gurudeo. I had read that people following the process or rather those who progress in spiritualism get such experiences. There was no way of judging my own progress and I was in a way indifferent to it. I was doing earnestly what I was told by Gurudeo to do. Anyway I had decided to continue my practice with great zeal and energy as I had no other occupation excepting my service and there was nothing to disturb my mind. I thought I would discuss these things or what was happening to me with somebody well versed in the line. Being placed in a quite different atmosphere of officialdom, I could not come across anybody whom I could consider an authority in the line. There were some people belonging to various religions, cults, societies, advocating various faiths, but all of them advocated their own line of thinking, quoted various scriptures and books written by various authorities. It seemed to me that everyone of them wanted to convert inquisitive persons to his own faith, prove that only he, his Guru, his books, his findings, were correct and the rest of the world was either in the wrong or being misguided. I had no use for such persons, where free thinking was neither understood nor conceived of. They would not understand that a man can live without any background of the past or planning of the future. They did not care to know what it would be to be free from the past, patterns, books, dogmas, theories, scriptures, religions, classes, castes and creeds. They had no idea of complete mental freedom without any shackles; without Guru or following any particular religion nobody could make any progress in the line of metaphysics - was their conviction. I, therefore, could not explain to them my difficulty nor did I require their help; but I was in a mental condition that would welcome discussion with somebody who would understand me. During this period I remembered Gurudeo much as I wished that I should narrate to him my experiences and seek his guidance which was ever available.

It was Saturday morning and we had a holiday. I returned from my tennis and had no other engagement during the day. I, therefore, decided to relax and take complete rest. I had hardly changed myself when I heard my telephone ringing.

My servant came to tell me that Mr. Gupta was at the other end. I was rather surprised and took the receiver. Mr Gupta asked me whether I was going out or had any immediate engagement. When I told him that I was free, he said that they were all coming and would be at my residence within half an hour. I asked him whether they had any fixed programme or whether they were coming casually. He said there was nothing in particular; but they were invited by a friend of theirs and they wanted me to accompany them. I told him that they would be most welcome to my place as I was in no mood to go out and had decided to take complete rest. I added that it being a holiday it would give me great pleasure if all of them stayed with me for lunch and in the afternoon I would accompany them to whatever place they desire. Mr. Gupta said all that could be decided when we met.

I instructed my servants to keep tea ready for Mr. Gupta and his family and I also hinted that they might stay for lunch.

In about half an hour's time I saw Mr. Gupta's luxurious car entering my compound. It was a surprise to me to see Mr. Gupta dressed in an Indian style and Mrs. Gupta as well as Vinodini as if they were going to visit an orthodox Hindu religious family or attend some religious function.

They all made themselves comfortable in the verandah instead of drawing room. I asked Vinodini what was it all about and where they were bound for? Was it a function that they were attending or were they going to visit a temple? Mr. Gupta said: "Raibahadur Hiralal, a famous businessman of Delhi and an intimate friend of mine, has invited us all to meet a saint who has come to his place. This saint, who happened to be his Guru, is supposed to possess extraordinary spiritual powers. I personally do not much believe in such powers and do not bother about saints and sadhus but my wife has a leaning towards such things and she always desires to meet such people. It was as a matter of fact she who accepted the invitation. Myself and Vinodini had to respect her desire. Vinodini said she was curious to see the man and also the feats of his spiritual powers. She added that your company would add to our pleasure as you are supposed to be in the line of spiritualism and you have met people of that type. That is why we are here and we have decided to take you with us."

I was rather hesitant to go and suggested that it would look awkward if I were to accompany them uninvited. Mrs. Gupta produced an original note of invitation received by her which contained invitation to the family of Mr. Gupta and their friends. I, however, told them that I would better stay at home and take rest than to meet the unknown sadhu as I had no curiosity to see him or to witness any miracle. Vinodini and her mother were so persistent that at last I had to give in and I consented to accompany them. Immediately after tea and refreshments we left for the house of Raibahadur Hiralal. It was about 10 o'clock when we entered the palatial building of Raibahadur.

Number of cars were parked in the compound and large number of people had gathered there. Arrangements were made to receive guests in the big spacious drawing room which was packed to the full. At the entrance Raibahadur and his wife were receiving guests. Raibahadur received us most cordially and he was pleased to see me; Vinodini and Mrs. Gupta were taken charge by Mrs. Hiralal. We were ushered in the hall by Raibahadur and offered seats in the front row. The sadhu or rather Guru of our host was sitting on the specially made dais on which velvet bed was spread which was covered with gold embroidered silk cloth. Cushions of the same material were arranged for him. He had a grand personality and was clad in silken robes. He was white-skinned with handsome face as well as proportionate figure. He looked about forty to fifty years of age; was clean shaven and had lustrous eyes. He was talking to the people round about him when we entered and did not take much notice of us. When he was little free Raibahadur took an opportunity to introduce Mr. Gupta, his family and me to him.

As soon as he looked at me he gave a start and I could see that he was bit puzzled. He looked at me again, smiled and got up from his place. He caught hold of my hand and asked me to sit by his side on the dais. Everybody including myself were greatly surprised at this. I thought he mistook me for somebody of his acquaintance. Mr. Gupta as well as Raibahadur were also puzzled and they did not know what to say. The sadhu laughed and he again told me to come to the dais which I most respectfully declined. Raibahadur tried to tell him that I was his friend but the sadhu said: “Please do not trouble yourself to tell me anything about this gentleman. You may not be knowing who he is, but I know something about him of which you are all ignorant. He is one of those who have right to sit by my side.” With these words, he caught hold of my hands once again and made me sit by his side. In order to avoid any more confusion and without waiting for any more explanation I accepted the invitation and occupied the seat offered. People were pouring in for his darshan and he was blessing them in the routine way as the people of his type do. He was completely at ease and to me it seemed that he was used to this sort of congregation as well as function. People asked him many questions pertaining to their life and troubles and he answered them with ease without any confusion. He suggested to them many ways and means to overcome their difficulties. To me there was nothing new or original in the way in which he handled the people. He talked to the people in Hindi as well as in English. He wielded both the languages fluently. At about 12 noon he rose from his seat and with folded hands requested the people to permit him to retire as he was feeling tired. He told them that he was staying in Delhi for a few days more and he was available every morning to those who wanted to meet him. With these words, he left the hall and asked me to follow him. A sort of curiosity and desire to know more of this man prompted me to obey him. I requested Mr. Gupta to come with me.

The sadhu was given a complete suite of rooms on the first floor.

With curiosity on their faces, Mr. Gupta, Mrs. Gupta, Vinodini and Raibahadur followed me upstairs. The sadhu did not much like all the people to follow us upstairs to his suite, as I learnt afterwards that he wanted to talk to me alone. When we were all comfortably seated in the drawing room on the first floor, Raibahadur asked his servants to get refreshments that were ready for the guests. The sadhu took only fruits while we did full justice to the sweets and other niceties. After tea was served, the sadhu rather bluntly told Raibahadur that he wanted to talk to me alone in private. With these words, he took me to the other room which was spacious and nicely furnished. He asked me to close the door, offered me a seat and made himself comfortable on the diwan. He was all the while smiling and seemed to be in good mood. I was curious to know what all these meant and what he was going to tell me in private. I also felt that Raibahadur and Mr. Gupta and his family may have been even more curious to know than myself what he was going to tell me.

As soon as we were alone, he looked into my eyes and said: "You have made a wonderful progress; and I am extremely pleased to see that your labours are meeting with great success." Before I could reply, he asked me when did I meet Gurudeo last? His question took me by surprise and instead of replying him straight, I asked him how did he happen to know about Gurudeo and that I had acquaintance with him? He smiled and said: "It is very easy and I can see what wonderful change the great Gurudeo has worked in you. You are very fortunate, I may say, amongst those very few who have received favours from so great a man as Shri Gurudeo." He further added that I was in the best hands than any fortunate man can ever possibly be. I should not, therefore, worry about anything in life as it was being moulded by a master like Gurudeo. He said : "You should have implicit faith as well as complete reliance in Gurudeo." He looked a bit thoughtful but immediately started smiling and said: "Oh, you can't escape from the hands of Gurudeo who has decided to make you great for reasons known to him only." I was rather stunned by what he said and asked him if he knew the whereabouts of Gurudeo and had I any chance of meeting him in near future. He said : "You will know his whereabouts in a couple of days and he will meet you shortly. I could see that you are anxious to meet him, and tell him your experiences and to seek his advice. Without going into the details of your experiences I may tell you that they are common to those who are in search and you should have no misgivings on any account. You are only to obey the instructions of Gurudeo and leave the rest to him. I don't think that you have anything to ask me and Gurudeo will solve your difficulty when you meet him." He stopped speaking. There was nothing more for me to ask and I was not in a frame of mind to carry any discussion. I, therefore, got up and before leaving the room I tried to touch his feet, but he embraced me and said that I should not do it. I was really puzzled by the behaviour of this man and I could not understand him. From his behaviour, clothes, appearances and the way in which he was living in the house of Raibahadur, I had formed an opinion that he was a professional Guru and not a genuine stuff. But the way he treated me, talked about Gurudeo, his knowledge as to what I was doing, about my relations with Gurudeo and all the rest that he said, convinced me that he was not an ordinary man but a person who not only possessed spiritual powers but had made a great progress in the line of mysticism. He created great impression on me but as he assured me that I was going to meet Gurudeo shortly, I thought I would ask Gurudeo about him.

When I came in the drawing room I found Raibahadur and Gupta family were waiting for me. They were all curious to know what the sadhu said to me and were disappointed when I said that it was only a casual talk. I could see from their faces that they disbelieved what I said. Vinodini said: "Please do not tell us if it is a secret but we do not believe that he took you to his room and closed the doors only for a casual talk." I said: "You don't know the ways of these people who are very eccentric." Mr. Gupta said: "We have nothing to say more in the matter, Madhav, and we are pleased to see that he has taken you in confidence. One day when it suits you, I am sure you will tell us of your own accord what the sadhu has told you." We left the house of Raibahadur in the afternoon and Mr. Gupta on their way dropped me at my residence.

Next day I received a letter from my father which ran as under:

My dear Madhav,

You will be surprised to receive this letter from me but as a matter of fact I am writing to you in short so as to tell you what has taken place in your absence. Instead of writing to my two sons, I am particularly writing to you because, I am sure, you will understand me as you happen to be the joining link between Gurudeo, myself and your mother. Last year, to be precise, exactly thirteen months before, Gurudeo suddenly came to Ahmednagar. Your mother and myself were extremely pleased to see him. He stayed with us for about a week. For reasons unknown, he had not only come to shower favours on us but had actually come to free us from all sorts of bondage, that is to say, to completely release us. By his grace, we got experiences which the words are too inadequate to express. He gave us various "Darshans" and completely changed not only our outlook of life but convinced us by experiences the purpose of life itself. He told us to observe and practise certain things so as to attain a sort of harmony between the body and mind. This harmony is definitely required to attain a sort of thoughtless condition and in a way to be free enough to get or rather have various as well as varied experiences and to understand them in their right perspective. Keen observation, state of perfect understanding are the conditions necessary to have the experiences. Gurudeo has, by his blessings, teachings, discussions and guidance, dispelled our ignorance and has made it possible for us to understand the truth. Myself and your mother are under his great obligations and to us he is our Guru, guide or God. He told us to observe complete silence on this point for twelve months, I think, in order to avoid growth of ego or consciousness. That period being over now, I have taken this opportunity to acquaint you with what the great Gurudeo has done for us. We both have understood the mistakes we have committed; or rather the honestly mistaken life we led so far. Of course, it was due to ignorance and we suffered for it. At least at the fag-end of our life, we have been able to see the truth by the grace of Gurudeo. Had it not been for you we would not have met Gurudeo during our lifetime. We are, thus, under your deep obligations and have no hesitation to express it, even though you happen to be our son. We are both convinced that you will be definitely happy, attain peace, realise the truth and experience that Unknown, or what may be called God, under the able guidance of Gurudeo.

What we now desire is your rapid progress and ultimate realisation, under the tutelage of Gurudeo. Your mother is not keeping good health, and I think we both have come to the end of our journey. We are in excellent frame of mind though bad in health. We are not afraid of death, not as an unavoidable evil but we see in it not only a change but transformation. It has ceased to have any fear for us. The fear of death is generally due to our fear of losing what we have acquired during our lifetime, what we possess at the time of death – our fame, name, family prestige, our children, kith and kin, etc., etc. It is also due to losing or keeping behind our ideals, ambitions unfulfilled, not attained. The fear is also due to ignorance of what is going to happen to us after death. We are used to a particular style of living in a particular society and set-up. We are, therefore, afraid of an unknown condition after death. From our very childhood or to the period our memory could be stretched back, we always have been in company or in association with somebody or things known to us. We die alone leaving behind all our relations, friends, associates and the things known to us. We are, thus, afraid of being alone after death.

By the grace of Shri Gurudeo, we have lost all attachment to possessions and we do not any more identify ourselves with anything on earth. We have now no ambitions, ideals, desires and cravings left in us. We have experienced by his favour a condition wherein no thought whatsoever of past or future arises; no memory of the past remains. We know or rather have the experience of being totally alone. We now know what is a still mind in which everything dissolves, disappears and no fear of any sort remains. Except joy and pleasure nothing remains in this condition. This has been possible by the grace of great Gurudeo.

As to the physical ills and pains, they have an unavoidable nuisance value, so long as there is ignorance.

Hope this finds you in excellent health and cheerful mood.

With kind regards to you from your mother.

Yours affectionately."

I read my father's letter many times over. It made me very happy to read that he had received the favours of Gurudeo. I did not know what we had done to receive Gurudeo's favours to so great an extent. I wanted to meet Gurudeo so much but did not know his whereabouts. I thought I should take leave and go home to meet my parents. I was rather eager to meet them. The pressure of work at the office kept me busy and it was not possible for me to get leave for some time. I thought, I was getting homesick.

CHAPTER IV

SIX months passed like that and I could neither meet Gurudeo nor go home. It was some time before X'mas I received a letter from my father intimating me of mother's illness. The pressure of work at the office was also reduced. I availed myself of the opportunity and applied for one month's leave. It was sanctioned. I left Delhi the next day for Ahmednagar.

When I arrived at Ahmednagar, I found that my entire family and gathered there. Both the brothers with their families had arrived a day before. I was expected and all were pleased to meet me, particularly mother and father. Father had gone down in health while mother was confined to bed. I could see that her sickness was causing anxiety. My brothers proposed that she should be taken to Bombay for treatment and consultation, where best medical help was available. Mother, however, was not prepared to leave Ahmednagar as she said that no medical treatment would now be of any use and she was more peaceful and comfortable in her home than she would be in Bombay. My father looked undisturbed. He was naturally by the side of my mother giving her all possible encouragement. Surprisingly enough, I could see a great change in both of them. As if by miracle, both of them had attained tranquillity and calm. Neither of them seemed worried and they were taking things in a matter of fact way. All the rest were, however, very anxious.

I sat near my mother, took both her hands in my hands and asked her how she felt. She smiled weakly and said: "Madhav, you may be knowing that my days are numbered. It may be in a few days or even in a few hours that I have to leave you all. I have the blessing of great Gurudeo who was here last year and stayed with us for a few days. I have now nothing to worry about and I am happy. By his grace and only due to his favours, your father and myself have attained that happiness and peace within a short time, which we could not get even if we had struggled throughout our life to find it. Even at the time of leaving you all, I have no regrets, nothing to live for, nor worry about. Gurudeo has blessed me with everything that could be desired. He loves you and I am sure he will make something great out of you as he seems to have decided. I have, therefore, to ask you to stick on to him under any circumstances, any conditions in life. He is something next to God and he will fulfill the purpose of your life. As your mother I have to give you this last advice to follow Gurudeo and have complete faith in him. If you could do this, he will manage the rest."

She drew me near her, kissed me on both the cheeks and blessed me. My father also blessed me and said: "What your mother has said is truth and I thoroughly agree with her." Tears were rolling down my cheeks and I was sobbing. My father said: "Madhav, you are now fully grown up. We have given you education and everything that we could possibly give.

You have proved worthy of our love, confidence and have also attained position in life. As your mother said the great Gurudeo has completely changed our angle of vision and consequently the outlook of life. We all had been trying to search for happiness as well as peace, where it did not exist, and that is why we had to struggle to the end of our life without success. It is not material to say what would happen to the world if all people stop work or the entire family life is disturbed. Nothing like that is going to happen with you, without you or inspite of your joining it or remaining away from it. What we are concerned with is our individual peace and happiness, which may be called emancipation from everything. The words and the terms are immaterial; it is the substance that only matters. The permanent as well as perpetual joy which is the aim and object of life has to be attained by one way or the other. Surely the set patterns do not lead to it and of that we are convinced. Everything that is seen, touched and felt is perishable and so is the body. When you accept or rather are convinced of the perishability of a thing the time factor is not material when considered in terms of perishability. The degree of perishability and the time involved depend upon the factors that govern the objects. We identify ourselves with them, attach importance to them only out of ignorance. Once this is understood conviction comes in and the attachments melt away. I do not know how much you have received from Gurudeo but I trust that you will not be grieved at our passing away. Long associations and the memories of the past may make you uneasy but Time, which is the great healer, will, I am sure, heal the scratches. We have both grown old and have discharged our duties towards all of you to the best of our abilities.

You have to remember the best we have done for you all and forget the rest." I was sitting with them till late in the evening. My brother came to give my mother some medicine. I came out with him in the hall when he told me that mother was going from bad to worse and that there was little hope of recovery.

The atmosphere in the house was tense with anxiety and everybody was aware of what was going to happen. After dinner at night we were all sitting in the hall, nobody seemed to be in a mood to talk, my elder brother Ramakant tried to ease the tension by asking me how was life in Delhi and whether I had joined any public activity. I answered him in a casual way and the topic again turned towards the sickness of mother. It was my brother's wife who suggested that some famous doctors from Bombay may be called for consultation. My doctor brother said that he had already talked to them over the phone and that they were expected next morning. He, however, sadly said that he had no hopes as mother was not responding to medicines. However, he had asked his friends to come down and see if any other line of treatment could be suggested. My brother, however, said that he was surprised at the psychological condition of mother as well as of father; particularly the peaceful way in which she was facing the crisis; and father did not look either upset or nervous. Ramakant said: "Gurudeo whom he had an opportunity to meet once seemed to have done a marvellous thing in bringing about the mental peace to both of them even during so great a crisis."

Our topic, therefore, naturally turned towards Gurudeo. My brother's wife who had no occasion to meet Gurudeo was curious to see him. They all asked me what was my opinion of Gurudeo as I was supposed to know him intimately. My brother asked me that with all my education and position in life, how was it that I could have faith in occult powers, and spiritual attainments of a man. I told them that I knew little of Gurudeo and with whatever associations I had with him, I have not been able to understand him or assess his real worth. To me he was a great saint who from my point of view has attained perfection. He seems to possess an extraordinary knowledge of everything. He is very simple, full of energy, joy and possesses tremendous powers of which he seems to be entirely unconscious. He is above passions, greed and everything that could be condemned. He does not seem to have any attachment to worldly possessions and has neither longing nor desires. Both my brothers said that this did not appeal to reason and the life of such a person seemed illogical. I told them that they could find this only when they came in contact with him. I also told that my reasoning, logic as well as education all fail when I see Gurudeo and I consider my intellect too poor to understand him. My brother's wife told her husband that he should not talk lightly of saints. She said that she had read from books and heard of many saints who possessed powers that astonished the world. My brother said that ignorant people have given undue importance to persons who pose themselves as saints, sadhus, sanyasis, spiritualists, etc. It is not possible for any human being to possess supernatural powers which could not be understood by an educated intelligent man or in terms of science. We talked for some time and when we saw that our parents went to sleep, we retired for the night.

Next morning my mother looked cheerful and seemed to be making progress. My brother had gone to the station to receive his friends. By the time we finished our tea, he returned with two of his friends who happened to be eminent doctors of Bombay. They were known to all of us and were in no way strangers. Immediately on their arrival they examined my mother and said that though she looked cheerful, there was no change in her physical condition. They, however, said that the line of treatment prescribed by my brother was correct.

I was sitting in mother's room since morning and I could see from her face that she was feeling better. Everybody excepting doctors was feeling that she was improving and may survive the crisis if the improvement continued. Father, however, was not very optimistic. He cordially received the doctors and talked to them very freely. The tension in the house was a bit relieved by the improvement in mother's condition and partly due to the presence of doctors from Bombay.

It was about three o'clock in the afternoon when we were having tea when we saw to our great surprise Gurudeo entering without any prior intimation. He was in his usual jolly mood, and entered without any formalities. I rushed to him and fell at his feet. I felt great relief at the sight of him. He picked me up and embraced me. All the members of the family stood up to receive him. My brother introduced his friends to him who were rather taken aback not at the sight of Gurudeo but the way in which he was received by us; Gurudeo asked how mother was feeling and without waiting for our reply made towards her room. I ran to the room of mother and said: "Mother, Gurudeo has come." Mother as well as father was full of joy and she could not restrain tears at the sight of Gurudeo. She wanted to get up but he told her to lie down. he sat on the bed by her side and gently took her hands in his own. All including the guests came to the room to see what was happening. Gurudeo asked my mother how she was feeling; she said: "Gurudeo, you know I have come to the end of my journey." With a smile on her face she added that she was neither sorry not afraid of death. She was expecting him and there he was. She knew that he would come and he had come. She was not concerned with the rest. My father also put his head on Gurudeo's feet and he, too, seemed highly pleased at his coming at the nick of time when he felt that Gurudeo's presence was desired.

Mother said: "Gurudeo, I can't express my pleasure and have no words to express my gratitude to you. I am too poor to offer you anything. Myself and my husband are under your great obligations." Gurudeo said: "Mother, I am here as I had promised you; please tell me what I can do for you and your husband. I am highly pleased to see that you are in cheerful mood and good spirits. I need not assure you that Madhav will be taken care of and you need not worry about the rest of your family. I have already told you what I had to tell and you have my good wishes as well as blessings." Mother enquired whether Gurudeo had his cup of milk and all of us remembered that we had forgotten even to offer him that. Gurudeo smiled and said that she need not worry about it and he would make himself comfortable without any formality. I therefore, requested Gurudeo to have his wash and in the meanwhile milk would be brought for him. As usual he had no luggage with him, so I took him to my room and provided him with necessary requisites. In about half an hour Gurudeo joined us in the hall. He took a cup of milk and did not partake of any refreshment. My brother asked him about mother's condition. Gurudeo was serious for a moment and said: "Eminent physicians from Bombay are here and they are more competent to give opinion about the patient than myself." One of the doctors said: "Excuse me, sir, the condition of the patient is critical, more so because there is no response from her to the treatment. We have done our best but in spite of that her condition is deteriorating and I am afraid she may not get over the crisis."

My brother said: "Gurudeo, you are supposed to possess superhuman powers and we think that you could save her life if you so desire." Everybody in the hall looked at Gurudeo with imploring and expectant eyes. Gurudeo looked at us all and said: "You say that there is no response from the body to the medicines you are giving her and that her condition is deteriorating. What do you expect me to do when her physical condition is beyond repair? To make it more clear, would you like to stay in a house which is in a dilapidated condition and beyond repairs, if you could help it? If you have a chance, opportunity and means to secure a better house, would you not leave the house that is crumbling down and not worth living in? Will it not be cruel and even criminal to force you to stay in the house because your relations desire so? The considerations of relations and love could be called foolish if they hold you back, out of ignorance, from the chances of getting better living conditions than what you are in. The problem is not what I can do but what best could be done under the circumstances. Our sentiments and feelings should neither come in the way nor bar the progress of your mother or whoever else he may be. When it is clear that the capacity of the body to hold life any longer has been exhausted and inspite of all this if the life is forced to stay in the body it will have to stay there without the body properly functioning. Would you, therefore, like your mother to live permanently invalid or continuously suffering from one ailment or the other? Will it not be cruel to keep a person who is happy and jolly at the moment continuously suffering? I would, therefore, like to know what all of you have to say. Please understand me clearly. It is not that I am shirking responsibility or parading knowledge or afraid to do what you desire, but I would like to know whether all of you have understood the problem correctly."

Gurudeo was serious and his clear-cut way of tackling the problem convinced everybody of his earnestness. My elder brother said: "You are the best judge of all and we have no opinion to offer. What we all desire is that mother should be saved and restored to health."

Gurudeo said: "You have still not understood what I have said. Everything has a time limit and so has the mortal body. The body has worn out because of age, mental worries and so many other factors which decay human body. Desires in this world have no end. If I were to save the life of your mother, are you sure she will be happy? Have you ever thought what constitutes happiness? If your mother survives, what about your father? Will his loss not make her unhappy? If she has to lead the life of a widow after his death, what about you all, who are growing in age day by day? What about your wife and children? You will thus see that to save the life of your mother is not the correct solution of your problem. If one has to save her life, to make her happy he has to take care of all her kith and kin, her health, etc., etc. I have, therefore, to request you once again to think honestly, leaving aside your feelings as well as sentiments and tell me what I should do under the circumstances. Everyone of us has to leave this perishable body one day or the other. Premature death may be a source of discomfort, annoyance as well as confusion, but death at a ripe age is a natural sequence and, therefore, should not be a source of worry as well as need not cause confusion. When death is an inevitable, unavoidable occurrence at a ripe age what one should desire is peace of mind and satisfaction at the time of such occurrence. You must have observed the psychological condition of your parents, particularly during this critical time. I myself am satisfied to see that they are not only indifferent to what is going to happen to them but they have attained a condition wherein they are full of joy, which is free from any remorse or pains and they are in a peaceful frame of mind. Don't you think it to be a great achievement? You are worried at the idea of separation of a permanent nature. But it is all out of sentiment and not an outcome of honest thinking." One of the doctors said: "Really we have been wondering over the psychological condition of the patient as if she has no concern with her physical body. Never did we witness such a wonderful psychology during our medical career. She knows that her condition is critical and has very little chance of surviving; even then it is not in the least disturbing the peace of her mind." Gurudeo asked: "Is it not a right condition, doctor, at the time of death if one has to die? I think mother as well as father are at this moment in a right condition to depart if that happens. Please do not misunderstand me and call me cruel. Try to look at the problem from the point of view I have explained."

All were silent and none of us said anything for a few minutes. We all knew what was going to happen, but even then the idea of her passing away was shocking.

Gurudeo said: "You are not in a position to give correct opinion as you are in a confused state of mind, being torn away by sentiments from the reality."

My brother said: "You are right, Gurudeo. Life would not be worth living in an invalid condition. It would neither be desirable from mother's point of view nor from ours. Life would not be also worth living if she has to face miseries and suffer in her old age. You have put before us things very clearly. We have understood the truth of what you have said. I would not desire personally to request you to save her life and to make her unhappy." One of the doctors said: "Excuse me, Gurudeo, I do not think that anybody could ever possess a supernatural power to stop the death. Of course, I do understand the reasons you have given and the way you have explained this particular aspect of life. But surely it would be a wonder or something really supernatural if ever a young life of a promising man could ever be saved merely by means of power where all other means have failed." Gurudeo said: "This is neither the occasion nor

I am here to demonstrate any such thing. But as regards supernatural powers, there is nothing like that in the world. The phenomenon which we do not ordinarily understand, the happenings for which we can't give plausible explanation are called supernatural. It is one of the ways of admitting our ignorance.

"Doctors have attained the powers of curing patients, diagnosing the diseases, performing surgical operations, etc., which may be called supernatural by a man who has no knowledge of medical science. Even reading and writing may be called miracles by a man who has not learnt to read and write. Abundance of money has also produced miracles from the point of view of the poor. Even the seven wonders in the world have been produced by man. Modern science has produced breath-taking miracles. Telephone, telegraph, wireless, are also wonders; but you don't call them miracles only because you are used to them or have elementary knowledge of them. All these things have been achieved by study, spreading over years, pains taken to attain insight and mastery over various elements and creations of nature.

"Those who have spent years on study of various yogas, their practices, the study of metaphysics in its true aspects have attained proficiency and mastery in their own way. Their acts, doings, performances are called supernatural by people because they don't understand them and have no desire to study them either. Such persons are given undue importance through sheer ignorance. But their performances are ordinary things from the point of view of one who knows them. Theirs also is a scientific study and it takes a good deal of time to master the various elements that form the universe. It is all so simple to those who have devoted their life to it. It is not possible for you or anybody to understand it merely by thinking, imagination, even if somebody gives you demonstration. You will not be able to understand how it was done and, to know that, you will have to spend years to study that particular branch of science. I know many have taken to the study of this science in its various branches and by various ways only with an idea of being able to perform miracles but when they went deep and learnt how to perform what you call miracles, they came to the conclusion that they had wasted a great part of their valuable time for knowing things which were either insignificant or unimportant. What is, therefore, most important in metaphysics is to understand the Truth, to realise or experience that which may be called Unknown. The idea of death is painful so long as one identifies himself with body. When one knows or experiences that one has nothing to do with the perishable body which has to be changed from time to time, that is to say, if one could understand or get the experience of how to live alone, quite separate and complete by himself without attachment to anything on earth including the mortal body, then only one can get experience of what may be called realisation. I am sorry you may not understand what I am saying and I don't want to give you a sermon on metaphysics. I have explained to you many things to the best of my abilities and I wish you should understand them."

Gurudeo spoke so earnestly that all were silent. Dinner was announced and we all left for the dining hall. Gurudeo took a little of fruits and a cup of milk.

After the meals we again assembled in the hall. Gurudeo was with mother. Everybody seemed highly impressed with the talk Gurudeo had given. My brother expressed his conviction that Gurudeo was an extraordinarily great man and was capable of doing anything one can think of. We are not able to understand him only because we are egoistic and not prepared to admit our ignorance. Just then I heard my father calling me and I went to the room. I found my parents in a happy mood and I was pleased to see them chatting with Gurudeo happily. Mother said: "Look here, Madhav, we are very happy at this moment and are prepared for what you consider the worst. Gurudeo has promised to take care of you and we are leaving you with great pleasure in more capable hands than ours. He will be your Guru, guide and we are sure you will attain that which very few of us have attained. The only thing we expect from you is to have implicit faith in Gurudeo and he will manage the rest." Tears gathered in my eyes, and I felt a choking sensation in my throat. I embraced my mother and found myself sobbing. She stroked my hair, kissed me on the forehead and said: "Madhav, you should not do it. There is nothing to be sorry for. We shall always be near you if you love what is within us." I was with mother for a long time when I heard Gurudeo saying: "Madhav, by now you have learnt many things and you should not lose your control like that. You understand what is permanent, what is perishable, and what is everlasting." I bowed at his feet, he touched my forehead with his palm and kept both his hands on my head for some time. I at once felt an electric current passing through my whole body and I was feeling immense pleasure. I became calm and had a feeling that all of a sudden a great clarity was dawning on me. I experienced a feeling of transformation and felt that something was actually taking place within me that I was unable to express in words. Gurudeo lifted me and I sat in a chair nearby as if in a trance. I could see that my parents were mightily pleased and said: "Madhav, your work is done and our ambition in life is fulfilled." Gurudeo stood up and said that he would be leaving us immediately. Father and mother touched his feet. He blessed them both, and took leave of them. We came out in the hall together. Gurudeo took leave of us all. Both my brothers and particularly their wives requested Gurudeo to come and stay with them when he happened to be in Bombay. At about ten at night, I saw Gurdeo off at the station. Our guests also left for Bombay that very night.

It was Thursday early morning. Gurudeo had left us a few days before. I heard the servant knocking at my door. I hurriedly left my bed and came out. The servant told me that mother was uneasy. I went to mother's room and found my brothers already sitting there. I could see that mother was breathing laboriously. Father was sitting near her and gently stroking her hair. She slowly opened her eyes. There was a smile on her face and a sort of lustre. A slight jerk to her body and she left us all indeed. Father took her head in his lap and very gently kissed her. Everybody started crying and we knew that mother had left us. It was difficult to control the ladies and we could hardly control ourselves. Father was very quiet. He only said that he lost his lifelong companion. He added that she was given an early start. We did not understand what he said then. We could see tears in his eyes and could hear his thick voice. The entire household gathered there and the neighbours started coming in. It was about 6 o'clock in the morning that mother left us. We took our father out of the room and helped him to a chair in the hall, thinking that he would fall. In a very clear voice he said to my elder brother: "I have made my will and you will find it in the safe, with the full inventories of my entire possessions. I have worked out everything in full detail and you have nothing to bother excepting the execution of it to its very letter. All instructions have been left therein for your guidance. You are the eldest son and have the responsibility of the family that is left behind. You shall take care of all as we have done. You belong to a family that has produced gentlemen of reputed nobility. You have inherited that and I am sure you will behave in keeping with the family traditions and the prestige. The keys of the safe are in the drawer of my table and you will find them there." We did not understand why he was talking thus. But we also knew that it would not be proper to interrupt him when he was giving vent to his feelings.

All of a sudden he got up from the chair and started walking towards his room. Hardly he took a few steps when we felt that he was unsteady on his legs and was not able to keep his balance. We rushed to help him and he collapsed. We lifted him up and he had fainted. He was carried to the bed and my brother rushed to fetch a bottle of smelling salt from his bag. When he returned with a bottle he said that it was too late and that father was dead. Thus hardly within an hour we were without parents. Both father and mother had left us and in a moment I felt myself to be an orphan.

The sad news spread in the town like a flash. People started calling in. Almost the entire town had turned up to have a last look of my parents. They were laid in state in the hall. It was considered almost a miracle that both died almost at the same time. Their bodies were profusely garlanded. At the cremation ground, almost the entire city was present. Speeches were delivered by citizens as well as Government officers, praising my father's brilliant career at the bar as well as for his social work. My mother was also paid high tributes for her social work. Courts and Offices were closed in honour of my father and the markets were closed as a mark of respect for him.

We passed the days of mourning with great difficulty. It was well-nigh impossible to stay in the house without parents which was full of their memories and associations. Without them it looked vacant and deserted. We were feeling as if we were staying in a strange house without the host. I can't explain how I passed my days. There was complete silence in the house on which great gloom was cast and everybody was moving silently with heavy feet and heart.

On the thirteenth day when we performed the last rites of our parents, according to Hindu scriptures, my eldest brother opened the safe of my father in the presence of all of us as well as my father's friend, a Government official, whom he had called to hear the will. The will was read. It was complete in all respects. The entire estate, property movable and immovable, was equally divided between three of us. Donations were given to educational institutions and various amounts were distributed among the servants. As I was not married a major portion of cash and securities was bequeathed to me and my father desired that I should invest the said amount in securities in consultation with my eldest brother so that I may get a good amount of interest throughout my life. I on my part, did not like this and wanted my brothers to take something out of my share. I tried to explain to them that I did not want so much as I had saved enough and I had decided to remain unmarried; but both the brothers refused to accept anything out of my share and said: "We have to respect the desires of our father and his will has to be executed to its very letter. We are happily placed in life and are more than satisfied with what we have." The reading of the will was over and all the wishes of our father were carried out.

It took about a week to transfer the properties in our respective names and make the necessary legal arrangements. Our family house which was passed on to our eldest brother was locked. Only two servants were kept to look after it. A gardener was kept to look after the garden and a man who was looking after our estates during our father's time was retained in service and was told to manage the estate as he used to do. My eldest brother, however, consented to look after the properties of all of us in our absence. I left for Delhi to join my duties.

CHAPTER V

IT was now six months over. The time was doing its work and making the memories of my parents faint. I was losing interest in life. My activities seemed without any purpose. The feeling of absolute loneliness was creeping over me and I had no heart in various activities that I was trying to keep myself engaged in. Gurudeo's teachings were working a sort of change in me but I was not able to understand what exactly was taking place. Mentally I was feeling more alert and a sort of new activity was springing within me but life outside seemed purposeless and uninteresting. The ambition to acquire higher position or to get increment in salary was fast disappearing. I was thus in a confused state as there was no harmony in the working within and without. I was expecting something to happen and had no clear idea of what that something would be. My friends in Delhi were puzzled over my psychological turmoil as they could not attribute it to any particular cause. I, therefore, managed to secure a short leave and went to Bombay to stay with my brothers. They also could not understand the reasons for my mental condition. They thought perhaps it may be due to the death of my parents to whom I was so much attached. They suggested that I should get married so that my feeling of loneliness would vanish. It would create new interest in life and I might get over the constant memories of my parents. I told them marriage was out of question and that I had decided to remain a bachelor. I also hinted that I was thinking of resigning my present services and to take to some social work or touring round the world. I also said that if possible I would like to spend the rest of my life in company of Gurudeo or devote it to the cause of humanity. They could see the truth in what I was telling them but were not sure whether I would be gaining anything by leaving the present life and taking to purposeless activities. They were also not sure whether I would be a successful social worker or I was fit enough to undergo the sufferings of patriots, and resigning the high government job was too great a sacrifice from their point of view when compared with the gains that were not certain and vague. Staying with Gurudeo for the rest of my life did not appeal to them at all. They said that the idea was foolish, childish as well as ridiculous and was, therefore, not worth thinking about.

I, however, decided to leave the services at the first opportunity but not before meeting Gurudeo and taking his advice. While in Bombay I consolidated all my funds and in consultation with my brothers invested a major portion of them in gilt-edged securities and deposited the balance with my banks. My brothers fully approved of the arrangements I made. The change had done me good and I was feeling much better when I returned to Delhi than when I left it. I was now eager to meet Gurudeo and was earnestly trying to find out his whereabouts.

It was Sunday and I decided to remain indoors. Mr. Gupta and his family came to my place for lunch and spent the day with me. It was really a jolly good company but somehow or other I was feeling completely detached. Vinodini was all the while trying to engage me in talk and to rouse me from the state of detachment. Mrs. Gupta suggested that it was high time that I should get married and Mr Gupta supported her. He asked me the reasons for my not getting married. I told him that not only had I decided to remain a bachelor but I was thinking of renouncing worldly life and devote my life to the studies of philosophy and metaphysics. He was shocked to hear this and said: "What would you gain thereby? You are thinking of leaving something concrete and running after illusory things. You have a great career before you. You are competent and born to be a great man. It would be sheer madness to leave a bird in hand and run after two in the bush. I would even understand a gambler staking everything for gaining more but in your case you have no idea of gains for which you are prepared to sacrifice your great career." I smiled and said: "You have no idea, Mr. Gupta, of what is concrete and what is illusory. You have no idea of what is permanent and what is perishable. I have seen and have achieved success to a degree in that walk of life which you call solid. I have thoroughly understood what you call career and achievements. I have now decided to tackle the other side of life which is quite differrent from what I have been pursuing so long. I hope to get success in that too as I have done so far." Mr. Gupta said: "What I desire is that you should not take any hasty step that may give you cause for repentance. You know your inclinations and I hope you will take your decisions after mature consideration." Mrs. Gupta changed the subject and we talked of many other things. Soon after lunch they left my place though they had decided to stay with me for the whole day.

It was now more than a year since my parents died. Nothing in particular happened during this time. I was feeling tired of life in Delhi but somehow or other I could not get out of it; with all my efforts I could neither trace the whereabouts of Gurudeo nor contact him personally.

One day in the office, I received a telegram that my eldest brother was seriously ill in Bombay and I was called there. I secured the necessary leave and left for Bombay. When I reached Bombay, I found my brother down with typhoid and his condition was serious. With all the best medical aid at his disposal there were no signs of improvement. I could see a feeling of anxiety on the faces of all and despair on the face of my brother's wife. This was a calamity for which none of us was prepared. My ailing brother could understand what was passing in the minds of everyone of us. He was not prepared to die though he knew what was coming. He called me by his side and said with great difficulty: "Madhav, I understand my condition is serious and doctors need not tell me that. I could also see that they are trying their level best to save my life. Nobody can change the fate and the will of God is supreme. The only possible thing that could be done at this time is by Gurudeo. I am confident that he is the only person who could save my life, if he happens to be here. Could you possibly call him? The time is very precious and I would like you to contact him if possible." I told him that I would see if I could trace his whereabouts; with tears in her eyes his wife also told me to help them in the crisis. I was deeply moved and thought of my helplessness to contact Gurudeo at that moment. I did not tell them anything but went to my room, bolted the door from within and sat in silence. Tears were rolling down my eyes and with all sincerity I said: "Gurudeo, wherever you may be, kindly come and save the life of my brother which is so precious to him and his family. You are the only person who could save his life which nobody else could do. We are helpless without your aid. Who else could help us if you do not?" I was, thus, in my room for about an hour praying to Gurudeo to save my brother's life when I clearly heard Gurudeo's ringing voice telling me that he would be there shortly and would see that everything is alright. I felt calm and in a way satisfied. I opened the door and went to the room of my brother and told him that Gurudeo had heard my prayer and had assured me to be here soon. He has also assured me that there is nothing to worry about his health. My brother's wife gave a sigh of relief and folded her hands as if in prayers. She said; "I have full faith in Gurudeo and I am sure he will do what he has said." My doctor brother, however, did not say anything. When I met him in the hall, he said: "Madhav, Vinayak is passing through the worst crisis. There are complications and his heart has become very weak. So far as we doctors are concerned, we have given up all hopes. We have done everything that is possible. I think you should not give false hopes unless you are sure about what you say." I said: "Look here, whatever may be your medical knowledge, you have not understood Gurudeo and what he could do. Whatever I have said is true and Vinayak will now survive." He said: "Madhav, I will feel greatly obliged if a miracle like that happens and let me assure you that I will ever remain grateful to Gurudeo."

In the afternoon my brother's condition became worse. Number of doctors had gathered there. They had lost hopes and they said it was only a question of time. The patient is sinking. I was all the while straining my ears to hear the familiar footsteps of Gurudeo and inwardly praying that he should come before the worst happened.

To my great relief, I heard the servant coming and informing me that a man looking like sadhu had come outside and desired to come in. With all possible speed I ran outside and found Gurudeo smiling. I fell at his feet and he raised me. I was crying like a child in his arms. All the people came out to see what was happening. My doctor brother touched the feet of Gurudeo and so did my brother's wife. Gurudeo entered the hall and asked the doctors about the condition of the patient. They were taken aback at the sight of Gurudeo and they did not like his asking them questions. My brother, however, in order to ease the situation told them that Gurudeo was a great saint and was the Guru of our family. Gurudeo without waiting for an answer from the doctors made straight for the room where my brother was lying. We all followed him. My ailing brother's wife fell at the feet of Gurudeo with tears in her eyes. "Gurudeo has come," I said. Vinayak understood what I said, tried to open his eyes but was too weak to do so. Gurudeo slowly went to him, put his hand on his forehead and patted his head gently. He said: "Vinayak, you are alright and there is nothing to worry about." My brother understood what Gurudeo said and a smile flickered on his face. Gurudeo sat on his bed and was silent for a few minutes. The doctors assembled in his room to see what was being done. In about ten minutes' time Gurudeo rose from the bed and left the room. My brother closed his eyes as if in fast sleep. Gurudeo said: "Kindly don't disturb him till he wakes up of his own accord." He left the room and all followed him out in the hall. My brother's wife very anxiously asked me: "Madhav, what do you think?" There were hopes in her eyes and anxiety on her face. I assured her that her husband had passed the danger. "He is definitely going to recover and there is no danger to his life as Gurudeo has assured." When I came in the hall, I saw Gurudeo sipping a cup of milk that was offered to him. Gurudeo asked me to sit by his side and said: "Madhav, why are you so nervous? I came here immediately I received your call." I said: "Gurudeo, how could you come in so short a time? Whence did you come?" He said: "I happened to be in Bombay and thought of coming to see your brother. I could hear your voice calling me and naturally I came to see what was the matter." I did not believe the explanation given by Gurudeo as I thought he did not want to tell us from what place he had come. It was, however, obvious that he heard my prayers wherever he might have been and had rushed to save the life of my brother. One of the doctors said: "Excuse me, Gurudeo, do you think Vinayak will survive? Could you do anything to cure him? So far as we are concerned we have done our best. We do not think that there is any chance of his surviving." Gurudeo smiled and said: "Vinayak is not going to die and you will know it from the condition of his health. Let him rest for some time and when he wakes up you may examine him if you so desire." There was a touch of finality in his voice and nobody asked him any more questions. He said: "Madhav, show me your room so that I can rest." I immediately got up to take him to my room where he had his wash and made himself comfortable on my bed. I asked him whether he wanted anything but he said he was a bit tired and wanted to be alone. I left him in my room and came down in the hall. I went to my brother's room and found him fast asleep. The doctors were waiting in the hall and the main topic was Gurudeo. One of the doctors asked me: "Madhav, could you tell us something more about Gurudeo? We have no faith in miracles and we do not believe that anybody could defy death. We have heard many stories of supernatural powers possessed by sadhus, sanyasis and fakirs but had no occasion to witness them personally. If anybody could save people from death, there would be chaos in the world and the whole machinery of nature would come to a standstill. Let us see now what happens in the case of Vinayak. Do you think Gurudeo is capable of performing the miracle of saving Vinayak's life?." I said: "It is no use arguing about a thing which both of us do not understand. I have implicit faith in Gurudeo and I am not in a position to judge his spiritual attainments, as I have no knowledge of them. So far as the life of Vinayak is concerned, I am sure that it is saved."

It was now more than two hours that Vinayak was fast asleep. I heard my brother calling me. I went and saw Vinayak slowly opening his eyes. He was smiling. He called me by his side and I went near him. In a faint voice he said: "I am under your deep obligations. You do not know what Gurudeo has done for me. He has saved me from death. Life that was fleeting away has been brought back by him. He is not only a superhuman being but a God who deserves to be worshipped. I cannot find words to express my gratitude towards him." I stopped him from speaking further and said: "Vinayak, please do not talk. You have already grown weak and talking may further affect your health. You are asked by Gurudeo to take rest and you have to respect his words." He said: "As you wish I will obey the commands of Gurudeo." In the meantime, my brother entered with his friends and they were pleased to see that Vinayak had opened his eyes. They asked him how he was feeling. He said that he was feeling great relief and that he had passed the crisis. They expressed their relief and felt his pulse as well as heart. They were really surprised to find improvement in his condition. They told him to take rest and we all came out in the hall so that he may not be disturbed. I asked my brother what he thought about the condition of Vinayak. He said: "There is some change but we are not sure whether the progress will be maintained. If he progresses like that, I am sure, he will be out of danger in day or two." His friend said: "Even as it is the change is wonderful. It may be due to the psychological effect of Gurudeo's presence." The other doctor said: "The psychological effect can't last long and I do not think that it could have such a marvellous effect on the sinking heart and the semiconscious state of the patient." I told them that whatever change you might have seen is all due to the grace of Gurudeo and as he has already told, you will see Vinayak completely recovered. The doctors left our house promising to come early next morning to see the condition of the patient. They, however, told my brother to continue the treatment. When I went to call Gurudeo for dinner, I found him fast asleep on the bed. I sat in the chair and thought of what he had done for us. I thought how great were our obligations and how we could ever repay him. We had as a matter of fact done nothing which deserved his kindness; obviously he had no expectations from us but even then we had been of no service to him. Why he was going out of way to oblige us was also a problem. While I was engrossed in the thought, Gurudeo opened his eyes and said: "Madhav, you will not understand things merely by thinking." I got up, put my head on his feet and said: "Gurudeo, you are so kind to us and you have done so much for us, that it is beyond my power of expression to express my gratitude and say what I feel for you. I have found it impossible to understand you by the power of intellect; the more I think of you, the more I am puzzled. You have changed the entire course of my life and I do not know what I am heading for. I have only the satisfaction that my life, future or whatever is completely safe in your hands. I do not bother about the consequences nor do I care for them. The only thing I am worried about is how to be of service to you and whether I would ever be able to repay the debt." Gurudeo patted me very kindly on the head and said: "Madhav, you are still a child. You have still to learn many things. Understanding will automatically dawn on you as you progress. I have done nothing particularly for you and you should not think about it. We have still a long way to go together as I have already told you before and you have not to worry, either about the future or the past. You have only to make the best of the present and if that is done, let me assure you that you have done much." He got up and we came down to the dining hall. After meals we went to the room of my brother and Gurudeo was pleased to see that Vinayak was fast progressing. He opened his eyes and folded his hands to pay his respects to Gurudeo. Gurudeo said: "Vinayak, you have nothing to worry about now. You have passed the danger; have complete rest. We will meet in the morning."

A room was prepared for Gurudeo to rest and I led him to it. I was satisfied to see that the condition of Vinayak was improving. We all retired early. I had a sound sleep and I got up fresh early next morning. I went to Gurudeo's room to see whether he was still asleep. To my surprise I found his room empty. On enquiry I learnt that Gurudeo had taken his bath early morning and had gone out. My brother's wife told me that she had given Gurudeo a cup of milk and that he had gone to see somebody. She further told me that she had given him the car for his use. Gurudeo had promised to come back by 10 o'clock. I asked her why I was not called. She said: "Gurudeo told us not to disturb you."

At about 9 o'clock, the doctors came to see the condition of my brother. They were surprised to see the rapid progress my brother had made. He was not only out of danger but was fast recovering. They said: "Vinayak, let us congratulate you on your wonderful recovery. Let us admit that it is not due to our treatment. You owe this to the grace of Gurudeo. It is something that baffles us completely." Vinayak who could now talk said: "I owe my life to Shri Gurudeo." There was a great joy in the house and my brother's wife was hardly able to control her feelings. Doctors, however, advised my brother to take utmost care and to maintain the progress till he was completely recovered. Tea was served in the hall and we all assembled there. Just then Gurudeo entered the hall. Everybody stood up in reverence. Gurudeo had his usual smile on the face. He straight came in and occupied a chair. He asked the doctors whether they had examined the patient. They all bowed down and said: "Gurudeo, it is all your pleasure. We admit our defeat. It is something which is really supernatural. So far we had heard about the powers possessed by man. We have now seen them. We were confident of our knowledge and we had come to a definite conclusion that Vinayak was beyond recovery. We now know that there is a force unknown to us, rather to the science, that could restore life in a dying man. It is not only a wonder but beyond intellect to understand how it could be done." Gurudeo said: "There is nothing like wonder, supernatural or unscientific. By association, education, circumstances and environments, we have developed an ego in us that makes us or leads us into thinking that we can understand everything; our intellect is capable of knowing things and has capacity to grasp everything. The things, incidents, and phenomenon which are not understood by us or which do not come in the range of our intellect are called wonders, supernatural or superhuman. In other words, we hide our ignorance by using these words. In the field of education and science, we always follow set patterns or go round trodden paths. As we advance, we make researches and discover or invent many things. We generally do not try to know unknown things and try to understand that which has remained unrevealed. Anybody who has probed into this is called superhuman and his actions are called supernatural. When you try to find out, labour to unfathom the mystery of what is called supernatural and unknown you know that it has a science of its own and the findings are scientific. The application of the same may not be universal for reasons of its own. It is not possible for me to tell you in a short time what has taken people hundreds of years to learn and it will not be possible for you to understand the same without seriously going in or undertaking its study. But the only thing I can tell you, there is nothing like supernatural or superhuman. Whosoever desires will have it by serious application, studies and labour which may extend to a number of years or even the whole life."

One of the doctors said: "Gurudeo how long are you going to stay in Bombay? Can we have an opportunity to hear you on this subject." Gurudeo smiled and said: "I will be leaving Bombay shortly. Next time when in Bombay I would be pleased to give you more information on the subject if you so desire." In the afternoon, Gurudeo informed my brother that he would be leaving Bombay that very evening. My brother requested him to stay for some days more and his wife implored him to stay till her husband was cured. Gurudeo said: "Vinayak, you will take some time to be completely cured." He bowed down in obedience. With these words, Gurudeo left the room and I followed him. When in the room he bolted the door from inside and occupied a chair, while I sat down at his feet. Gurudeo said: "Madhav, listen to me." I was all attentive and naturally curious to know what instructions he was leaving behind for me to follow.

Gurudeo said: "I am extremely pleased to see your progress. But this is not enough. You have to go a long way and have, therefore, to hurry up. You have been practising what I told you and have also developed the great psychological observation; but there is no co-ordination betweeen the two so as to get experiences and interpret the same into understanding or knowledge, the reason being you have decided to do what I told you without observing and understanding the relation between what you are doing and what you are experiencing. This is a defect in following, that is why I have been expressing myself against it."

I related to Gurudeo my various experiences since I met him last. He said: "I am glad to see that you are on the correct path; but these are very common experiences and you need not deceive yourself into thinking that you have attained anything worth mentioning. The attainments, whether small or big, have very little importance excepting to show that you are progressing on right lines. They should not in any way distract your attention or be able to induce you to slacken your efforts. This is the most critical period in your life and you have to be very careful. I had every confidence that you will succeed in the effort and I am doing my level best to see that you come up to expectations." I bowed to him and he placed both of his hands on my head. I closed my eyes and felt a sensation, rather a current passing through my body.

I was in that happy state for some time and, when I opened my eyes, I found Gurudeo still sitting in the chair and I with my head on his feet. Gurudeo said: "Madhav, you need not worry about your present occupation and your mode of living. It will be changed in due course in a most natural way." We came down to the dining room. The whole family was there to pay their respects to Gurudeo before he left. He went to my brother's room, blessed him, took leave of all and left. I accompanied him to the station and handed him a ticket for Madras as he desired.

My brother made rapid progress and within a week's time I was able to leave Bombay for Delhi. However, before leaving I told them that I have decided to resign my services and devote the rest of my life in search of truth and eternal peace. I told them that there was no purpose in my carrying on with services as I had no ambition to rise any further in service nor any desire for family life. If I were to lead a bachelor's life, I had enough funds at my disposal lasting till my death. I, however, assured them that I would inform them before I take the final decision in the matter.

CHAPTER VI

THE time went on. It was almost a year since I left Bombay. I was in excellent health and doing nicely. I was pursuing my progress with great zeal and energy. The purpose of life was unfolding itself to me. Great clarity was dawning on me with the result that I was able to see the truth in its various aspects. I was feeling pleasure in leading a secluded life. The social activities had lost their interest for me as I found them to be purposeless. My friends were naturally surprised at my changed outlook of life; of course, that did not disturb me at all.

One Sunday morning I had hardly finished my morning papers and was about to take my tea when I saw Vinodini entering the bungalow. She seemed to be in the best of health and excellent spirits. She was on her way back home from the tennis court. I offered her a chair and asked my servant to bring tea for her. I could see from her face that she was eager to tell me something interesting. She said: "Madhav, whatever may be the reasons, but we have come to the conclusion that you are avoiding our company. Could you tell me in confidence the reasons for the same? I do not believe that you have found more interesting company than ours; or that you are so much engaged in your work or official duty that you do not find time to see us. I have purposely come to see you to know the reasons that keep you away from us. My parents suspect that I am responsible in one way or the other for this. You are not visiting the club now-a-days, and everybody seems to miss your jolly company."

I laughed loudly and said: "Miss Gupta, you have asked me so many questions that I find it difficult to answer them all at once. Believe it or not, I have so much work to do that I hardly find time to stir out of my bungalow from four in the morning to ten at night, when I go to sleep. I have hardly any leisure to go to the club or visit my friends." Vinodini said: "Madhav, could you tell me what work after office hours you are engaged in that prevents you from meeting your friends?" I said: "Listen, you won't understand what I am doing and if I were to tell you, you might call it even foolish. The seriousness of my work will never appeal to you. You are only a fondled child and have never thought seriously of life."

She said: "All right, grand old man, tell me something about it and let me see whether I understand." I said: "To put the whole thing in short, I am preparing myself to be a Sanyasi and obviously I have to avoid the company of a most charming girl like you. You may not be knowing how dangerous your charms are to a young Sanyasi. You will now appreciate that what I am doing is only a safety measure." Vinodini said: "I don't believe a single word of what you have said and you are avoiding to tell me the truth by paying compliments. Now to come to the most important part of my visit this morning. I have come to invite you for dinner tonight and my parents have asked me to take you forcibly if you do not come voluntarily." I said: "If these are the orders, I certainly shall obey them." We talked for an hour or so about our friends and acquaintances and she left me with definite instructions to be at her place at 7 p.m.

When Vinodini left, I started thinking about what she said. It was true that I, intentionally or otherwise, did not meet my friends for a long time; nor did I visit my club for the last so many days. I was drifting away from company and, somehow or other, losing interest in society.

During this period of about an year, what I had achieved was also a problem. When started reviewing this period, I could see that there were many experiences to my credit of which I had no idea. There was definite change in my outlook on life and consequently there was a vast change in my assessment of values. I had experienced strange aspects which I could not have ordinarily done and which were definitely beyond my intellectual capacities to understand. They were, of course, the outcome of various practices I was doing as directed by Gurudeo. With all these, I could not understand where I was being led, what the objective was and where I was drifting to. Of course, when once I had placed myself entirely in the hands of Gurudeo, it was immaterial what was in store for me in future. I was happy with the idea that I was following instructions of Gurudeo thoroughly and I was least concerned with the results. Strangely enough, in spite of strenuous work at the office, the physical efforts and the mental strain at home, I was neither tired nor exhausted. I was keeping quite fit and was in excellent frame of mind. There was no eagerness to meet Gurudeo as I had confidence that he would come at the right time. One thing I could mark was that I had inexhaustible energy which was ever increasing with the efforts I was doing. The only thing I had to do was to direct it to the work I had undertaken. I, therefore, had to curtail other activities. Since the death of my parents, I was practically cut off from my family. It may be that there was nothing to worry about them. My financial affairs were so nicely arranged that they gave me no troubles. I was, thus, completely at ease and without any botheration on whatsoever account.

That night I went to Mr. Gupta's house for dinner at about 7 p.m. Mr. & Mrs. Gupta were genuinely pleased to see me and both of them asked me the same questions that Vinodini had asked. Mr. Gupta believed to a certain extent that I was trying to fathom the depths of spiritualism under the guidance of an able guru. He very earnestly told me that it was something more dangerous than to play with fire. He said that he knew many intellectuals who had completely ruined their career by following these illusive ideas. He also added that one need not sacrifice his material life to understand spiritualism and to attain peace. He said that he knew many people who have made a substantial progress in spiritualism, leading at the same time a worldly life. "A man of your abilities and resources should concentrate on achieving success in life rather than to follow something that does not appeal to reason. To leave the tangible, concrete and definite for something which is unknown appears to me to be idiotic. I would, therefore, like you to think very seriously of what you are doing."

"I am not advising you only as an elder but I have a very soft corner for you and I wish that you should not sacrifice your achievement and success for a thing about which you have no definite idea." The dinner was nicely prepared and our talk was general.

Mrs. Gupta asked me a number of questions about my Guru as well as the practice that I was doing. I was not in the mood to satisfy her curiosity; so I answered her questions in a general way. It was about 10-30 when I returned home.

I could not get sleep for a long time. Mr. Gupta's remarks that I was leaving the tangible and running after something vague started a chain of thoughts in my mind. Was I really running after something illusive and wasting my time was the problem. What is tangible as a matter of fact? The thing which is considered as tangible is past with its memory. Was Mr. Gupta himself with all his self-earned wealth and limited family happy? If the individual achievements in the material world do not make a person happy then it should be considered a folly to strive for the material achievements. A person has to spend his entire life, all his energies to achieve, to get on, to succeed in the material world and at the end has to disillusion himself for not attaining that happiness and peace for which he wasted his life. Is it, therefore, not more rational to make efforts to get that peace and happiness by following a path which is less trodden by the majority? I have at least seen or met two persons, Swamiji and Gurudeo, who not only seemed happy and peaceful but they honestly claim to have been so. So far I had no reasons to disbelieve them and they do not seem to have any motive in telling me a lie or to misguide me. I had already drifted away from my family and there was nothing to tie me down to the worldly life and fancy-fed pleasures. If the idea of pleasure could be only through senses, I think I was getting more by inward process than what I would get otherwise. The pleasure of senses is temporay while that of inner ones is definitely more lasting if not eternal. So far I had no regrets of what I had been doing since I met Swamiji and Gurudeo. My worldly life, therefore, was without any purpose and the only thing that I could do was to devote the remainder of my life to spiritualism. Somehow or other, probing into the mysteries of spiritualism and search for the unknown had so taken hold of my mind that it was quite impossible to go back. I did not think that I was taking a leap into the dark but instead I was feeling that from the dark I was taking a leap into the light. I had full confidence that the day would come when I would succeed in getting that which very few might have achieved. With these thoughts in my mind I must have slept some time past midnight.

Next evening when I returned home, I saw Mr. & Mrs. Gupta waiting for me. I could not guess why they had come, but thought they might have casually dropped in on their way. After exchange of usual formalities I asked them whether their visit had any particular significance or was a casual one. Mr. Gupta said: "We have come with some definite purpose and I would like to discuss with you a very important matter." He further added: "We have decided to get Vinodini married at the first opportunity. She has been given enough education and I have spent a lot on her. Myself and my wife are now getting old and we desire that she should be married and settled in life. We had given her all opportunities to find a suitable husband but it seems that she is not able to make her choice. Any way, we have now decided to find a suitable husband for her." "My own marriage," he said, "was settled by us and you may not be knowing that myself and my wife belong to different castes. Ours in an inter-caste marriage of which very few people are aware. I am an outcast and my parents, who did not like my marrying outside the caste, disinherited me and I had to leave my father's house at an early age. For years, we had to live on scanty means and slowly I made my way in the world with great efforts, striving day and night for success. In his old age, my father tried to reconcile but it was too late and I had already made my life a success to a certain extent. I, therefore, desire my daughter should marry a promising young man belonging to any caste or creed. Myself and my wife have formed a very good opinion about you and we are here to know whether you would consent to marry our daughter, whom you know so well." I said: "You have really obliged me by paying compliments and I have really a high opinion about Vinodini. But as I told you yesterday, I have decided to lead a bachelor's life and have no desire to be bound in wedlock." I explained to him the reasons and told him that my decision to remain a bachelor was neither out of disappointment nor frustration but was an outcome of mature thought. I further said that I, too, would be pleased to see Vinodini happily married and would try to help them to find out a suitable husband for her. Mr. Gupta then asked me my opinion about one Mr. Sen from Bengal who was working in the same office with me occupying a position a little inferior to myself. I told him that Mr. Sen was a promising young man who would suit Vinodini admirably. He was very well educated, belonged to a well-known rich family from Bengal. He was healthy, good looking and spoken well of in the circle that he moved in. He had met Vinodini on a number of occasions and I think he knows her well. Mr. & Mrs. Gupta requested me to sound him about the proposal and inform them what he has to say in the matter. With a promise that I would help them, they left me late in the evening.

Next evening I went to the club and met Mr. Sen. Over the tea I casually asked him whether he had decided to get married and settle in life. He looked at me with surprise and said : "Be frank, what is on your mind? Your questions can't be out of a mere curiosity or an idle enquiry. You must have something up your sleeves and that is why you are here after an absence of so many days." I said: "Mr. Sen, it is high time that you should marry and settle in life. Of course, I have no right to give you any advice as I am still a bachelor; but mine is quite a different case as I have decided to remain a bachelor for the rest of my life." When I told him about the talk I had with Mr. Gupta the other day, he was more than surprised and would not believe me. He said that everybody in our circle looked upon me as a prospective son-in-law of Mr. Gupta. But I told him that not only had I decided to remain a bachelor but also resign my services and devote the rest of my life to the study of spiritualism. He was shocked. He said he was sorry about my decision and advised me to think what a great sacrifice I was making and the chances I was throwing away. He said he had great respect for me but this decision of mine was nothing short of madness.

I, however, told him that we would discuss my career at some other time but wanted to know from him whether he would consent to marry Miss Gupta if such proposal comes from her parents. He said that he would think over the matter and would meet me at my residence on Sunday morning. In the evening,

I told Mr. Gupta over the phone about the talk I had with Mr. Sen. A couple of days later, I met Vinodini at my residence and she asked me how much I knew about Mr. Sen. I asked her why, of all the persons, she was interested in Mr. Sen, and the reasons for the enquiries. Colour rose to her cheeks but without any embarrassment she said: "Mr. Sen has proposed to me; naturally I would like to gather as much information about him as possible." I asked her what she thought about the proposal. She said: "Mr. Sen seems to be a decent fellow but I must know something more if I were to accept him as my husband.." I said: "Apart from his being my best friend, I can confidently say that he is jolly by temperament, well behaved, possessing sober habits, has a promising career before him and comes from a well-known family that is supposed to be financially sound. I would like you to accept him as your husband and I am sure yours will be a happy married life."

Sunday morning Mr. Sen came to me and said: "Sir, I have thought over what you told me last week and also talked with Miss Gupta. I consulted my parents and I am pleased to inform you that myself and Vinodini have no objection whatsoever to join into wedlock." I congratulated him on his very wise decision and told him that he would be very happy in life with Vinodini. Next day their engagement was announced and Mr. Gupta celebrated the same with pomp and an expensive dinner to all of us. I don't know why, but I felt a sort of relief, of course psychological, over Vinodini's engagement.

Within a fortnight of this incident, I received a letter from Miss Malati Gokhale. She had returned from England and was now happily placed as an officer in the Educational Department of Government of Bombay. She also informed me that my friend Ramesh had also returned from America and joined one of the Bombay colleges as vice-principal. She further informed me that she was very pleased to announce her engagement with Ramesh and very shortly their marriage would take place. She very cordially invited me for her marriage adding that my presence was absolutely essential as I happened to be an intimate friend of both of them.

Couple of years passed. Vinodini and Malati were happily married and were happily placed in life. I had not gone to Bombay for a long time though my brothers used to write to me from time to time. I was, I think, drifting away not only from society and friends but also from my relations. The pull that I was feeling for them was getting less and feeble by now. I had completed what Gurudeo had told me to do and I was experiencing a peaceful clarity. Things which looked to me supernatural before, were clear to me now and I knew their causes and effects. Much of my time was now spent in thinking and what could be called meditation. The concentration that looked to me difficult was a simple thing now which did not require any effort. Books had no interest for me excepting as a reference. Thinking was only a process to observe and the mind ceased to exist for me as a ruling element. I was now awaiting a change in life and expecting Gurudeo to effect the same.

After years I again experienced a dream in which I met the saint whom I had met on the top of snow-clad mountain. I recognised him immediately I saw him. He seemed highly pleased. He said: "I am pleased at your progress and you will soon come to occupy your place in the cave." I woke up with a start though not surprised. I thought the dream was foretelling the change in my life.

A happy day dawned. I saw early in the morning Gurudeo entering the compound of my bungalow. Words are too inadequate to explain what I felt, at seeing him so near and at my residence; I was overjoyed and could not speak anything for some time. He lifted me up and embraced me. He was with me for a couple of days. I knew not how the time flew in his company. He gave me some instructions and I discussed with him about my future. I had a lot to tell him about my experiences and he most willingly solved my doubts and difficulties. We had perfect understanding and he was so clear about everything concerning me that I had not only nothing to think about myself and my future but a clear way was open for me. This time he did not meet anybody in Delhi but spent all his time with me and I, too, did not inform anybody about his arrival. He left for Rishikesh in Himalayas.

Within six months I tendered resignation of my service. With great difficulty government consented to relieve me. In appreciation of my services, I was granted a pension though, in fact, I had no desire for it. My friends and acquaintances were extremely sorry for the step I had taken. Everybody, excepting myself, sincerely regretted for what I had done. I packed my things and bade good-bye to Delhi. The parting was difficult. Mr. & Mrs. Gupta, Vinodini and her husband and the entire circle of my friends were there to see me off. I left them with an assurance that, being free from the shackles of service, I would meet them often. I left Delhi for Bombay.

CHAPTER VII

I HAD informed my decision to my brothers and, before leaving Delhi, I intimated to them that I was coming to Bombay. I went to Bombay straight and my eldest brother met me at the station. I stayed with them for a few days. It was rather difficult to convince them of the wisdom of the decision I had taken. In consultation with my brothers I made my financial arrangements complete and I went to Nagar. I decided to stay there till the arrival of Gurudeo and the final course to be decided. My old house, full of memories of my parents and the happy days passed with them, was now completely changed. It was difficult to stay in the house without the loving mother and father. House was kept neat and clean by the servants and the old servants had returned at the news that I was to stay there. The house was full of memories and it was difficult to lead isolated life in the house of my beloved parents. I could with great difficulty overcome the sentiments and engage myself in the routine of my process. The news of my resignation from the service was known to the people before my arrival. My friends, well-wishers and relations were very anxious to know the reasons for resigning so promising a job. They were not satisfied when I had told them that I had no interest in service and that I had decided to lead a retired life. Some took it as an idiotic act while others suspected my sanity. However, soon the commotion was over and it was accepted as a fact.

After about a month both my brothers with their families came to stay with me. It was again a family gathering and the empty house was full. The subject of my future was again discussed and I told them in clear words my final and firm decision to follow Gurudeo and to find out for myself everlasting peace and happiness. I wanted to know or rather understand what is spiritualism and what exactly is meant by realisation. I also wanted to find out and experience the truth and real love. Seeing me adamant, the subject was not pressed any further. Myself and my brothers wanted to settle the affairs about the property and thus I gave final touches to arrangements for leaving the family life. They took assurance from me that I would take due care of my health and acquaint them from time to time of my whereabouts and if possible of my progress as well. I was, thus, a free bird with no bonds left to go anywhere I liked.

A day or two before my brothers were to leave for Bombay, we had a pleasant surprise in the arrival of Gurudeo at our house. I knew that he would come and I was expecting him at any time and my brothers felt great relief when they saw Gurudeo entering our house. They were very anxious to see Gurudeo so as to get clear idea of what he had decided for me. Needless to say that Gurudeo was received very cordially by one and all without exception. When asked by my eldest brother Gurudeo said that he had not chalked out any programme and added: "Madhav is master of himself and is fully capable of deciding his mode of life. I am on my way on tour around India and he may accompany me. Let me assure you that

I will take due care of him and you should have no misgivings about his safety or health." My brothers said: "Gurudeo, we have full confidence that Madhav would be properly taken care of . What we are anxious to know is about his future. He has now resigned his service and we do not know what he is going to do next. When asked Madhav said he had decided to spend the rest of his life in your company and under your guidance. We have not understood what he exactly means thereby. We think he is running after something which is vague and indefinite. He is our beloved brother and we naturally desire that there should be no frustration in his life and he should be happy, wherever he may be and whatever he may be doing. We are confident that you will look after him properly and shall thank you to let us know if ever our assistance is required. It was the desire of our parents that the destiny of Madhav should be left in your hands and we have no objection whatsoever to entrust him entirely to your care." Gurudeo's face was serious. He said: "I am glad that you have confidence in me. If you have what is called faith in me and in my capacity to do good, you need not be anxious about Madhav and his welfare. Your parents have, as you say, entrusted Madhav to my care; like good sons of theirs you have fulfilled their desires. Madhav has accumulated enough of worldly experience and I have no desire to gain anything from him. He has decided, I understand, to fathom the depths of mysticism, understand spiritualism and know what is reality. If I could help him in any way to attain his objective, I would have discharged my duty or rather done the work entrusted to me by his parents. I will take due care of him so long as he is with me but I may not come in his way if he decides to leave me and live an isolated life. Under no circumstances, shall I force my decisions on him or compel him to act according to my desires. All I can assure you is that any change in his mode of living, or otherwise, will be intimated to you immediately. You must have by now observed that Madhav belongs to quite a different category from the rest of you all. Everybody in this world is assigned to play a different role, if I could say that. Destiny also plays an important part in the life of a being. One may believe it or not but one has got to admit it by observation and the results. If you think that Swamiji or myself have anything to do with the life of Madhav, let me tell you we have absolutely nothing to do with it. He is being guided by quite a different force which is much superior to ours and you may call it a destiny or anything else. Nobody knows what is in store for him but I am confident that it is something much greater and it is far more important than one could ever imagine. I can't say more at this stage but I wish him a very successful and glorious life in whatever sphere it may be." My brothers said nothing. In a couple of days they left for Bombay. Before leaving both of them had a talk with Gurudeo for about two hours while I was not at home. Both my brothers had tears in their eyes when they left me though I assured them that I would meet them immediately on my return from tour. Somehow or other I felt that they did not believe what I said. The day following my brothers left for Bombay, I locked the house and left for Bengal with Gurudeo. Nothing much happened during the journey and we arrived safe at Calcutta.

PART - IV

CHAPTER I

CONTRARY to my expectations we did not go to stay with any Bengali gentleman or Marwari merchant but instead Gurudeo took me to a temple where a Sanyasi was staying in a well-built house. This house was called Anandashram and was frequented by many Sadhus and Sanyasis. Our host Krishnanandji Maharaj was a well-known figure in Bengal; he was a bachelor and happened to know Gurudeo intimately. He was really pleased when he saw us and was anxious to make Gurudeo as comfortable as possible. Gurudeo was completely at ease in the company of various Sadhus and Sanyasis who seemed to respect him. I found the atmosphere very strange and was rather ill at ease. To me it was a new experience and I had never met fellows like that. I was really uncomfortable and thought the way they led their life rather unclean and dirty. I was doubtful whether I would be able to put up with them for a long time. This was due mostly to my education and the way I was brought up.

Gurudeo understood my thoughts and feelings but did not say a word about it. I did not take any part in the discussions that took place between various groups of Sadhus and Gurudeo on various subjects. Slowly I was dragged into discussions by those who came in contact with me and, in about a week's time, I found myself interested in whatever they were doing. I also got used to their mode of living and found that it was not based only on simplicity and circumstances but it at least helped to reduce the ego in man, lessen the "I" process and had definitely an educative value from the point of view of spiritualism. I could now guess the reasons why Gurudeo brought me there and why we were staying in the Ashram instead of a palatial building. A number of wealthy persons came to have darshan of Gurudeo and invited him to their houses but Gurudeo was very firm in refusing their invitations on some grounds or other which, of course, I thought flimsy. We were in Calcutta for more than a fortnight. I was told by Gurudeo to mix freely with the inmates of the Matha as well as with the Sadhus and Sanyasis who came there from time to time. He was all the while staying with our host and did not stir out much. I think he was watching my reaction to the new atmosphere and mixing with the people who I had no occasion to meet in my life. I found that almost all the people I met there were the followers of some particular Guru and owed their allegiance to some sect or creed. It was interesting to watch the various aspects of life and the multifarious ways in which the life was being looked upon. Somehow or other I felt that though many of them claimed perfection and were supposed to have acquired what may be called supernatural powers, they had not understood what spiritualism was and none of them had attained the clarity which I found in Gurudeo and Swamiji. I think this was due to their following somebody, following a pattern and trying to attain that which they had either heard from somebody or read from some books. Intelligent search or free thinking was totally absent in the people I met there. By various practices, worship and devotion many of them had attained some powers but they had no idea whatsoever about the reality and spiritualism. Some of them with whom I became closely acquainted tried to gauge my knowledge and tried to know how much I had learnt from Gurudeo. Almost all of them were unanimous on one point, that Gurudeo was a great master and I was fortunate in having a teacher like him. Some of them tried to teach me various mantras and demonstrated to me the performance of certain miracles. They were rather disappointed when I told them that I did not give much importance to miracles and mantras and believed that the miracles could be easily done without them. I tried to impress upon them that if one could understand and realise the *"LIFE FORCE"* and the *"TRUTH"*, one would not be required to make efforts to attain powers. They could least understand what I said and thought that I was an inexperienced person in the line. Anyway, I was passing a very happy time.

Since coming to Calcutta I wrote twice to my elder brother about my whereabouts as well as my health. One evening during our stay at Calcutta, after the meals, we were sitting and talking about various saints known to many in the line. One of the Sadhus who had taken a great fancy for me said to Gurudeo who was sitting there: "Excuse me, Sir, this young disciple of yours has been talking to us about *"LIFE FORCE"* and realisation. He does not give any importance to the process and practices which are absolutely necessary from our point of view. Do you, Sir, believe that the processes and practices are waste of time and energy? Do you think that the knowledge and realisation could ever be attained without process and practice? Do you think that the person who has attained what you call realisation could acquire powers without the aid of mantras?" All of a sudden the hubbub in the room gave place to pindrop silence. Every ear was strained to hear Gurudeo's opinion on the subject. Gurudeo said: "You have asked the questions without understanding what is knowledge and what is realisation. Similarly, you have not understood the meaning of mantras, their causes and effects. Have you ever tried to understand why they are effective though many of you may be possessing powers by their practices? The subject on which you seek my opinion is not so light and trifle as the way and manner in which you have asked me. My answer either in the affirmative or negative will not give you the correct perspective of the subject and will not sstisfy you either. To understand the subject, we have to start from the beginning of the world, the creation of the world, what is called God, what is called Maya and the rest of the creation down to you and me. It will naturally take time to explain what it all means. I would rather suggest, if you ask me particular questions relating to a particular thing or phenomenon, it will be easy for you to understand and convenient for me to explain."

Our host Shri Krishnanandji Maharaj said: "Excuse me, Gurudeo, so many of us were waiting for the opportunity to hear from you and we would consider ourselves fortunate if you enlighten us on the subject." He further requested Gurudeo to take his seat in the hall and asked us all to occupy our seats. A word was sent round, that those who wanted to hear Gurudeo should assemble in the hall. In a short time the hall was packed to the full. Majority of the audience was Sadhus and Sanyasis and a few outsiders who happened to be there in the temple at that time. Gurudeo, in a very clear voice, started speaking which was audible to all.

Gurudeo said: "I am here as desired by you to answer your questions and to explain or rather solve your difficulties to the best of my abilities. Let me, at the outset, tell you that my talk is confined to those only, who are in earnest search and who have a sincere desire to understand things. Now I would request you to let me know what are your difficulties and doubts." Somebody from the audience said: "Excuse me, Sir, could you explain to us what is Brahma and Maya? If Maya is an illusion, how Brahma who is supposed to be the knowledge is enticed and covered by Maya? How could it be possible for human beings to cast off the spells of Maya in which the so-called all powerful Brahma is entangled?" Gurudeo said: "To understand Brahma and Maya, you have first to understand what is real and what is unreal. Maya and Brahma, both being in a sense unreal, could only be understood, of course, verbally by similies and metaphors. What leads to the understanding of Maya and Brahma is only an experience which definitely goes with the individual. To give you an example, I may say that many of you have seen the mirage created by the heat of the sun. It is so realistic that one who has no knowledge of it before would consider it a reality. He would not only be deceived by it but anybody, who would try to dissuade him from thinking it a reality, would be considered a fool or an idiot. The only thing that would convince him of his folly would be knowledge, experience, and nothing else. Similarly, this Maya has been caused by the living force called Chaitanya or Brahma.

"The only thing that would convince one of its illusory existence is knowledge or experience, whatever you may call it. As the mirage is seen when the sun is in the sky and not before or after sunset, similarly this Maya is caused by Purush that is Brahma when the living force is at his best. It, therefore, follows that Maya has existence only when the Purush or Brahma is at his best and not at any other time. To make it more plain, when Brahma is active, there is the existence of Maya. In the mirage you see the creation of the nature and its various aspects. The whole of it disappears without leaving a single trace, as the sun is not shining full, when it is not active. Similarly the entire creation of Maya disappears, when Brahma is not active. To carry the simile further for the purposes of understanding, the sun, as a matter of fact, never sets or rises but it is all along moving round its orbit. It is, therefore, permanent and imperishable but the mirage is perishable; it has its birth and destruction. You will thus see that Brahma is a living force that has neither birth nor death; but that is not the case with Maya. Is it not very clear that everything which has birth and death, beginning and end, perishability and destruction is in short, Maya?

"Coming to the second part of your question that Brahma is enticed and entangled by Maya. You will find the mirage is caused by the sun, its existence depends upon the sun; so also its end. Not only that but you can see the sun reflected in the mirage as well as the entire mirage works on the power radiated by the sun. Consider for a moment this whole aspect from the point of view of one who happens to be one of the subjects of mirage itself. To him it will look that the sun is involved or entirely engrossed into the working of mirage and that it has particular pleasure and specific interest in the mirage. In short, he would feel that the sun is completely entangled in the entity of the mirage. Please tell me now whether the findings that the sun is entangled in the mirage could be called correct? Certainly not. The sun has nothing to do with the mirage which is caused by the rays radiated from it. Not only that, but the sun is not aware of the mirage or number of mirages created by it at one and the same time. It has neither pleasure nor any interest in it. It does not care whether mirages are created, maintained or destroyed. Similarly the Brahma, Purush, Paramatma or Chaitanya, whatever you may call Him, can't be either entangled or ensnared by Maya as it has no interest in it and does not take pleasure in its creation or become sorry when it is destroyed. Nor is it aware of its existence.

"Now what is it that entangles human beings into the folds of Maya and how to get out of it is the problem. Once again, consider the simile of mirage and the sun. You will find that a mirage is a reality to those who have no experience and knowledge of it. You must have also observed that when sun or moon is reflected in the pond or a bucket full of water, children think that the sun or moon has fallen into the water. This clearly shows that the knowledge with experience is the only instrument which dispels Maya. It is, therefore, quite obvious that the only way to get rid of Maya is knowledge and experience. Please understand that the above similes are given to explain the relationship of Brahma and Maya and, therefore, do not waste your time to examine them any further. You thus see that the creation of Maya has never been the object of Brahma. Brahma is the power and life all pervading. The entire creation of Maya is out of this power and energy. Therefore, the power and energy of Brahma pervades through all animate and inanimate objects, that is to say, throughout the entire creation of Maya. It is, therefore, obvious that this pervading energy of Brahma is the only one complete by himself, irrespective of various forms, and millions and millions of created objects. This energy, power, or Chaitanya is present either subjectively or objectively and may be perceived or not. It may be present or may be dormant but there can never be any space or void without it. You are all familiar with electricity. In this very hall where we are sitting, so many lights are burning. Ordinarily we don't know the exact amount of power generated at the power-house but we are familiar with the various purposes for which the power generated is utilised. When you switch on the power becomes visible either through the bulbs, electric appliances or the machines it drives. If somebody says that electric power is only at that point where the lamp is burning, or appliance is working or the machinery is running and is not present at any other point throughout the wiring, will that be a correct statement? Obviously not. It is running throughout the entire wiring and is visible only there, where it has means of exposure. Similarly, Brahma, Chaitanya, Power or God, is omnipotent, pervading throughout the entire creation but its existence is felt or known wherever there is a created object to manifest His existence. You will thus find that the Brahma is exposed by Maya or, in other words, Maya is the exposure of Brahma. You will also find that the object or a number of objects that expose the existence of Chaitanya or Brahma have a limited existence from the point of view of time depending upon the material they are created with; but their perishability irrespective of the time factor is definite. Whenever an electric bulb fuses or an appliance goes out of order, we do not bring in a new electric current but we replace the object. This means that the power or the current remains the same and it re-exposes itself through the replacements. What is, therefore, of importance is not the object, through which the electricity is exposed and which is the subject of repairs, renewal and ultimately thrown out as unserviceable or dead, but the power and current. You will thus find that in the creation various forms, objects, animate or inanimate are of little value when considered in relation to the power or energy that keep them living or that pervades through them.

"You might have also observed that the light of electric bulb varies with its capacity. This means that the capacity to expose energy or power depends upon the material of which the object is made and this capacity may vary with different objects. Even in the creation the persons who expose more of this pervading power are called "AVATARS", Saints, etc. The capacity to expose more, naturally, depends upon the finer material of which the object is made.

"In the case of human beings, the exposition of Brahma, Chaitanya or God depends upon their experience, their knowledge and understanding."

One of the listeners said: "Excuse me, Sir, for the interruption. You said that the Maya is created by Brahma when it is active or at his best and it disappears when Brahma is inactive. Do you mean to say, Sir, that Brahma changes its phases and is active sometimes and is at other times inactive? Do you, Sir, mean to say that the life force or Chaitanya has ebb and flow like a tide?"

Gurudeo said. "I am sorry, you have not listened to me properly. I have already told you not to examine the similes but to understand the subject under the discussion for which the similes are used. If you cover your understanding with your imagination, fund of information and the intellectual consciousness, then it will be impossible for you to understand the subject. In short, your problem will remain unsolved. However, if you all desire to know or have the same question I may tell you that the heat of the sun remains constant but we feel it differently and it helps the creation in various ways because we receive the heat of the sun from different angles owing to the different movements of the earth, atmospheric changes and variations and so many other factors. All these do not affect the sun so far as its capacity to radiate the heat is concerned. Similarly Brahma, Chaitanya, or living force is perfect and constant and has no variations.

At the same time owing to certain factors a sort of activity is created by the power that radiates from Chaitanya into the void or space, whatever you may call it, and that forms the existence of Maya. The heat radiated by the sun gives birth to mirages only at certain places depending upon various factors and not all over the universe nor on every inch of ground. Similarly, the creation of Maya into the void depends upon certain factors not related with the Brahma but with the void and space."

It was more than two hours that Gurudeo was speaking and his ringing voice was heard from one end to the other in pindrop silence of the hall.

Just then our host Krishnanandji Maharaj said: "Gurudeo, you have been talking to us for more than two hours and I don't think that we should trouble you any more today. It is also getting late and some people have to go a long way to reach their homes. I, therefore, request you to continue the talk tomorrow at 7 p.m." Many people looked disappointed at this interruption as the great subject under discussion was being handled by Gurudeo very ably and with mastery over it, but they also thought that what our host said was correct. Anyway, the meeting was postponed to next day evening. There was a rush for darshan and everybody got an opportunity to touch Gurudeo's feet before leaving.

CHAPTER II

NEXT evening there was a great rush to hear Gurudeo. People came in by hundreds from the city when they learnt that Gurudeo was to give a discourse on Metaphysics. The arrangements for the meeting were made in the open compound instead of hall. A dais was erected for Gurudeo to sit and address the gathering. Exactly at 7 p.m. Gurudeo occupied his seat. I was rather doubtful whether his voice could be heard by all in the big compound, but I could see that everybody could hear his voice from one corner of the compound to the other without any difficulty. He was completely at ease and appeared to be speaking without any effort. Gurudeo said: "To continue yesterday's talk further, please let me know if you have any difficulty regarding the subject we have already discussed." A sanyasi from the audience said: "Gurudeo, we are highly obliged to you for yesterday's talk in which you have made clear about Maya and Brahma. It is also clear that the knowledge only can dispel ignorance, that is the only way to know the truth.

"Could you tell us why different persons, who are supposed to be or called "Avatars" or incarnations of God, have founded different religions and have been advocating different ways to attain the spiritual goal?

Don't you think, instead of making matters clear, they have added to confusion and it becomes difficult for an ordinary man to keep faith in the teachings of the so-called great men?" Gurudeo said: "Those that have attained clarity, knowledge, truth, could be called "Avatars", incarnations, saints etc. They have attained this achievement if it could be called one which is the result of their having developed a way of understanding. The factors that cover the knowledge or the reality are of our own creation and one has to study or observe one's own working so thoroughly as to arrive at the real understanding of the thing. In the cases of a few, this understanding has dawned upon them accidentally and in many cases it is the result of their sincere search for the truth and the efforts in that direction. In almost all the cases, the experiences and findings based on it remain the same while the methods of approach are different.

"The individual methods differ because of circumstances, environments, atmosphere, social set-up and many other factors. What is, therefore, of importance is the problem of understanding and not the methods of approach. Unfortunately we see that the methods are given more importance than the problem itself; and that is why there is confusion. The teachings of the persons who are called Saints and the broad principles advocated by them are practically the same. Their followers, who give more importance to the methods and practices, are responsible for the confusion created and have covered the objective with methods and practices. The great men, of whom we speak, had no idea that their followers would confuse the real issue and give prominence to forms and formalities, practices and methods.

"Now the problem would be: Have these saints

served any purpose, or, in other words, so far as human emancipation is concerned, have been of any use to humanity in general or to those who are in search for the truth in particular? You all know that the person who has an experience or knowledge of mirage may try to disillusion those to a certain extent who have illusion about it. It means that an experienced person may be of use to prepare an ignorant one for a stage of disillusionment but the disillusionment is an experience which is to be attained by the individual. A saint or master can only help him to attain a stage wherein the experience may be possible. To make it more clear, let us take an example of a person who is asleep and who is experiencing a dream. The state of dream is so realistic that unless something happens or somebody wakes him up, he moves in a dreamland as if it were a real thing. This means that to shake off the dream, something is required to happen or some outside help is required to wake the subject of the dream or the dream should exhaust itself.

"Similarly, in this life, for the attainment of knowledge or ultimate realisation, three factors are necessary. Something must happen in the life of a subject, which completely would transform him from the state of sleep to wakefulness. That is to say, from ignorance to knowledge or ultimate realisation. It has so happened in the case of a fortunate few individuals but such cases are rare and they may be called accidents or exceptions.

"The second factor of an outside help is of great importance and requires careful listening. The saints or the great ones, that is to say, the experienced ones are there to help humanity in general and in particular those who are in search to bring about the state of wakefulness. How far their help has been of use depends upon the intensity of sleep and the receptive condition of those who are asleep. Those who are benefited by the teachings and guidance of the saints would naturally be grateful to them for the help rendered. Some may consider them helpful while others may even treat their efforts as nuisance. It would, therefore, be wrong to give judgment on the work of the saints by those who are still not awake. The judgment given by persons in sleep on those who are awake could be considered as absurd. Is it not, therefore, clear that those who have attained knowledge have been helpful to humanity in whatever state it may be and have definitely helped those who are really in search?

"The third factor that the dream or the state of sleep should exhaust itself when the subject under it would naturally wake up, is a true one. In this case, there cannot be any consideration of time and space and the subject may have to wait till eternity, till the entire dream of life is exhausted."

At this stage a question was asked: "Do you mean to say, Gurudeo, that the saints are not able to render any help to those who prefer to remain in the state of sleep, that is, those who ignore the saints and their teachings completely?

"If such persons have to wait till eternity for their emancipation, then what purpose the saints could be said to have served for the humanity in general?"

Gurudeo said: "As we have not considered the cases of those few fortunates, similarly let us not consider the cases of those who are mere exceptions. When the great hubbub and noise goes round about you, you feel disturbed even though you decided to ignore the noise and remain in the state of sound sleep. A time comes when this continuous disturbance round about brings you to a state of wakefulness, whether you desire it or not. Similarly, the teachings of saints, the intensity of their messages and the influence created by them directly or indirectly on the atmosphere round about, help the humanity in general to attain the truth. Of course, for such, time and space have no consideration. Your statement that the so-called great men have added to the general confusion and their teachings generally have confused ordinary human beings is not correct. The confusion that exists is due to the misinterpretation of their teachings, which is wilful in some cases while in the others, to suit a particular cult, a religious propaganda etc. the teachings of the great men are profusely quoted to suit the purpose of exponents, propagandists and others who are interested in the cause. The object behind this obviously is to enlist the support of the general public or to effect mass conversion. At such times the teachings of the great are generally misinterpreted to suit the purpose. It would, therefore, be unwise to accuse great men for the confusion created by the people interested in creating such confusion."

Gurudeo said: "I think I have answered your questions to the best of my ability. Please let me know if you have not understood what I have said or any part thereof. If you have any particular question to ask, I would be pleased to answer the same." Gurudeo stopped speaking. No questions were asked and after some light talk, the meeting was closed at about 9 p.m. Everybody seemed satisfied with Gurudeo's talk.

It was about 8 o'clock next morning. I was sitting in the temple and Gurudeo was in the garden. Two Bengali youths looked at me and straight went towards the idol and stood there for a few minutes in reverence. For no reasons I was watching their movement. They straight came to me and asked: "Are you the sanyasi who is called Gurudeo?" I smiled and asked them in return: "Do I look like a sanyasi, with loose pyjama and kudta on? I thank you for the compliments, but do I look like one fit to be called Gurudeo? Please sit down, let me know who you are and the nature of your business with Gurudeo." One of them said that they have heard that Gurudeo was a great saint and they have come to see Gurudeo out of curiosity. I said: "You may not tell me the nature of your business but it is quite plain that nobody would come so early in the morning to see Gurudeo only out of curiosity." One of them said: "Are you Mr. Madhav, the educated disciple of Gurudeo?" I said: "You have come with full information about me, which naturally gives you advantage over myself. Will you please let me know your names if you don't mind?" They were, however, not inclined to divulge their identity and so without pressing the point, I said: "Let us go to Gurudeo, who is in the garden."

Gurudeo was sitting under a tree with eyes partially closed and looked as if he was having a nap. At the sound of our footsteps, he opened his eyes. I told him that two young boys have come here for his darshan. Gurudeo regarded them for a moment and said: "Please sit down. Do not mind Madhav being here. He is a man of my confidence, who is fully capable of keeping your secrets." At these words, the youths not only seemed surprised, but looked rather nervous. Gurudeo smiled and said again: "Please have no fears either from Madhav or me. I know who you are and why you have come to me." There was a sudden movement on the part of the youths. Gurudeo said: "Do not trouble yourself to touch the revolvers in your pocket. The fire arms have a nasty habit of going off at any moment without warning." Expressions were changing like searchlights on the faces of the youths when they heard Gurudeo's remark. They stood speechless for a moment or two and fell at the feet of Gurudeo. "Now be calm," said Gurudeo, "and out with your troubles." They said: "Gurudeo, we are here for your darshan as well as for your blessings. You know the task we have undertaken and we need very badly blessings of saints like you." There was nobody in the small garden and there was no possibility of our being disturbed. In his usual way Gurudeo said: "You are but children and you do not know what you are doing. You are trying to free your country by means of violence. You think that yours is a perfect organisation and that you would be able to drive away the foreigners from your country. I fully appreciate your sentiments and your struggle for freedom. No doubt your patriotism is of high order and deserves respect. Your willingness to sacrifice your life for the cause of your motherland is not only praiseworthy and noble but something more than that. Have you ever thought how your country has come to be ruled by an alien government? Did you ever think why a handful of foreigners are masterly ruling millions? Desire to achieve your goal, merely by wiping out a few foreign individuals of whatever status they may be, would not either shatter the organisation or help you in your goal. You have lost freedom because of nationwide disunity, enmity, jealousy, greed for power and number of religions and creeds, etc. Unless there is unity of purpose in the entire nation, common goal to achieve freedom, dominating every other feeling, sentiments and consideration, freedom will be impossible. When your entire nation will be united for achieving the freedom at all costs, the working of foreign Government would be impossible and they will have to pack off with or without grace.

"Violence would breed violence and your present struggle would be taken up as a challenge by the present rulers. They will try to crush it with all their might and they would be so ruthless in doing so that all efforts in the direction of freedom would be paralysed for some time." They said: "Gurudeo, do you mean to say that our motherland would never be free?" The question was asked with a depth of feelings and sincerity that immediately I felt a sort of respect for the two young boys who looked hardly beyond their teens. Gurudeo said: "You need not worry. Your motherland is definitely going to be free. He who would free her from all bondage would be able to unite the entire nation under the banner of truth and non-violence; with this weapon of truth and non-violence and the entire nation behind him to attain freedom, he would successfully be able to fight the mightiest Government. Let me assure you that India would definitely be free in three to four decades, but I am not sure whether you would be there to see that glorious day. Let me also assure you that a time will come when your names will be written in golden letters in the history of your country. You would not listen to my advice I know. But understand it once for all that sacrifice made for a noble cause is never a waste." One of them said "Gurudeo, what you said may be true. We are glad to learn that India is going to be free; may be, as you say, after three to four decades. It is immaterial whether we are there to see the glorious day. Our struggle is for the entire population and not for any personal gains. We know what would be our fate in case of failure." One of them said: "We have not been able to understand, Gurudeo, whether you love your country and what the people like you are doing to free her from bondage."

Gurudeo said: "Patience is the virtue and your being impatient does not help the cause. The thing which is going to happen tomorrow will not take place today, howsoever you may desire. If you want to see the sunrise you have to wait for another twenty-four hours. All your desires, sentiments and impatience would not make the sun rise earlier. Similarly, the events that are destined to take place some time hence would not take place today, whatever may be the intensity of your desires and magnitude of your efforts. Of course, the struggle that is being carried out, having a noble cause as its objective, will never go waste and it has definitely an immense value from the point of view of the achievement of the goal. As regards my love for the country and the people, let me tell you that with the growth of knowledge and experience, the sphere of love increase in dimensions. When you were small children, your love was centred round your parents and was confined to the four walls of your house. Today with the increased in knowledge the scope of your love has also increased dimensions and it has covered the entire country and the millions of people. Now if someone were to ask you whether your love is confined to your particular house or village, you would think that the question is ridiculous and say that your love has now expanded so that innumerable villages and houses have come within its compass. When you are engaged in the struggle for the freedom of your country, you feel the dispute in the villages for lands, properties, etc. as petty things even below your dignity to consider them seriously. Imagine for a moment that a person who has attained still higher knowledge, gained much wider experience, naturally in consequence, his sphere of love would vastly increase and the entire humanity may be embraced by it, irrespective of caste, creed, religion, nationalism and geographical boundaries. To such a person, freedom of one group from the domination of another may not be so important as you think. Of course, even such a person would not like a stronger unit to enforce slavery on the weaker one. He would, therefore, like to find out means by which stronger unit would be convinced of the futility of imposing slavery or bondage on the weaker one. Under no circumstances, such a person would encourage violence or bloodshed as he happens to love the whole humanity. It is the love for the entire creation that will one day bring peace to the whole earth. A day will dawn when humanity will understand the real meaning of the word 'love'. This is the purpose of the utility of the so-called great saints. Don't misunderstand me but carry my love with you wherever you go." With these words, Gurudeo stood up and started walking towards the temple. The youths bowed again and left the garden by other exit.

CHAPTER III

In a couple of days, we left Calcutta for Jagannathpuri. Our host Shri Krishnanandji Maharaj as well as a number of other sadhus accompanied us to Jagannath. The journey was uneventful in a way but the company of sadhus made it comfortable. The Head Priest of Jagannath temple was informed beforehand by Shri Krishnanandji Maharaj and there was a big gathering to receive Gurudeo at the station. Gurudeo was profusely garlanded. We were the guests of the Head Priest and the arrangement for our stay was made in his palatial residence. Gurudeo, Shri Krishnanandji and myself stayed together while arrangements for the rest of the people who accompanied us were made at various Dharmashalas.

Soon after our arrival we all went for sea-bath. The seashore at Jagannath is attractive. It is spacious as well as most inviting. We were in the water for more than an hour and everyone of us enjoyed the bath. Immediately after the bath, we went to the temple for darshan. The temple has an historical background and is standing there for centuries. It is a well-known place of pilgrimage and it is visited by millions during the year. Our host explained to me the importance of the temple and told me in short, the history of donations and jewellery given to the temple by various Indian princes and millionaires. After spending some time in the temple, we returned to our residence. As per the practice in vogue our meals in the form of prasad of Shree Jagannath came from the temple. It was very rich food and of the best quality. Gurudeo took some of it while we had hearty meals.

After resting for some time I went to see the town and make some purchases. It was almost evening when I returned home and on enquiry learnt that Gurudeo has already gone to the temple. I, therefore, made for it and met Gurudeo and our host there.

As we were coming out of the temple building, we saw a lady belonging to a decent family, shouting loudly and behaving wildly, being forcibly dragged by some people towards the temple. I was rather shocked at the sight and could not understand what it was all about. On seeing us standing at the doorsteps, some people came to us and bowed down to Gurudeo with folded hands. They said: "Gurudeo, you are a great saint, the lady whom you see behaving like a lunatic is a relation of ours. She is possessed by ghost and we have brought her here with full faith that you will cure her completely." In the meanwhile, the lady was brought near the temple where she stood shouting and behaving in a lunatic way. People gathered and many sadhus and sanyasis who were nearby came to see what was happening. All eyes turned to Gurudeo with expectant curiosity.

Gurudeo sat on the steps of the temple and asked all of us to sit down. He addressed one of the sadhus who accompanied us from Calcutta, saying: "Please try your mantras to cure the lady of the possession." Everybody looked at him and he looked confused. He said: "Excuse me, Sir, how did you know that I know mantras which are effective in driving away the possessions?" Gurudeo smiled but did not reply. Addressing the lady he said: "This sadhu knows mantras that control the spirits. He, I am sure, will help you to drive it away."

The sadhu, thereupon, took some water, sprinkled on the lady and started chanting his mantras. The lady started abusing the sadhu, behaved more wildly than before and adopted a most defiant attitude towards him. This went on for some time and the spirit in her would not come under control for some reason or other. The more he tried the wilder the lady grew. At last he said: "Gurudeo, the spirit seems rather difficult to be brought under control immediately. It will take at least a day or two for me to drive it out. I am quite confident that I will be able to master the spirit, however great it may be." The relations of the lady who were watching what was being done by the sadhu said: "Gurudeo, we have tried all this before and number of mantriks have tried their hand but they have admitted that the spirit that has taken possession is strong and naughty, whatever you may call. We have come to you with confidence that you will be able to drive the spirit away if you so desire. The lady is suffering for a long time and if you could oblige her, we shall ever be indebted to you." The condition of the lady was so pitiable and the sight painful that going out of way I requested Gurudeo to cure the lady of the agony she was going through. Even Krishnanandji Maharaj and our host supported my request. Gurudeo asked the sadhu who had tried to cure the lady whether he would feel offended if he tried the cure. The sadhu was a good man and he said: "Gurudeo, you are a master. I would not feel anything like defeat or smallness if you cure the lady. The problem is to cure the lady as quickly as possible and not one of my prestige. The condition of the lady is really pitiable and I would personally feel obliged if she could be cured early." Gurudeo, thereupon, looked at the lady and in a very stern voice asked her to sit down. She looked at Gurudeo with stern eyes for a moment and sat down heavily on the ground grumbling something between her teeth. Gurudeo fixed his eyes on her face for a minute or two and said: "I know who you are! But I do not know what is your object in troubling this poor being." To our surprise, the woman who looked to be out of senses, replied in a gruff voice. "This lady has offended me and as a revenge I have taken possession of her. I have decided to make her unhappy throughout the life. She is doomed and nothing on earth would cure her." Gurudeo laughed loudly and said; "You are a fool. You don't know what you are talking about. This lady has come under my protection. There is nothing on earth and beyond that can trouble her any more. Will you leave the lady immediately before I decide any course of action? Think twice before you answer me and let me know if you have to say anything before you leave her. My orders are final and you have to forthwith walk out of her."

The lady looked at Gurudeo for fraction of a moment and in a meek voice said: "You are a great saint and you should not be partial to anybody, even to a spirit like myself. At your hands I expect justice." Gurudeo smiled and said: "You have already left your worldly possessions, relations and friends. Now does it not look absurd that you should stick to feelings like vengeance which is detestable in the worldly life and much more in the life you are now in?"

"As a matter of fact the earlier you get rid of your ambitions, desires, expectations, etc., the sooner you will be free from the life which you are leading at present."

The lady spoke: "The present life of mine is neither of my choice nor I am in love with it. It was none of my fault that I did not come in contact with people like you before I left my earthly belongings. Great men like you should take pity on us and release us from the ties and bondages that keep us bound to the life in whatever form it may be. It is no use giving sermons which I had plenty when I was a human being walking on earth. I am still rotting in this wretched life in spite of my having learnt and read plenty of philosophy. What is needed is transformation or salvation, whatever you may call it. You are supposed to be in a position to release, transform or give salvation to me. I, therefore, request you to favour me and I assure you that I will leave the lady immediately." Gurudeo said: "Is it not absurd that you bind yourself to the desire of revenge and ask me to relieve you? Think for a momnt what you are doing. Drop the load of revenge, leave the lady alone and you are free. Your time is up and you shall have what you desire." The lady all of a sudden rose and fell at the feet of Gurudeo. With both hands spread he blessed the lady on her head and patted her on the back. She got up, tried to stand up on her legs but she was unable to support herself. Gurudeo gently took her in his arms and she became unconscious. Cold water was sprinkled on her face and in about five minutes she opened her eyes. No sooner she opened her eyes, she got up and looked at us all with surprise. She was confused and seemed shocked at the condition of her clothes and hair. Gurudeo said: "My child, do not worry, you are completely cured," and asked her people to take her home.

Without a word Gurudeo got up and straight walked towards the seashore. He did not seem to be in mood to be disturbed. I therefore, requested everybody to let Gurudeo alone and I followed him.

I joined Gurudeo on the sands and we had a long walk. I asked him whether he was annoyed at something or was feeling unwell. He said that he was quite well and was neither annoyed nor disturbed. He said: "Madhav, you know little of the world and much less about spiritualism. What one has to avoid in the pursuit of metaphysics or spiritualism is the publicity, or the act of being famous. We have got to make a move from this place; otherwise hundreds and thousands of people will gather round about us requesting us to cure them of their various complaints. It is not possible for anybody to change the wheel of destiny and nobody can give a permanent relief. People in general do not want to understand the things. They do not want to make sincere efforts, lead a disciplined life, take trouble to learn, suffer privations for knowledge but they desire to have things as gifts, desire to see miracles only for the sake of curiosity and lead life in their own ways without any change for avoiding their troubles or sufferings."

We returned at about 7 p.m. After meals our host requested Gurudeo to give a talk similar to the one he had given in Calcutta. Gurudeo said that he was neither in favour of giving talks nor was he in a mood to talk at length that night. However, he said he would be pleased to answer the questions if the people so desire but would not be in a position to carry the conversation for a long time. Our host therefore, arranged a sort of infornal meeting on the terrace of his building. Jagannath is famous place of pilgrimage and quite a number of people are present there every day, to pay their homage. A word was sent round that Gurudeo would be giving a talk and by 9 o'clock the terrace was full to its capacity. Gurudeo as usual said: "I am here as desired by you. Please let me know what you have to ask. Kindly make your question as brief as possible." Somebody from the audience said: "Gurudeo, we have seen you curing the possessed lady this evening. Would you be kind enough to tell us what is this possession and how it takes place? Why the spirits desire to take the possession of human body and how is it that they express their desires through human medium?"

Gurudeo said: "It will take very long to answer your question in all their details, but I may try to explain to you in short and I hope you will listen to me carefully. I am not going in for explaining the process of rebirth, but I may tell you that the stage in between the death and rebirth is a spirit world. For some the spirit world is a mere passing phase but others have to pass long time in it before they could take rebirth. Do not misunderstand that every dead being has to visit a spirit world but some of them have to and I will only refer to them. What is it that leads to spirit world? These problems are altogether different and they will be dealt with later or on some other occasion if I get time to explain to you. When a person dies, the conditioning that has formed in his person during the lifetime, consisting of multifarious desires, sentiments, likes and dislikes and so many other things leave his perishable body. This conditioned thing, let us call it substance for the sake of understanding, takes its place in the spirit world.

Human bodies could roughly be divided into two sorts, solid and porous. You can easily understand that it is difficult to pass anything through a solid body, while you can easily pass through a porous one liquid or gaseous things. Though all human beings look alike, the body fibre of which they are made materially differs from each other. Generally speaking, the female bodies are more porous than male ones but even in the males, you come across bodies which are porous. The spirits which are invisible beings, much finer than the air or gas, pass into porous body easily and take possession of it. That is why amongst the possessed persons, ladies form a majority. Spirits take advantage of their porous soft bodies and equally soft mental structure. The females in general possess an impressionable mind and that helps the spirits to behave in the way they like. I have come across a number of males who are also possessed by spirits. As I have already told you, the spirit world is formed of unfulfilled desires and conditioning of various elements. The spirits, therefore, when they take possession of human bodies, express their desires through them. They trouble the subjects of their possession till their desires are satisfied. They sometimes take their vengeance on the subject till he or she meets with a tragic end. The spirits could be controlled by various processes. Mantras form one of the ways to control the spirits. The power of the mantras could be judged by their effects on the subjects."

"Do you mean to say that the mantras are not effective in all the cases? Will you be kind enough to explain whether you cured the lady in the evening by the mantras or otherwise?" said someone from the audience. Gurudeo said: "A mantra has a power like an axe. An axe is able to cut anything into pieces but when it is struck at a hard substance like flint it is not only ineffective but sometimes it breaks also. That is to say, the efficacy of mantras depends upon the substance of which the subject is made and over whom the mantras are used. Referring to the episode of the evening, I may tell you that there are other ways than mantras to control the various elements of the Universe. One who has a knowledge of universe and elements, may not require the aid of mantras for doing such things. I think I have answered your questions and if you could excuse me now, I should better retire." With these words, Gurudeo got up from his seat and came down the terrace. I followed him down and asked him whether he wanted anything. He said "Madhav, let us go out and sit on the seashore."

On the sands I found Gurudeo was in a mood to talk. He said: "Madhav, people waste their time in learning mantras and other practices by means of which they are able to do or create certain conditions which in the natural course can't be done or achieved. These are called or considered miracles by those who are ignorant. This is a sheer waste of time and leads one nowhere. It only creates an ego and much energy is wasted in performing tricks like that. It also leads to a sort of an exhaustion from which a performer may not recover even to the end. With the coming of exhaustion the mantras or powers so acquired become gradually ineffective and in the end they become completely impotent. He then finds it difficult to concentrate and has to lead a miserable life. I have seen hundreds of persons who have ruined their promising career in this line by pursuit of mantras, and the practices, done only for the sake of acquiring mastery in order to be able to perform miracles which in turn lead to publicity, fame, wealth, etc. This, as a matter of fact, is a hindrance to the understanding of truth or acquiring knowledge. I have, therefore, to impress upon you to strictly avoid the performance of that which may lead to the aforesaid evil.

I said: "Gurudeo, do you mean to say that when one uses his power for performing a miracle, or curing a person, he has to use his physical strength? Otherwise, how could there be exhaustion as you say?"

Gurudeo said that in a being a physical exhaustion depends upon the mental strain too. In instances like these a person has to use his mental strength to a great extent. Constant mental strain brings about a mental exhaustion which impairs physical health in many cases. Those who are in pursuit of spiritualism or knowledge do acquire powers and are also capable of performing miracles or bringing about a cure. Such persons are really more powerful as they are in pursuit of something which is great and noble. But even such persons come to grief if they fall into evil ways of using the powers for the sake of publicity, fame, wealth. etc. The reason being, in performing such things they lose sight of their objective, the pursuit of which has given them powers. It is, therefore, important that one has to take utmost care while pursuing this particular line. One should not allow his attention to be diverted from the objective till it is reached. I said: "Gurudeo, is Guru required to part with his power while giving guidance to his disciples? Would it be correct to say that a Guru can have a limited number of disciples depending upon his capacity to impart knowledge? Would he be exhausted if he does it on a mass scale?"

Gurudeo said: "What you think is not correct. In giving guidance to his disciples, the Guru is neither imparting any of his physical or psychological powers nor such guidance would be a miracle or a cure. It is, therefore, obvious that the capacity of giving guidance is not limited by the number of disciples but by the time limit of his physical existence. A lamp has a limit to burn for a certain number of hours depending upon the quantity of oil. It certainly does not depend upon the number of persons that take advantage of the light. The lamp will even remain burning even if nobody takes advantage of its light. The sun shines for a limited number of hours of the day and its rise as well as setting does not depend upon the number of people who are affected by it. Similarly, a person who has attained truth or knowledge, who can only be rightly called Guru, has no limit for giving guidance. A question may arise in your mind why different disciples of the same Guru do not attain the same level. The simple way to understand this is: it rains everywhere, while there exists difference in crops, quantity of yield and even with the same quantity of rains, nothing grows on the rocks or on unfertile soil. Every human being is moulded with different kinds of ingredients, their physical as well as mental structure differs from each other. Therefore, with the guidance of the same Guru, the development of each disciple is different from the other."

It was late at night when we returned to our residence. Next morning, when I came to the drawing room I found some people talking in a familiar manner with our host. On seeing me entering the hall, our host introduced me to them. They were big landlords from Bengal and had come to Jagannath. They learnt that Gurudeo who was already known to them was here and had come for his darshan. They had brought with them baskets full of garlands and some other presents. They asked me when Gurudeo would come down. Assuring to look up, I went to see Gurudeo in his room. I saw him sitting in the chair and on the table by his side an empty cup of milk. I said: "Gurudeo, people are waiting for you in the drawing room, and I have come to enquire how long will it take you to come down."

He said: "Madhav, you can go and have a talk with them and I will join you in a few minutes."

I returned to the hall and told the waiting persons that Gurudeo would be there within a few minutes. Within half an hour's time, Gurudeo came. He was profusely garlanded and was presented with many things including a woollen shawl and a basket full of sweets and fruits. One of them tried to put a garland on my neck but I refused to accept the same politely telling that I am neither a saint nor a great man. Gurudeo was talking to them in Bengali. I could follow their talk with great difficulty. Gurudeo told them that we were shortly leaving Jagannath for Darjeeling. One of the merchants requested him to stay at his bungalow at Darjeeling which was then vacant and he undertook all arrangements to make our stay comfortable. Gurudeo hesitated for a moment but accepted the offer after great persuasion.

Next morning we left Jagannath for Darjeeling.

CHAPTER IV

INSTRUCTIONS were given beforehand by the gentleman who had placed his bungalow at our disposal and his servants were at the station to receive us. From the station we went straight to the bungalow which was very well maintained and we were its sole occupants. Every arrangement was made to make our stay comfortable and a number of servants were there to look after us. Darjeeling is a hill station in that part of Himalayas which is most picturesque. It being the place where the Governor of Bengal resides in summer, is naturally well kept and well looked after. The climatic conditions are ideal, one feels energetic to the point of buoyancy at all hours of the day. Nights are naturally very cool.

The first two days of our stay were spent in visiting various points and enjoying the scenery at various times of the day. There were no visitors, no rush for darshan and no fixed programme. We were, therefore, completely at ease and in two days' time I found a marked change in my health. I said to Gurudeo: "Here is complete peace and perfect calm which we never had almost since the time we met. I would therefore, desire to take as much advantage of your company as I could possibly do." I narrated to him my experiences so far and the work I had done and explained to him my numerous difficulties. He listened to me patiently and said: "Madhav, I have brought you to this place precisely for the same purpose. I wanted to know from you your experiences. The experience is the only correct criterion of the real stage of knowledge or understanding. The rest of your difficulties are either imaginary, fancy-fed theories of the desires of what you wish to become. Desires of this sort spring up from what we read in books, what we hear from people or are sometimes product of fund of information that has been collected in the past."

"Some years back, I told you to practice certain things at Vriddeshwar which were necessary for bringing about an harmonious condition between physical and mental states. You have already seen the advantage of it. I am now going to give you a lesson in what is called Nirvikalp Samadhi. In this state the knowledge and memory of physical existence completely merges into a mental state in its vast expansion, drowns the entire world created by the inner senses. Further the mental aspects develop to that vast extent in which everything within and beyond merges to the point of complete dissolution wherein the mental consciousness completely disappears. The experience and the one who gets experience do not remain as separate and, therefore, there is no experience either to relate or to narrate."

Next day early in the morning after bath, Gurudeo started his lessons. I do not know for how many hours I used to remain in that particular condition. Sometimes it was days and even a week. I never felt hungry nor any particular physical strain. I had gone a little thin but vastly improved in appearance. We were at Darjeeling for three months. Only once during this time the gentleman whose bungalow we were occupying paid us a visit. He was surprised to see my condition and told me in confidence that there was a wonderful change in my appearance and health. He said: "I do not know much of you but you look to be a greater saint than Gurudeo." I thanked him for the compliments and said: "You do not know what Gurudeo is and I have not attained even a fraction of Gurudeo. I am still a novice and I am trying to learn something at his feet."

When alone, I thought over the days I spent in the company of Gurudeo and the change that had taken place in me. I could hardly see in me the big Government Officer of a few months back. I thought, my own people would not recognise me when I meet them again. There wasn't any physical change in me nor a radical change in my dress. I was still putting on clean freshly pressed pyjama and kurta with woollen jersey on, whenever necessary. I was still clean shaved, westernised in manners. The change in me was in the outlook, thought, mental attitude and understanding of various problems. It seemed that clarity had dawned on me and things which I considered problematical some time back were so clear to me that I no more considered them as problems. I was fully satisfied with the present and there was a feeling of complete satisfaction. A feeling was there that I had come very near to my objective and it was within my reach. Gurudeo was generous beyond words and he wanted to teach or rather give me everything that he possessed. I could see in him a real Guru who gives fully without any idea about the magnitude of his gift. He was giving it for no considerations, or without any idea of gratification. It was just like the sun shining or the rains pouring or the earth giving out its all to make the world happy.

I was living every moment and had no regrets for the past or the worries for the future. With the present I was moving almost with the same speed. Every moment was new and full of pleasure as well as joy. There was no consideration of future. There were no barriers and no schools of thought. The entire creation within and without, in sight and beyond, was one of pleasure.

One day Gurudeo said: "Madhav, I am satisfied with the progress you have made. I have done my best and have given you everything that I could possibly give. Now let me lead you to a secret. You may not be knowing that our contact was not accidental. It was deliberately brought about. I was asked by my Guru to take charge of you and to train you up before you meet him in person. I do not know how far I have succeeded. It is for him to judge and not for me. The time has come and we shall be going to meet him in Himalayas." This was rather a revelation to me and it did surprise me to a certain extent. All of a sudden I remembered the dream I had in my college days. I remembered the Himalayas, meeting with a sanyasi, his snow-covered cave and I could clearly remember his words that the cave belonged to me and one day I had to go there. I related the dream to Gurudeo in all its details. He smiled and said: "Madhav, you are going to meet the same personality and may stay in the cave. You will be in the hands of the greatest of all the saints on earth. You do not know how fortunate you are to be one of those very few who are favoured by him, who is like God.

"You will thus see that a great personality, for reasons known to him, has taken interest in you as well as decided the course of your life. Not only this but he had made all arrangements, created all opportunities, managed various incidents in your life in such a way that you have to follow the way chalked out by him for you, whether you like it or not. Of course, this is all for your good which you must have realised by now. I have been only an instrument but the entire credit goes to him." I was greatly moved when Gurudeo said this. I fell at his feet and could not help weeping like a child. I said: "Gurudeo, I do not know who this personality is nor do I care to know him. I am ever grateful to you for all that you have done for me, the transformation in my life would not have taken place, but for you. It is impossible for me to express my feelings, but let me tell you that even God would not have been able to work miracles in my life which you have done so easily." Gurudeo lifted me up and kissed me on both the cheeks.

A couple of days after, we left Darjeeling and returned to Calcutta. During the journey Gurudeo said to me: "Madhav I brought you to Bengal with some purpose and you know that my object is served. You are now at liberty to decide the course of your life. The only thing that I am now concerned with is to accompany you on your journey into the Himalayas. I now leave it to you to fix your programme and meet me at Hardwar. You take your own time to meet your friends, relatives as well as settle your affairs. I shall meet you the day you arrive at Hardwar." I left Gurudeo at Calcutta and proceeded to Bombay. I intimated to my brother that I was coming and it happened to be Sunday when I reached Bombay. My brother and his wife met me at the station. They were highly pleased when they saw me. Both of them said: "Madhav, we see a great change in you and we are pleased to have you in our midst." We reached home. The children made a great noise about me and I could see a genuine pleasure on their faces. After shave and wash when I came down, tea and breakfast was ready and my brother and his small family were waiting for me. My brother's wife said: "Madhav, let us hear how you passed time in the company of Gurudeo and what progress you have made towards becoming a saint." I said: "Gurudeo is hale and hearty as usual and I spent almost six months in his company in Bengal. You must have observed that I have neither become a saint nor a sanyasi and I am still my old self." My brother said: "Don't try to deceive my wife. The change in you is quite apparent. Physically you have lost weight but you look to be in excellent health and your face looks full of energy and beams with a sort of lustre. Particularly your eyes give you away. Somehow or other I feel that though you are so near to me now, you are far away from us; call it psychological, mental, or whatever you like." I smiled and said: "Nothing of the sort; you may be feeling that because I was away from you for about six months." His wife said: "You are avoiding or rather suppressing the truth. Somehow or other we feel that you have attained some superiority, at least over us." I narrated to them how I spent my days in Calcutta, Jagannath and Darjeeling without going into details. My doctor brother and his family were invited for lunch. We all, therefore, met for lunch and it was a sort of a family gathering. They also practically expressed the same opinion about change in me. My brother asked me what was my next move. I told him that I have already decided about my future and I would put before them my plans in a day or two. I spent about a week, meeting various friends and visiting a number of places. After a week or so, I called both my brothers and told them that I had decided to go to Himalayas and I was not certain when I would meet them again. They both were surprised and in a way shocked at this. I said: "Please listen to me carefully. During the six months when I was with Gurudeo, I have tried to understand a great deal of spiritualism. I do not know exactly what percentage of success I attained but let me tell you with confidence that I have understood to a great extent what spiritualism is. I have lost complete interest in the struggle for existence, to be or to become somebody or to attain something. I am, as you see, completely happy and satisfied with whatever I may be having. Your world and mine are quite different, in a sense that things which are more important from your point of view, essential from your consideration, aims and objectives in your opinion have lost their importance, value and significance, so far as I am concerned. Materialistic attachments, worldly attainments, have fallen down in my estimate; in short, I have become a complete misfit in your world. I would, therefore, consider it impossible for me now to lead a society life. You are in a way chained to this life and you have ambitions as well as aspirations in the world. You have your responsibilities and the obligations to fulfil. Fortunately, I am free from all these and there is nothing to hold me back. You are pursuing your ways to become happy and attain prosperity. Allow me, therefore, to pursue my own way and attain whatever may be my objective. You have taken care of me so far and have in a way guarded my interests. I do not think that I will be having any more interests in this world to be guarded. I, therefore, request you to permit me to go to Himalayas in the quest of my objective and with your blessings, I am sure, I will succeed." I could see tears in the eyes of my brothers as well as in those of their wives. I said: "There is nothing to be sorry about; on the contrary, you should be pleased that I am happy and I am going in the quest of perfect happiness. I am sufficiently able to take care of myself under any circumstances and let me assure you with confidence that no harm will ever come to me. The only thing of which I am uncertain today, is the time when I would see you again. By some means or other, I will try to contact you whenever you need me badly, of which please be sure. I do not think that I will require money and my estates have no value from my point of view. I, therefore, desire that they should be equally distributed between you two." They did not agree to this and my eldest brother said: "Madhav, leave the things to me and on no account the arrangements that have been already made be disturbed. Please do not disturb yourself about the things for which you have no attachment, and as you said, let your affairs be managed as they have been so far."

While in Bombay I could not meet my friend Ramesh and his wife Malati. They were holidaying somewhere in Northern India but were expected back any moment. It was Saturday morning and I had a pleasant surprise in meeting Ramesh at the house of my brother where he had come to inquire about me. They had returned only previous evening and had learnt that I was in Bombay and had called upon them during their absence. Ramesh had grown up now into a fine gentleman and had put on weight. He looked happy and cheerful. He was highly pleased to meet me and invited me for dinner at his place that night. I enquired about Malati and learnt that she was in excellent health and by now they had two children who I would be meeting for the first time. In the evening I went to their place at 7 o'clock. They were staying in a well furnished nice flat in an aristocratic locality of Bombay. As expected, I saw signs of wealth and affluence. Everything was neatly arranged with artistic eye. Malati was there to receive me and introduced me to her children as uncle Madhav. Both the children were handsome, healthy and well looked after. After preliminaries were over, we went to the dining room. The children had already taken their meals and were taken to their bedrooms by their attendant. A table was laid for three of us and everything that could be desired was there. Over the dinner I said: "Malati, you look happy and prosperous. You have found in Ramesh an ideal husband. I wish you both all prosperity and everything best." Ramesh said: "Madhav, you are talking in the language that grandfathers generally do. Do you mean to say that you are completely retired from worldly life and have no more interests left? Since I met you this morning, I have not been able to understand the change that has taken place in you." Malati said, "Madhav, we have heard so much about you and your Gurudeo that I am afraid you might turn a sanyasi any moment. I had a feeling of that sort for the last so many years but I think that matters had come to such a stage that you may take a decision in that direction any moment." Ramesh said: "Now be frank and tell us how you have chalked out your future. You have already left Government service and have taken to aimless wandering so far as we understand. Now let us know what is your next stunt."

I said: "There is nothing like stunt but as Malati has already said, I have decided to follow the footsteps of Gurudeo. Perhaps this might be my last meeting with you. I am going to the Himalayas and do not know when I would return. It may be that even for years I may not come to Bombay." At these words they both became serious and I could see tears rising in the eyes of Malati. Continuing, I said: "I had cherished a desire to find the real truth, real happiness and attain peace in life. I may tell you that I have almost succeeded. You might think it strange or may not even believe but with the present life I am completely happy. I may tell you that I have no regrets and have not missed anything that could be said worth having. My looking at life is quite different from yours. We are looking at the same thing from different angles of vision. I am not finding fault with you or the life you lead but let me assure you that mine is also faultless." Ramesh said: "Do you think that you cannot attain your objective by remaining in the midst of your friends and relations? Do you think that it is absolutely necessary to relinquish this world and take resort in the Himalayas? Supposing for the sake of argument that you have attained something great in the realm of spiritualism, of what use is it to humanity in general and your kith and kin in particular?" Malati said: "Madhav, I think you can serve the society still better by remaining here in our midst rather than leaving us all." I said: "I fully appreciate the feelings of both of you for me but let me tell you that for the completion of my present mission I have got to stay in Himalayas for the present. With age, experience and knowledge, you must have observed a constant change in the values of life. Many things to which we used to give importance in our childhood have ceased to have any value now. Similarly the society, social service, kith and kin, friends and relations have their values changed with the growth of understanding. Today, so far as I am concerned, there is a material change in the values of all these things; and in a way I am free from all such considerations." Ramesh said: "Madhav, as you know, I am also a student of philosophy but, unfortunately, I have not received that touch which you have. I could see that no arguments or pleadings would prevail upon you to change your decided line of action. I would like you to communicate to me if possible your experiences and attainment if they could be ever put into words." It was almost 10 o'clock when we left the dining hall. Both of them were really sorry when I left them.

CHAPTER V

NEXT day in the evening, I left Bombay for Delhi. A number of persons were there to see me including my friends and relatives. I had intimated to Mr. Gupta about my arrival at Delhi. He was there on the station with his wife to receive me. I straight went to their place, met Vinodini, her husband and her child. She had a nice little baby, beautiful like a doll and intelligent. I was received there very cordially and it was really a great pleasure to meet them after a long time. Mr. & Mrs. Gupta looked advanced in age but cheerful, Vinodini in excellent health and as jolly as ever. I stayed with them for a couple of days. Next evening after dinner when we met in the drawing room, I told Mr. Gupta about my going to Himalayas. He very patiently heard what I had to say without comments. He said: "I think you have taken decision after mature deliberations and you know what is best for you. I wish you success in your undertaking, whatever it may be. If ever you need any help you can count on me as your friend and let me assure you that I will help you to the best of my abilities." Vinodini said: "Madhav, I do not believe that the life of an ascetic will ever suit you. You have taken a very wrong step from my point of view and your going away into seclusion will neither benefit you nor help the world in any way. It is not only wrong but a foolish action, if I am permitted to say so. I would be pleased to see you come back and settle in society." I simply smiled and did not encourage her any further. Mrs. Gupta said: "Madhav, I do not understand much about Yoga and knowledge. I am a simple woman as you see and have throughout my life been believing in devotion, and performing some religious practices as per family traditions. I have heard from a number of persons and read from sacred books written by saints that one gets salvation or can meet God by devotion. In devotion one is not required to renounce the world or take to sanyas. One can go on developing devotion even by leading a normal worldly life. If this were true, may I know why you have decided to renounce the world and take to sanyas? I think you are making too great a sacrifice which is not necessary." Mr. Gupta also supported his wife's argument. I said: "What you say may be true to a certain extent. I have never handled that line but I can tell you one thing that the worldly life is full of complications and presents various manifold problems. The entire life energy is wasted in solving these and hardly any time is left to devote for concrete work. One is so much entangled in day-to-day problems that devotion becomes a mechanical thing or part of duty without any substance. I have doubts whether it would lead to any tangible results. I, too, have read lives of many a person who made great progress towards the attainment of truth through devotion; but in almost all such cases, they had to draw themselves completely out of what you call their worldly life. Their life in society was reduced to mere farce and in no case it could be called successful. It looked like a picture with no shape. It is, therefore, obvious that even in devotion what is required is to renounce the world at least internally. I would consider it to be living a life of a hypocrite. Is it not, therefore, desirable for one who has to attain truth, to straightforwardly renounce the world? It would not be possible for everybody to live a double life which a devotee has to. Many a time it meets with tragic results, and at no time it is harmonious. It may be good for people like you who are not very serious about it and do not desire to attain concrete results. But it definitely does not suit me, who is after a definite achievement and fulfilment of particular objective. Excuse me, I do not desire to offend you and injure your feelings in any way nor do I desire to criticise your devotion but what I want to impress upon you is that devotion is a long process full of pitfalls and complications and would never suit my nature. We men are made of hard metal and when we are in pursuit of our objective, we do not rest until it is achieved. All other aspects of life and any other consideration have no place while we are in pursuit of the real truth." Mr. Gupta said: "Madhav, I fully agree with what you say." Mrs. Gupta also said: "You have my blessings and wishes for success." I spent a day or two in Delhi in their sweet company and left for the Himalayas.

It was early morning when I got down at Hardwar station. I was thus in the Himalayas. Though extremely cold, the morning was pleasant. The horizon was lit with prospect of the rising sun. I felt a sort of thrill and with long strides I came out of the station. I was thinking about finding a place to stay. Just then I saw a familiar figure coming towards me, and with an expression of joy, I ran towards him. He asked the porter to carry my luggage to a place known to him. Gurudeo knew the place very well and he was known there. We stayed at Hardwar for about a week. It is a holy place visited by people from all over India. There are many sadhus as well as hundreds of people who stay there permanently practising various ways which are supposed to lead to salvation. The great river Ganga, considered to be most holy, flows here with its majestic pomp. On its banks, number of ashrams are there; but somehow to me the place looked much crowded and uninteresting. Gurudeo took me round and showed me many places of importance. Excepting a dip in the Ganga, twice a day and wandering in the hills, I did not take any interest in Hardwar. I felt that so nicely situated a spot remote from cities and towns where one can easily rise to any height by simple meditation or concentration, was being spoiled by beggars, professional Brahmins, hawkers and traders. By erecting numerous temples without understanding the importance by lavishly spending wealth for attaining fame and publicity the rich community of India has done more harm to this place than any good. From Hardwar we moved to Rishikesh. Here arrangements were made for our stay in an ashram. This big building is exclusively built for sadhus and sanyasis to stay. It is ideally situated and commands a nice view of Himalayas. I liked the place immensely. The inhabitants of the ashram knew Gurudeo intimately. We were received with a sort of deference and Gurudeo was treated with respect. Here I met various persons, highly educated who were staying there in search of truth. We were at Rishikesh for about a fortnight. Gurudeo left me completely free and asked me to do whatever I liked. He was busy in his own way. He used to meet me only in the evening. I passed best of my time in company with a number of persons who had made remarkable progress in spiritualism. Here I could get an opportunity to compare notes, exchange experiences with the people in the line. One day Gurudeo said to me: "Madhav, we are leaving Rishikesh tomorrow, keeping all our belongings here. On the journey onwards, you will require hardly anything excepting the woollen clothes you have on your person and a blanket. I brought for you a staff that you would require while ascending and descending the hills. It will also help you to keep your balance while walking on ice. You have also to carry with you a jug which will be of use to you on the journey. Hand over everything you have to the manager of the ashram." In addition to the things that Gurudeo told me, I took with me in the knapsack, my diaries, fountain-pen and such other things which I thought I might require during the journey. Next morning we left Rishikesh. It was the 13th day of January and there was a great rush of pilgrims to have a dip in the Ganga as it was considered to be an auspicious day as the sun enters Capricorn. Soon we left the road and started following footpaths. Gurudeo was leading. We were soon passing through jungles where footpaths also disappeared under the snow.

This wasn't my first experience to probe into the interiors of jungles on foot. Many a time I had combed the jungles in pursuit of animals while hunting. That time I had a rifle or a gun on my shoulders but this time I had a staff instead. I was not hunting the animals but now the mission was quite different. In a way this was a novel experience and it was exhilarating. Gurudeo was in a communicative mood and was telling various incidents in his life in a vivid way. It was a treat to hear him and the incidents too were interesting. We walked the whole day almost without any food. We did not rest in the afternoon as we did not feel tired and Gurudeo showed no inclination for rest. In the evening we came to a very small colony in a deep valley covered at many places by thick snow. It consisted of a few huts here and there. Some children were playing and Gurudeo enquired with them about somebody he knew. Luckily the person he was inquiring about came out of a hut at the very moment. At the sight of Gurudeo he came running towards us and fell at his feet. Soon the people of the colony learnt of Gurudeo's arrival and almost all of them came to meet him. A hut was kept at our disposal, mats and blankets were brought from various places to make our stay comfortable. A big fire was lighted to keep the hut warm. We had our meals of bread, fresh milk and some vegetables.

After meals I hardly laid on the mat when my eyes closed. I had a very sound sleep and by 6 o'clock in the morning I was fresh as ever.

Gurudeo asked me whether I would require tea. I told him that with all my belongings I left my tea at Rishikesh and I did not need it any more. With a glass of steaming hot milk, we took leave of the people of the small village and proceeded further. We were thus travelling on foot in the Himalayas for about a week. We stayed at various places only for meals and rest at night. I did not feel any strain of the journey because of Gurudeo's entertaining company. On the way he enlightened me on various subjects and I learnt many things from him during this period. Our journey ended when we entered a cave in a snow-clad mountain one evening. During the last twenty-five hours, we had not seen a single village or a colony. The last night we had spent under a bush. Though it was my first experience to undergo such hardships, I did not feel anything excepting complete exhaustion. When I saw the cave, I was so tired that I literally dragged myself to the entrance, while what surprised me most was that Gurudeo, in spite of all the walking was as fresh and energetic as ever. This was a secret of which I was curious to know.

Gurudeo entered the cave first and I followed. We had hardly taken a few steps when I saw a tiger and tigress lying there as if in wait. I shouted, caught hold of Gurudeo and tried to pull him back. Strangely enough, Gurudeo did not move an inch but quietly said: "Madhav, do not be afraid of them. They are our friends. They are the sentinels of this place." I must admit that this was an experience for which I was not prepared. I was not exactly nervous but I must admit that I was ill at ease in the presence of the king and queen of the jungle in their own den, without my fire-arms. Gurudeo straight walked to them and both the animals roared loudly as if in joy. Gurudeo very tenderly stroked their heads and the king of the jungle stood up resting his huge paws on Gurudeo's shoulders. I was ashamed of my uneasiness and happily surprised at the sight of the ferocious animals so tenderly loving Gurudeo. I could now understand the power of love which Gurudeo explained to us during our stay at Madras. It was not only a theory but I could see its practical demonstration which convinced me beyond doubt that love could achieve anything beyond imagination and power of thinking provided it is without any idea of consideration or gratification. At the sound of the animals roar, I saw a white head peeping through the thick creepers that covered the further entrance of the cave. At the sight of Gurudeo, a very old man came out extending both of his hands and embraced Gurudeo most lovingly. Gurudeo asked me to take his darshan and I fell at his feet. In spite of his age he looked very strong and he lifted me up with ease. He blessed me with great affection, caught hold my hands and led us in.

CHAPTER VI

THE cave was very spacious inside; it extended long into the hill and was broad enough to accommodate a large number of people. It was well ventilated and I could see sufficient light pouring in from various holes. There were about a dozen people in the cave, occupied in one way or other. They all hurriedly stood up to see us and at the sight of Gurudeo, bowed down in reverence. I found a very friendly atmosphere and felt that I was amongst my old friends. The old gentleman asked us to sit down and make ourselves comfortable. The grass mats were spread on the floor and a big fire was burning, which kept the cave warm. The cave was divided into compartments. I followed Gurudeo in the next compartment where I found arrangement for bath. In one corner, there was a small storage, which contained enough hot water. After a long tiresome journey, I found the hot water bath most welcome. I took my bath and felt completely refreshed. By the time we came out to the main drawing hall, we found food ready. It consisted of hot bread made of some flour tasting like wheat and liberal quantity of hot milk. I think I must have consumed number of breads and good quantity of milk. The people in the cave told us that they were expecting us this morning. They were informed by the old gentleman that we were coming. They rarely had visitors; so they were happy to receive us. Gurudeo was talking to the old man and I joined the company of the rest. To my surprise I found the cave to be much bigger than I had expected. At the end, there was a cow-shed or rather a compound where more than a dozen cows were grazing. The sun must have set sometime back and it was getting dark in the cave. The drawing room was poorly lighted by a torch and I found quite a number of sticks wrapped with cloth, dipped in oil to be used as torches, kept ready in one corner. I was feeling sleepy, I think, due to exhaustion and partly due to the quantity of food I had taken. Gurudeo said: "Madhav, you are tired; you may go to bed." A bed prepared of soft grass on which a mat was spread was shown to me. Immediately I stretched myself on the bed, closed my eyes.

When I opened my eyes next, it was already morning. I was in the bed with a couple of blankets on. Gurudeo was standing near and with a beaming smile he extended his hand to me to get up. "Madhav," he said, "how do you feel? You were completely exhausted and you had sound sleep. It is morning and everybody has started his work." I at once got up, folded my blankets and arranged them at a place where other blankets were kept. We left the cave together. Gurudeo led me to a place about a mile away from the cave where there was a small stream coming from the mountain. The water was icy cold. After wash, I took a dip in the icy water and found it refreshing. Finishing our bath and washing, we returned to the cave. Gurudeo said "Madhav, you have to help yourself here. There are no servants and no formalities of any sort." I found everybody fully occupied in his own work. There was hot milk kept near the fire. I gave some of it to Gurudeo and helped myself to a glassful. Gurudeo told me that the old man was the head of the cave and the rest were his followers. They were practising whatever he told them to do. When I asked him what could be the age of the old man, Gurudeo said: "I am unable to tell you. For more than fifty years, I have been seeing the old man exactly as he looks today. He is much older than myself, that is certain. The number of people who have learnt under him is great. He stays here permanently and gives knowledge to those who seek guidance." I asked Gurudeo how long we are going to stay here.

He said: "Madhav, we shall stay here for some time and now you start your usual routine."

It was after a week we came to the cave. Gurudeo said: "Madhav, tomorrow morning, you are to be in Nirvikalp Samadhi and have to be in it till I wake you up." Though Gurudeo had taught this to me, he had strictly forbidden me from going into it without his prior permission. I was, therefore, extremely pleased at the prospect of going into it. Next morning we got up early and when we returned to the cave after bath, I found arrangements were made for me to sit at a particular place, where flowers were spread and incense was burning. The whole atmosphere looked fresh, pervading with sweet scent of flowers and incense. I bowed down to everybody and touched the feet of Gurudeo. I took my seat on the grass matting. Gurudeo sat before me and within a few minutes I closed my eyes.

The state of Samadhi can be only experienced and not explained. When I opened my eyes, Gurudeo was sitting before me and everything was exactly as it was when I went into the Samadhi. I tried to get up but found it impossible. Gurudeo rushed towards me and embraced me most lovingly. He said: "Madhav; do not try to get up." The old man of the cave asked his disciples to massage my body with some oil that he had with him. I saw a sense of great delight on the face of the old man and also on those of his followers. After about an hour's massaging of the body, I could stand and walk about with difficulty. I was rather surprised at my physical condition and could not understand the reasons. I thought I must have been in Samadhi for a very short time, at least not long enough, to stiffen my limbs. To my surprise I also found that my body looked much emaciated and had lost whatever flesh I may be having. In spite of thin body I was neither feeling weak nor exhausted. On the contrary, I was feeling full of energy and a sense of happiness. The old man said: "Madhav, I am fully satisfied with your progress; your achievements are really great and the entire credit goes to your Gurudeo." I was then given a glassful of lemon juice to drink. In a couple of hours, my movements were completely free. Gurudeo said: "Madhav, do you know that the whole year has passed and you were in Samadhi state without being aware of time?" I then became conscious of tremendous growth of hair on my head and that I had grown a very respectable wild beard and thick bush of moustaches on my lips. I was curious to see myself in the mirror but had to be satisfied with my reflection in the clear water of the rivulet. My whole face had undergone a change and I was hardly able to recognise myself.

After bath I took some milk only and did not feel inclined to take any solid food. Gurudeo told me that during the period I was in Samadhi he had gone on his travel and had returned only a day before. The old man and his disciples took care of me in his absence. The people in the cave were so nice towards me that they would not allow me to express my gratitude to them. A couple of days later Gurudeo said to me: "Madhav, we are now moving toward the last stage of our journey. I will leave you there in charge of the Supreme Being who is my Guru. I think I have done the work entrusted to me. In you I found an ideal subject." I said: "Gurudeo, I do not know your Guru and have not had the pleasure of meeting him. I shall, however, follow your instructions to the last as I have done so far. I have no interest in life left."

Early next morning we left the cave, had our bath at the usual place and started on our journey. We were moving about in the Himalayas treading on snow at various places, taking rest wherever possible. We walked for about a week through jungles and snow. Gurudeo knew his way very well and hence there was no disaster or accident. One fine morning when the sun was about to rise we left our place of rest and started moving. The whole snow-clad mountain round about seemed to have been made of gold due to the tender rays of the sun. Everywhere there was calm and peace and it was really a pleasure to walk in the cold atmosphere. We had hardly walked a mile and half when Gurudeo, who was walking ahead of me, stopped all of a sudden. With a start, I looked at the direction he was looking, and saw a person coming towards us. As he came nearer, Gurudeo rushed towards him and fell at his feet. My memory, in an instance, flashed back to the dream I had seen years back. In him I could recognise the person I saw in the dream twice over. I followed Gurudeo and fell at his feet. He lifted me up and very tenderly embraced me. In his sweet voice he said: "Oh Madhav, you have come. I have been waiting for you." Gurudeo said: "Oh Divine, I have brought him to you as per your instructions. I think I have carried out your orders to the full." He said to Gurudeo: "I am pleased with what you have done. Now let us go to our place." In a short time, we arrived at the cave I had seen in the dream and those two huge dogs came to receive us at the entrance. The dogs showed a great familiarity towards me though I thought myself a stranger. Gurudeo was naturally known to them intimately. The cave I could see, was really very big, accommodative and comfortable. We all sat down there, Gurudeo went inside the cave and brought hot milk for all of us. The Divine one said to me: "Madhav, you shall stay here with me and Chidanand whom you call Gurudeo will go his own way as he has got some work to do. He will of course stay with us for some time as he requires rest and till you are familiar with the conditions here." Gurudeo said: "Madhav, this day next week I will leave you. If you want me to carry any message to your relations and friends, I will be pleased to deliver the same." I said: "Gurudeo, before you go, I will complete my diary and hand the same over to you." My last possessions consisted of fountain-pen, wrist watch and letters to Vinodini, my brother and fountain-pen and diaries to Malati.

I think I have come to the end of my journey and I do not know whether I will write any diary hereafter. I had formed the habit of writing diary from my very boyhood. I think I had hardly entered English School when our teacher told us to write a day-to-day diary of the events of the day. For reasons unknown, I continued the same to this day. I do not know whether I would miss it henceforth. Before completing it I would like to note down my last observations, if at all they could be called last.

Reviewing my past, I have to say that I passed a very good life. I have no regrets and have nothing to be ashamed of. From my very childhood I had the tenacity of purpose in carrying out my decisions. Never had I developed any inferiority complex or superiority consciousness. I would not accept anything as impossible. I had confidence that I was capable of achieving all that which a human being could achieve. Fortunately, I was happily placed in life and therefore, did not know any struggle for existence. That gave me ample time to pursue my objectives. In my school and college days academic career and proficiency in games were my objectives. I did achieve marked success in both the spheres. Somehow or other I felt that there was little peace and happiness in life being led by people at large. On careful observations of the day-to-day life of my friends and relations, I was convinced that I was right in my surmise. I started thinking that everlasting peace and happiness was possible. I came in contact first with Swamiji and then with Gurudeo. Swamiji impressed me well but when I saw Gurudeo I felt certain that here was somebody who was really happy and peaceful. I had read a lot on this subject but thought it all to be a theory. When I met Gurudeo I felt that it was possible. I accepted it as a challenge and determined to attain that, of which I had no idea, knowledge or information. It was easy for me to lead what is said to be a happy married life, but I thought it would tie me down hand and foot to the family life. I would thus be deprived of absolute freedom needed for my purpose. I, therefore, got over the temptations, allurements and comforts of worldly life. I do not think that I would have covered such a big distance in so short a time had I allowed myself to be shackled to the world. Compared with the gains my losses were microscopic. When I came under the direct guidance of Gurudeo, and started following his instructions, I could see that a guidance was neither superfluous nor a trash for those in search of truth, leaving aside exceptions, and the fortunate few who realised truth instantaneously. The majority of the truth-seekers do need guidance. The word process has been misunderstood and misinterpreted to such an extent that it has lost its real meaning. Serious thinking to understand the working of the inner system leads the mind to its working and experience and is also in a sense, a process that looked to me essential. Mere intellectual convictions, all accepted truths, the teaching of books, the lectures, and the talks of the so-called realised persons do not seem to me to be capable of controlling the ever moving mind. The mind in its movements does not recognise the barriers of distance, ethics, laws of decency, culture and education, choice of subjects etc. Its movement is so swift and sporadic that mere understanding, of course, verbally or watching it is in no way capable of controlling it. Physical fitness and hence discipline in that regard is absolutely necessary to bring about harmony between within and without. Gurudeo had a wonderful understanding of human psychology and he knew the pulse of each individual so thoroughly that he was capable of giving him a correct guidance or process, whatever one may call it.

My real search for truth or unknown started when I was able to understand in terms of experience of what is called the mind. Say, when there is a movement in an atmosphere we call it wind but when the atmosphere is still we say there is no wind. We also observe ripples, or waves, when water is disturbed but there are no waves or ripples when it is still. As a matter of fact, nothing comes or nothing goes. There are no additions or subtractions but we call it wind and waves to the disturbed atmosphere and the disturbed water. Similarly mind comes into existence, only when there is a movement or an inner activity. What causes this mental activity is a separate subject by itself. With the help of Gurudeo all my difficulties were solved. I felt myself ever free and fresh without any burden of the past and any anxiety about the future. The eternal truth and what is called "Unknown" is an experience beyond words.

I have nothing but joy, peace and happiness. I started in search of the Unknown but I find that today I have lost myself in the Unknown. That "I" in me has completely vanished and it has remained only symbolic without any meaning. The physical existence has very little to do with the "I" and the person once known to the world as Madhav has little to do with me excepting as vanished symbol of identification. If this could be explained to some extent, I may say that a river has an existence or a separate identity so long as it does not meet the sea. The moment it merges into the sea, its identity is completely lost in the vast ocean and there does not remain any separate existence for it. In the vast ocean it is impossible to distinguish the waters of different rivers that merge into it. Similarly I was in search of the "Unknown" and today I am "Unknown" even to myself.

I think I have nothing more to write in the diary. Side by side with my diary I completed a notebook of experiences as well as letters to my brother, Malati and Vinodini, and I handed all these with my watch, and fountain-pen to Gurudeo who left us.

THE END

IT was almost two years since Madhav left us for the Himalayas. No news about him was received so far. According to him he had gone for good and he had promised us no communication. On his mission of finding the truth or realisation, whatever one may call it, he was accompanied by Gurudeo in whom we had confidence and faith. But even then as time passed, myself and my younger brother were growing anxious about him. Our anxiety was also shared by Prof. Ramesh, Malati, Mr. & Mrs. Gupta and their daughter. It was not possible to communicate with Madhav by any means and our helplessness in that respect was adding to our uneasiness.

It was Sunday morning. I was having tea in the garden of our house with a casual caller who had just dropped in. My wife was busy inside the house and children with their studies. I heard our garden gate being pushed open and I half rose in the chair to see the visitor. With a hasty excuse to the surprised visitor I started running towards the figure that had hardly entered and was closing the gate. It was Gurudeo. Meeting him after years filled my heart with joy and I fell at his feet. For a moment I lost control over myself. Gurudeo lifted me up and embraced me. In the meanwhile my wife came and bowed down to Gurudeo. I hardly regained my control when I remembered Gurudeo was alone and where was

Madhav? Gurudeo knew what was passing in my mind and smilingly said: "Do not worry, Madhav is hale and hearty. He is in Himalayas and I have brought with me his letter for you." My wife interrupted and said: "Won't you ask Gurudeo inside?" I was ashamed that I had forgotten the ordinary courtesy. Gurudeo laughed loudly and said: "It is alright. Let us all go in together." By now our visitor had already departed. I did not know what impressions he might have carried. In the drawing room, children were called and introduced to Gurudeo. My wife went in to bring milk and refreshments for Gurudeo and I opened Madhav's letter. I asked my son to inform my brother by phone to come down to our place with his family to meet Gurudeo. Madhav's letter ran as under :

My dear Vinayak,

I am writing after a very long time. You all naturally would have been anxious about me. Let me rest your fears by stating that I am in excellent health and perfectly happy in all respects. You need not worry about me on any account — you know throughout my life, after I met Swamiji and Gurudeo, I was in search of Truth and real happiness. You will be pleased to know that my efforts have met with success and my search has ended. Today I am with no problems, no worries and have no regrets. The entire credit goes to Gurudeo who did the greatest miracle ever possible in leading me from ignorance to knowledge, from darkness to light, from misery to everlasting happiness and peace. It is not possible for people to understand Gurudeo with their intellect trained in different ways of thinking, brought up in different environments, educated in a particular setup, society, political schools, economic conditions and considerations which completely shackle the mind. You can, therefore, understand him as something or somebody equal to God of your conception.

I have to request you all not to worry about me in any way. If possible kindly try to forget me. I know not when I would return to the civilisation of your concept from the deeply snow-clad mountains where I am at present. You will be happy to note that I am free from wants and need nothing.

With kind regards to you all.

Yours affectionately,
MADHAV

Gurudeo left us next morning with a promise to look us up whenever in Bombay.

I intimated to Mr. & Mrs. Gupta, their daughter and her husband. Malati and Ramesh had come to meet Gurudeo.

Exactly a month after, the friends of Madhav met at my place and it was then decided to publish the diaries of Madhav in a concise autobiographical form for the benefit of the public at large.